*Praise fo*

"*Showmance* is the most fun you'll have off-off-off Broadway! The zingers fly, the romance sizzles, and the dialogue sparkles like the best Dom Perignon. A novel so charming it somehow bursts into song. What more could you want? Patti Lupone? She's in here too!"

—Andrew Sean Greer, Pulitzer Prize–winning
author of *Less* and *Less Is Lost*

"No out-of-town tryouts needed here—*Showmance* is ready for the big time. *Stage of Fools*, the show within the novel, might open and close in one night, but Beguelin crafts a story you never want to end. *Showmance* sings."

—Steven Rowley, *New York Times* bestselling
author of *The Guncle Abroad*

PENGUIN BOOKS

# SHOWMANCE

Chad Beguelin is a six-time Tony Award nominee. His Broadway works include *The Prom*, *Disney's Aladdin*, *Elf*, and *The Wedding Singer*. Chad also cowrote the screenplay for *The Prom*, currently available on Netflix. Chad is a graduate of New York University's Tisch School of the Arts Graduate Dramatic Writing Program. He currently lives in Bridgehampton with his husband, Tom, and their rescue dog, Tucker.

# Showmance

## Chad Beguelin

PENGUIN BOOKS

PENGUIN BOOKS
An imprint of Penguin Random House LLC
penguinrandomhouse.com

BABY MINE

LIBRARY OF CONGRESS CATALOGING-IN-PUBLICATION DATA
Names: Beguelin, Chad, 1969– author.
Title: Showmance / Chad Beguelin.
Description: [New York] : Penguin Books, 2024.
Identifiers: LCCN 2024014069 (print) | LCCN 2024014070 (ebook) |
ISBN 9780143138396 (paperback) | ISBN 9780593512449 (ebook)
Subjects: LCGFT: Romance fiction. | Gay fiction. | Novels.
Classification: LCC PS3602.E3748 S56 2024 (print) |
LCC PS3602.E3748 (ebook) | DDC 813/.6—dc23/eng/20240329
LC record available at https://lccn.loc.gov/2024014069
LC ebook record available at https://lccn.loc.gov/2024014070

Printed in the United States of America
1st Printing

Set in Adobe Caslon Pro
Designed by *Christina Nguyen*

For Tom
*Forever*

# Showmance

one

# "Opening Night"

The thing about the opening night of a Broadway show is that it's supposed to be this glamorous, boozy, buzzy extravaganza. There's a red carpet before the performance for the creative types to pose in front of a step-and-repeat with the show's logo splashed across it. There's usually a huge party after the show, someplace criminally expensive with everyone swanning around in tuxedos and Academy Awards–style dresses. There's insanely loud music blaring so everyone has to shout over their canapés and glasses of champagne. And that's exactly how it is: exhilarating, glitzy, and fun.

Unless.

Unless you're the author.

If you're the author of the show, it's as if you've swallowed a ticking time bomb, but you have to keep smiling and shaking hands and filming interviews about what a magical night it is. When you're the author of the show, there is a very public reckoning coming that could possibly not only destroy your career, but close the show and throw countless actors, musicians, stage-hands, dressers, ushers, and so on out of work in the blink of an eye.

It all depends on the *New York Times* review. Unlike television or film, most Broadway shows need a rave from the *Times* if they want to keep running. And that review comes out right in the middle of the opening night party. So if you get panned, the magic turns into a nightmare of epic proportions. So, you know, no pressure. Have fun with that.

And I was doing my level best to do just that. Have fun. Celebrate the milestone. *Stage of Fools* was my first Broadway musical, and I was trying to focus solely on that achievement and not the possibility of a soul-crushing failure. And damn it, it *was* a milestone. An achievement. I nearly passed out the first time I saw the marquee at the theater. "*Stage of Fools*—book, lyrics, and music by Noah Adams." How did I go from being a small-town hick in Southern Illinois to having my name plastered across a Broadway theater? So no matter what the reviews were, I was going to have fun.

Fun, fun, fun.

I'd only had two musicals previously produced in New York. Both off-Broadway and both reviewed by the same *New York Times* critic. Carrie Payne.

The first one was called *The Docents*. Probably not the greatest choice of subject matter, I'll admit. I'm not sure why I thought that audiences would find people who explain museum exhibits galvanizing. Carrie Payne called the book "sitcom-y" and the score a "nothing burger."

My second show was a slightly pretentious experimental musical about a dying girl lost in a ghost-filled forest called *The Jade Corpse*. There might have been shadow puppets. Carrie deemed it "an avant-garde rabbit hole, except boring."

But here I am on the great big Broadway. At long last I've moved up from the kiddie table. This is my one and possibly only shot at the big time. If *Stage of Fools* is a hit, all of my childhood dreams will come true and it will be the kickoff to what I can only hope is a long career as a Broadway writer. If it's a flop, well, there really isn't a plan B. I guess I could start an OnlyFans? Become one of those manically gleeful people who sprays cologne at strangers in Bloomingdale's? No. This musical *has* to be a hit. But of course, the *Times* chose Carrie Payne to review it. The woman who vehemently hates every single thing I've managed to get produced. But I'm still trying to be, you know, smiley.

In the midst of all this insanity, I see Chase and my world steadies a little.

Jesus, that man has swagger. Why he's dating me, I'll never know.

He's typing furiously into his phone about God knows what. And he looks exactly like George Clooney if George Clooney decided to be slightly younger and more handsome. And he has this British accent, mainly because he's British. And the accent is there, even when he's just moaning. Which means every time I sleep with him, it's like I'm banging all of the Bridgerton brothers at once.

And he's completely out of my league. And he's my agent.

Stop judging, it's complicated.

With his usual psychic abilities, Chase notices me staring at him and nods to a nearby nook. I follow him, pushing my way through the frenzied throng and smiling at everyone like a brain-damaged idiot. I'm trying to give off an "isn't this just amazing" vibe, but I think it might be coming across as "which way is the electric chair?" at best.

Chase rests his forearms on a high table littered with abandoned drinks, still typing into his phone. "I want you to know that I'm here for you and that I am a very good boyfriend, but I am also trying to close a film deal and if I do, I will be able to buy you many pretty things."

"I don't feel much like talking anyway. I just . . . I don't know. I keep telling myself that there are wars and famine and hunger running rampant on this planet and I'd be an asshole if I worried about one little musical when there are bigger problems in the world."

Chase freezes. His cobalt blue eyes flood with surprise and then concern. "Oh my God." He actually puts his phone into his suit pocket. His very expensive suit pocket. No matter how much money he spends on tailoring, and it's a lot, his well-toned shoulders and biceps still look like they're trying to fight their way free from the Armani fabric. "Did you just get philosophical?"

"Just in a very selfish, 'make my problems seem small' way."

Chase looks worried. "You *are* nervous."

"Of course I'm nervous! Any minute now I could be denounced as a charlatan in *The New York Times*."

Chase gives a sexy yet possibly patronizing chuckle. "Relax, Noah. You've got Danielle."

Danielle Vincent. The most prolific and lauded director of musicals since Hal Prince. She could make orchids bloom in the Sahara. She has a string of bulletproof mega musicals under her belt and I'm pretty sure they had to reinforce the floor of her penthouse to support her massive collection of Tony Awards. Chase is right. Truth be told, Danielle and I have a slightly unbalanced working relationship. I'm the newbie and she's the Svengali. So any time I disagreed with her, I never put up a fight. I mean, who the hell do I think I am, anyway? Since the very first read-through my strategy was to smile pretty and let Danielle be Danielle. It had gotten me this far.

Chase, whose phone is inconceivably still in his suit pocket, goes sympathetic around the eyes. Those dreamy cobalt eyes. "You're very talented, Noah. And you work harder than anyone I know. You deserve to take this moment in."

And then he's enveloping me in a much-needed hug and our ears graze one another for a brief second. And though we've been together for almost two years, even ear grazing is still strangely hot. He gives me a brief peck on the lips and says, "Would it calm you down any if you were to give my bum a little cuddle?"

I consider his proposition for a nanosecond and decide it couldn't hurt. So I pretend that I'm putting my right hand around his waist, but secretively slide it down to his unbelievable ass and silently command my knees not to buckle.

"Well done, my lad. Stay above the trousers, though. We *are* in public."

I swallow a laugh. "How on God's green earth is your ass so fucking awesomely distracting?"

Chase nonchalantly pulls his phone back out and continues typing. "Goblet squats."

There's a sea change in the room. A shift in the vibe.

Everyone is getting a bit quieter and I'm wondering how much it will cost to get my tux cleaned if I vomit all over it. I remove my hand from Chase's ass and ask, "What's happening? Are the reviews coming out?"

Chase is frantically scrolling.

"Chase? Chase?!"

"I'm reading." His face is a mask completely devoid of emotion. I clamp onto the high table so intensely that the abandoned cocktails actually vibrate. They titter like nervous aunts. Chase takes an almost imperceptible swallow of air and looks at me with a renewed expression of Zen-like peace. "Just a couple reviews. From a couple of meaningless outlets. Nothing to worry about."

"But were they good?"

"They're meaningless."

"So they're bad."

"They're . . . immaterial. And I love you. And you're wonderful. And you just need to be a brave soldier for another hour or two. Then we can go home, and I'll let you reap the rewards of my countless goblet squats."

And his George Clooney lips are on my nose just long enough to make me forget my name for a brief second, but just quickly enough to be annoying.

Then he smirks. Chase is the king of smirks. They're devilishly handsome, like he's promising you that sooner or later you're going to be all his. "Now, I've got to go talk to some people."

I know he means talk to some people about the so-called "meaningless" reviews. But he's right. They are meaningless. The only one that has any sway over public opinion is the *New York Times*'s. Carrie fucking Payne. Of course her last name is Payne. She's like a Charles Dickens villain with the obvious surname to boot.

Before Chase can abandon me, we both hear an overly loud but gloriously familiar voice.

"There's my super sexy future Tony Award winner!"

I turn on my heel and almost squeal with joy to see Kiara. She's looking totally va-va-voom in a cherry red gown and heels that make her tower over me in a very selfish way. She envelops me in a hug and for a second I forget to be a bundle of twitchy nerves.

"Holy crap, Kiara! The Sharons are present and accounted for tonight!"

For reasons that we both have forgotten, Kiara named her breasts "the Sharons" years ago.

"I feel objectified and I love it. Although, stage right Sharon needs a little wiggle. My fault for going strapless." Kiara gives a little tug and a shimmy and the Sharons are back in place.

Chase gives her a very showy two-cheek kiss and whispers conspiratorially, "I've got to go work now. Can you babysit our scared little pony for me?"

"I am not a little pony."

Chase turns to me again with that smirk. "You very much are a little pony, except for one very important aspect where you happen to be a horse."

Kiara is not having any of this. "Nope! Uh-uh. I do not need to know these things about my best friend. Go off and be agent-y somewhere."

Another peck on my nose and Chase vanishes into the crowd.

I turn to Kiara and tell her she looks nothing short of a miracle because she does and respect must be paid.

She goes humble, but we both know deep down she's the most beautiful woman in the room. "Well, thanks for the compliment, but I've been mistaken for Audra McDonald twice tonight."

"And you're mad? Audra McDonald is a goddess."

"Audra McDonald is a goddess who is a quarter of a century older than me, thank you."

"Oh, please! She's got the skin of a newborn."

And then I stop, acutely aware that I have been old-fashioned hornswoggled. "Wait, did you just name-drop Audra McDonald so you could humblebrag about the fact that you were mistaken for said goddess twice?"

Instead of admitting any guilt, Kiara pretends to bob her head to the music.

"Also, I might point out that wearing such high heels is clearly a microaggression against me."

Kiara does a gagging face like only she can do. "Noah, you're taller than Tom Cruise *and* Tom Holland and hotter than both combined, you shameless thirsty queen."

"Okay, so we're both fishing for compliments, and we can both journal about that tomorrow when the pressure is off."

Always a mind reader, Kiara holds up a vodka and soda that

she's clearly wrangled to calm my nerves. I take a sip and almost do a spit take. "Damn, that is *strong*!"

"I told the bartender to pour the vodka until we *both* felt uncomfortable. So . . ." Kiara gives me a searching look before she says ever so carefully, "How are you doing?"

"Is it that obvious?"

"Only I would notice, because I know you so well. But you look about ready to spiral. Don't worry, though. To most onlookers and civilians, you look relaxed and blasé about this major life event."

My forced smile gets even bigger. "Can this review just come the fuck on out, already?"

Kiara wraps her pinky in mine like I'm a six-year-old afraid of my first day of kindergarten. "Don't worry, momma's got you."

And then our gruesome little routine begins.

I start, "I love you so much I would light myself on fire for you."

Kiara pauses, then, "I love you so much I would breastfeed a piranha for you."

I consider this, then counter with, "I love you so much I would throw myself in front of a whirling combine for you."

And this leaves Kiara confused. "What's a combine?"

"It's a farmer thing. They use them to cut down crops."

"Bitch, I was born in Queens. Vet your references next time."

I shrug and manage another huge gulp of booze. And then I quietly thank the universe for Kiara's friendship. She assumed the role of my personal guardian angel on the first day we met. Kiara was an RA at my NYU dorm a million years ago. No, she wasn't *an* RA, she was *the* RA. And she set my teetering world right back on its axis from minute one.

Instead of spending money we didn't have on airplane tickets, my parents drove me fourteen and a half hours to the big, scary city. Since they were double-parked, there was only time for a quick goodbye before Mom and Dad piloted their busted Dodge Charger off into a sea of traffic and vanished. I had never felt so completely and immediately alone. I was standing in front of an imposing dormitory building with only a couple of suitcases and a stomach full of roaring anxiety. I was a lost, Midwestern hill-billy who didn't know a single soul. As I was getting pushed back and forth on the busy sidewalk by heartless New Yorkers, some-one suddenly grabbed one of my suitcases. Certain that I was being robbed, I screamed out, "That's *mine*! That's *my* suitcase! Hands *off*!"

And that's when I saw the gorgeous and also obviously of-fended face that I would grow to worship.

"Bitch, I'm not trying to steal your raggedy-ass suitcase. I'm trying to help you," Kiara bellowed. "Have you been assigned to Brittany Hall? Because if you have, then the only two words I need to hear from you right now are 'thank' and 'you.'"

I could barely muster enough oxygen to whimper, "I'm sorry, I don't know anyone and . . . and . . . and I already hate it here!"

And then, to my eternal embarrassment, I exploded into a thousand tears. And with that, Kiara's cold scowl melted on the spot. And right there on the filthy sidewalk, she pulled me into an embrace and cooed into my ear, "Oh, you're just a lost little hummingbird of a thing, aren't you?"

And all I could do was cry into her magnificent hair and nod.

"That's all right. Let's get you all set up in your dorm room and then we can discuss why you showed up to your first day of college wearing acid-washed jeans."

And with that tiny act of kindness, Kiara and I practically became fused into one human being. While watching *Wuthering Heights* in Film History that year, I understood exactly what Catherine meant when she said, "I am Heathcliff!" I was so instantly enamored with Kiara that I told her I felt the same way. Before Christmas break I blurted out to her, "I love you so much, I am Kiara!"

Kiara grinned and took my little chipmunk-cheeked face in her hands and said, "I love you, too, baby boy. But never say that again, because it's weird as fuck."

She was right. It *was* weird as fuck. But she loved me, too!

Years later when Chase and I moved in together, he was a little taken aback by my Kiara shrine. Rows upon rows of framed pictures of Kiara and me popped up like toadstools on every flat surface available. Kiara and me on spring break riding a tacky banana boat down in Key West. Kiara's graduation photo from Columbia Law, her tam cap at a jaunty angle on her head. The two of us at the opening night of every musical I ever wrote. A candid shot of me as "Man of Honor" at Kiara's wedding, kneeling like a Disney footman as I straighten her elaborate train.

I'm not sure how our gruesome little game of one-upmanship began, but I absolutely would prove my love to her by throwing myself in front of a whirling combine. I also wonder how the rest of the world gets by without having a Kiara in their lives. Those poor, unfortunate souls.

"Hey, where's Stephen?"

Stephen. Wonderful, friend to the world, Stephen. I used to think he was lucky to have Kiara. Then I thought she was lucky to have him. Now they're in a dead heat and if I didn't have Chase, I would be riddled with envy.

Kiara pulls a sad face. "Oh, he's so bummed he can't be here. He's showing a penthouse on the Upper West Side, and the owner is this really kooky gazillionaire who only lets the apartment be shown after sundown. We think he might be a vampire."

I narrow my eyes at her. "So that's how it's going to be? You're going to lie straight to my face at my first and possibly last Broadway opening?"

Kiara's sad face turns dismissive. "You know he loves you, he just hates theater more. I told him I would take one for the team. Besides, we don't need him hanging around and stinking up the place with his uselessness."

"That's fair." I pause to consider not bringing it up, but self-control has never been my strong suit. "Tell me again about Thursday night."

Kiara throws her head back and stares at the ceiling in very dramatic frustration. Carrie Payne came to see the show on Thursday. In the old days, critics would come to opening night and then run back to their offices to type up their reviews for the morning newspapers. There are all these glorious stories of the days of yore where a bleary-eyed producer would read the rave reviews to the trembling opening night partygoers as the sun came up and the stars started to fade over Manhattan. Nowadays, critics come a few nights beforehand to write their reviews in advance because, I don't know, laziness?

I'd sent Kiara to spy on Carrie to see if there was any response to the show written across her face. I knew there was none, but I couldn't stop asking.

"Noah, she's like a professional poker player. Next to her, the *Mona Lisa* looks downright *frantic*. I don't know what to tell you. Her face is a locked safe. And I don't have the combination. And you know what? I don't even care! And neither should you. You wrote a kick-ass musical and people love it."

"I'm skeptical."

"People love it. Your score is fantastic and Danielle's staging, with all of those special effects? When you told me you were writing a musical based on *King Lear*, I was like, SNOOOOZE! I don't even get the show's title. I mean, *Stage of Fools*?"

"It's a quote from *King Lear*. 'When we are born, we cry that we are come to this great stage of fools,'" I explain.

"Well, I wasn't crying, I was in ecstasy! I mean, when I realized that you set the show in the far-off future and on a spaceship, I was like, mind officially blown. And when Cordelia's ghost hovers upstage during the last few scenes—"

"That was Danielle's idea."

"Who cares? It's brilliant. The whole thing is brilliant. And you deserve a hit. Do you know why? Because you're a very good person."

"We both know I'm a bitch, but I thank you for that very unfounded swing for the fences."

Kiara gets very solemn, which is not a usual look for her. "You saved my husband's life."

This again. "Kiara, I referred him to a therapist. It's not that big of a deal."

"No, no, no. I will not have you rewriting history here tonight. I told you I was worried that he was depressed, and you came over and threw me out of my own apartment so that you could talk to Stephen alone. You assessed the situation, which, technically speaking, you aren't trained to do, but we'll skip that. Then you called a therapist you used to see and not only got Stephen an appointment two hours later, but you went with him and sat in the waiting room and then brought him home to me."

"I was, I don't know, worried. He's still doing okay?"

"He's doing great. In fact, he's so confident and self-assured that he was able to ditch your big night. That's progress."

Kiara clocks Chase talking to someone in a pink blazer that is very attention grabbing, but maybe not in the right way. "Um, is your boyfriend trying to sign Aleister Murphy?"

Aleister. Blech. "I wouldn't be surprised. He's had two hit shows. One at the Public and one at Playwrights Horizons."

Their conversation ends and Aleister hurries to catch up to a cater waiter and his tray of free chardonnay.

Kiara watches him, then says, "Is it me, or is Aleister's walk not cute?"

"Oh, it's the opposite of cute. I have no idea why he has such a weird walk. It's like he slinks."

"He one hundred percent slinks. And the eyebrows are a little too curated for my taste. And I'm sorry, but who names their child Aleister?"

"Satan worshippers," I respond.

We both know what we're doing. Aleister's star is rising and mine could implode at any second. And my boyfriend is clearly trying to get on board the Aleister Murphy train. So Kiara is being the best friend ever and reading Aleister for filth.

Maybe I'm too paranoid about my star imploding. I *was* chosen as one of *Variety*'s "30 Creatives Under 30" list. Although, having just turned twenty-nine, I was cutting it pretty damn close.

"Oh no." My eyes have landed on Chase, who's now with his assistant, Anna Wong. "Chase is berating Anna Wong again." Chase doesn't yell when he gets angry. His eyes narrow and he talks quickly and quietly. Anna Wong nods her head so fast it's moving double-time to the blaring music.

"Maybe go stop him. That looks like some Scott Rudin shit."

"I agree." I push my way through the crowd toward a very chagrined looking Anna Wong. No one ever calls her Anna. It's always her complete name: Anna Wong. I asked her about this once and she simply shrugged and said, "Even my own mother calls me Anna Wong. I can't explain why things gain traction."

I'm close enough to hear Chase hissing, "You're in charge of transportation! My boyfriend and I are not going to end this night in a filthy New York City taxi!"

Anna Wong doesn't look Chase in the eyes. "I misunderstood. I thought you just wanted the car service to take you from the theater to here."

"Why would I want that? How does that even make sense?! How did you think we were going to get home? Did you think we were going to, oh, I don't know, levitate and float home? Do I look like Peter Pan to you?"

Chase sees me approaching and immediately switches back to the Chase I know and love. It's like a magic trick. Any trace of anger has evaporated. But the three of us obviously know that he was being a complete asshole seconds earlier.

I try to pull my most affable attitude. "You know, there's something really romantic about a filthy New York City taxi. It's like riding in a little piece of history."

Anna Wong gives me a relieved look, but mutters, "No, no. I'm on it. Sorry about the confusion." And she's on her phone and off into the crowd as quickly as possible. I turn to Chase and I can tell he already knows what I'm going to say.

"You have to be nicer to her."

His expression goes stone-cold. "I don't tell you how to write musicals, please don't tell me how to agent."

We both pretend to be interested in the ceiling.

But I can't let it go. "Chase. You know I'm right."

Chase is silent for a couple of ticks. Then he tries, "It's kind of an industry thing. A lot of people think they want to be agents and so they start as assistants. I like to make sure that if my assistants do get to move up the ranks that they can take a little toughness. I don't believe in hand-holding. It's as simple as that."

Before I can argue back, glasses are being clinked. The music is cut off and it appears that our fearless leader Danielle is going to make some sort of a speech. Statuesque, pantsuit-wearing

Danielle. Once during rehearsal I asked her if she thought we needed another reprise of a ballad from Act One. She turned to me and apropos of nothing, told me that she and her wife, much like Annette Bening and Julianne Moore in the movie *The Kids Are All Right*, sometimes enjoy watching gay male porn. Lost for an answer, I could only mutter, "Good for you! Now about this reprise . . ."

Even though Chase and I are possibly in a fight, I need answers immediately. "Do directors usually make big speeches on opening nights? Is this normal?"

"Absolutely not. I think she might be drunk."

Danielle does seem a little wobbly. And she's got lipstick on her teeth. But that might just be because she's not used to wearing lipstick.

"My fellow partygoers . . ." She starts off very grandly, sweeping her massive hands across the crowd. "I believe the musical we have opened here tonight is a truly groundbreaking work of art. With a top-notch cast, design team, and, of course, Noah Adams's soul-searing script and score." And there's a little smattering of applause as people look uncomfortably at me and I look uncomfortably back. Thankfully, Danielle thunders on.

"But as is true with most groundbreaking works, it may take the passage of time to reveal the piece's profundity."

I don't like where this is going.

"Now, I know it might be considered . . ." And Danielle looks, for once in her life, lost for words. I look around and realize Kiara has reappeared. We're doing the pinky-holding thing. Chase is wearing an expression of complete horror.

Danielle has unfortunately found her train of thought again. "It might be considered déclassé to speak of reviews, especially when they are unkind."

Ice water shoots through my veins. The floor beneath my feet feels precarious and unreliable. I turn to Chase desperately. "Is it out? Is the *Times* review out?!"

Chase swallows with difficulty. Kiara's pinky grip tightens.

"But Noah." Danielle is trying to drunkenly hold my gaze. "No matter what Ms. Payne says about your work, no matter how much she dismisses your talent, just know that everyone in this room believes that one day in the not-so-distant future, *Stage of Fools* will be considered a seminal addition to the musical theater canon!"

And then I run.

Well, first I drop my vodka soda on the floor, and then I pick up my proverbial petticoats and run.

There's a door with an exit sign and I beeline for it. It's embarrassing and cowardly, but I can't stop myself. I can't take the humiliation. I find myself on a gray stairwell and I start descending as fast as I can. Behind me I hear Chase and Kiara hot on my trail. Flop sweat is dampening my expensive shirt collar and I accidentally slip and fall a couple of steps onto the nearest landing. When Chase and Kiara catch up, I'm sitting on the ground like a sad, abandoned ventriloquist dummy in a tux.

Kiara sits down beside me on one side and Chase sits on the other. They both lean their heads onto my trembling shoulders. No one talks for a very long time.

Finally, I muster up the truth. "So. My career is over."

Chase's tone is more adamant than I have ever heard. "That. Is. Not. True."

My voice is pathetic and quivery. "Oh, come on, Chase. What producer is going to put money behind anything I write now? I'm done. And there's nothing anyone can do about it."

"Well, I'm gonna do something about it," Kiara says, fuming. I love it when Kiara gets all tough and defiant. "I'm gonna find out where this Carrie Payne asshole lives.

"She's going to find out how we handle little bitches like her in Jackson Heights, Queens!"

I laugh and pretend tears aren't spilling out of my eyes. "Oh my God, you would destroy her. She's like a million years old."

"I will destroy her. I will take her out at the knees. I will perform some mafia shit on her."

And we all three share a sad little laugh. And then my cell rings.

Ugh. It's Mom. I stand up to take the call, pacing the landing while I consider letting it go to voicemail. She's probably read the review and now I have to go through the embarrassing act of being consoled.

When I answer, she's crying. "Noah!"

"Mom, it's just a bad review. Those are the rules of the game. That's the gig. Wanna be a writer? You've got to get reviewed. Them's the rules."

"No, honey. It's your dad. He's had a heart attack."

And to my complete confusion, my legs give out and I'm falling into blackness.

two

# "Plainview"

always assumed that my first Broadway opening night would
end with Chase and me passionately tearing each other's tuxedos off the minute we got home. Instead it ended with my ass
hanging out of a paper hospital gown while I endured the world's
longest MRI. Not ideal. After a very dramatic overnight stay in the
ER and an even more dramatic bump on the right side of my head,
I was released from the hospital and actually didn't get my bearings
until I was in a cab heading toward LaGuardia with Chase.

Dad was stable and we were dutifully making the trip back to
my hometown.

Manhattan blurs by the car window as Chase pecks at his
phone. And I, true to form, pick at the wound.

"Have they taken down the marquee at the theater yet?"

Chase uses his gentle voice. Reserved for hurt animals and the
elderly. "It's only been a couple of days."

The rest of the reviews had been only slightly less vicious than
the *Times*. *Stage of Fools* had just joined the tragic list of musicals

that opened and closed in one night. And the embarrassment of it all made my skin hot with shame.

But I can't stop asking questions. "Do we know which show is going to move into the theater?"

"There are rumors."

He knows. He's just shielding me. I quietly appreciate it.

But, of course, I continue on.

"Do you think . . . ugh . . . do you think it would have helped if we had stunt cast the part of Lear? Some big movie star? Like Hugh Jackman?" I feel sick to my stomach for even bringing it up. The cast was filled with Broadway royalty. The kind of performers I had been obsessed with since I was a teen in very unfortunate braces. But I can't help it. "I mean, then the reviews wouldn't have mattered. Maybe?"

Chase puts his hand on my knee. His hand is very well manicured, yet somehow still masculine. Even during all of the drama, his touch still makes my heart leap a little. "We'll never know. Stop torturing yourself."

I've refused to read the *Times* review. What's the point? Still, I have to ask. "Did she hate everything?"

Chase pauses, considering how to answer. "She thought you had some very clever lyrics."

"But the tunes? And the script?" His silence says it all. "Got it. So I guess I'm just damaged goods now, right? And the cast and the crew, basically everyone involved with the show is out of a job because of me. Everyone's unemployed because I couldn't cut it."

"That kind of thinking will not be allowed by either your agent or your boyfriend. So. Let's focus on your family."

My family. I let out a slightly tortured sigh. What is posher-than-posh Chase going to think about Mom and Dad?

"About my family. I love them to the moon and back, but they're not . . ." I'm searching.

Chase gives me an inquisitive look. Even in the middle of texting, he can pretend to be present and interested. "They're not what?"

"Just . . . Mom and Dad . . . they're . . . folksy. In fact, my entire town is folksy. I mean, Dad runs a dairy farm."

"I'm aware."

"Yeah, but just . . ." I search for the proper instructions. "Just . . . gird your loins."

Chase is back typing into his phone. "I am very excited to visit this place called Plainview. Why is it called that, anyway?"

"I don't know. Some leather-faced, Native American-killing settler must have arrived on the land and asked his bucktoothed wife what she thought of the view and she said, 'It's plain.' And then they decided not to get all creative about naming things, because that might take up time from their butter churning and various hoedowns."

Chase gives me a look.

"What? I'm not being mean, I'm just trying to do some level setting here."

Chase nods. "Consider my levels sufficiently calibrated."

"But you're gonna be very judgy about it, I can tell. Our convenience stores are called 'Hucks' after *Huckleberry Finn*, so that kind of says it all."

"So it's a town that values literature."

I give him a weary look.

"I promise, I will put on my least judgmental face. I keep it wrapped in mothballs for just this sort of occasion. For now, let's just be glad the old pater is doing well."

"I can't believe he had a heart attack."

"Why? He's not exactly a spring chicken."

"I know. It's just weird to have any scientific proof that he actually has a heart."

Dad and me. Unfortunately it's textbook. When I was a kid I would catch him looking at me like I was somebody else's luggage he picked up at the airport by mistake. He's a man's man and I practically came out of the womb wearing a dance belt and tap shoes. We didn't have much to discuss. Thankfully, I always had Mom on my side. While Dad was dealing with the farm, Mom was busy with her bizarre paintings and generally cheering on my various backyard performances. And now Chase was about to meet them both. And the town that I had fled as soon as my high school senior year ended. But for now, Chase was right. I was glad Dad was doing well.

We sit glumly on the shiny Airbus A320 and Chase goes over contracts on his laptop for what I can only assume are other, much more successful writers. Glutton for punishment that I am, I plan to spend the flight mourning my career like a Sicilian widow. All of those years of struggling to be a professional writer. The endless shitty jobs. Waiting tables or answering phones. The bartending gig at a gay bar where they asked me if I could wear a vest without a shirt. And then a few days later, if I could ditch the vest. And then a few days after that, if I could go out and dance in the middle of the club every half an hour or so. It took my stupid brain an entire week to realize that I'd been demoted from bartender to go-go boy. But the humiliation seemed worth it, because it paid the rent and the electricity bill. It paid for me to write. To keep the fantasy alive that one distant day I'd make it to the flashing lights of old Broadway. And then the miracle happened. Against all odds, the dream came true. And then it was pulled out from underneath me in a matter of hours. And all the previous toiling away, the striving and the praying and the bartering away the precious years of my twenties added up to what? A big, fat disappointment. To use the words of Carrie Payne: a nothing burger.

Chase reads my mind and takes my hand. Without him, this would all be unbearable.

"Thanks for coming with me, Chase. I mean it. I couldn't do this alone."

Chase smiles and recites our favorite quote from E. M. Forster's *Maurice*, "We shan't be parted no more."

It's what he always says when I'm sad or worried. And it works every time.

Before I know it, we're in the rental car, starting the hour-long drive south to Plainview, Illinois. Even though he was brought up with steering wheels on the opposite side, Chase drives because we both know he's more capable at that sort of thing. That's one of the many dreamy things about Chase. He's always there to do whatever I suck at. He figures out the tip on every bill. He makes sure my taxes get done. He sees to it that my closets get organized and my credit card bills get paid. He claims that it's all so I can focus my brain cells solely on being creative. Handsome, helpful, and willing to keep the boring parts of the world out of my hair. No wonder I fell for him so completely. What I did to deserve him, I'll never know.

As we pull into town, Chase gives a low whistle. "This place is very . . ." And then he just stops talking.

"It's lost some of its former glory, I'll give you that." And then I feel something rise up inside of me. Am I defensive of Plainview? Because that would be beyond hypocritical. I spent my entire high school career making fun of how backwater the place was. But it was my backwater place. *Mine*, damn it.

Plainview. Population: twelve thousand or so. Where people spend their weekends fishing for largemouth bass or catfish. Where basketball is a religion and gossip is a currency. And where I stuck out like a sore, sequined thumb. I brush the thought away.

"Take a right up here, at the grimacing garden gnome."

The creepy little statue welcomes visitors to our long gravel driveway and Chase remains silent as we drive past the steel and wood barn that's painted fire engine red. When we pull up to the house, there stands Mom on the front porch in all of her Momness. Of course she doesn't take off her painting smock before meeting Chase for the first time. Of course she doesn't fix her hair, but just leaves it in a messy, curly bun. Of course she wears the hideous bright orange Crocs that I have forbidden on countless occasions. She looks like a crazy person and I wonder if she does this to embarrass me in front of my very polished British boyfriend. Some people mistake her for Sally Field. But they're wrong. She's one hundred percent Nancy Kay Adams and she won't let you forget it. Oh, and her eyes are constantly locked in full-on twinkle mode and it's endearing beyond words. And I find myself crying because she's exactly all the things I need in the world right now.

Chase notices me reduced to tears as he parks the car. "Those are happy tears, right?"

"Yep." I turn to Chase and say very seriously, "Before you meet her, you should know that my mother is completely and certifiably insane. And wildly inappropriate. And you will absolutely fall in love with her just like everyone else and probably run away with her to Rio."

Chase looks worried. "Does it have to be Rio? I think they require a visa and the waiting time might be a problem. I'm not a patient man."

Feeling that Chase has been sufficiently warned, I'm out of the car and up the front porch steps and Mom and I are doing our hugging-swaying dance, while she rains a million little smooches on my cheek.

Then, with what is probably a little too much pageantry, I gesture to Chase. "Mom, this is Chase."

Mom gives my glossy boyfriend one of her biggest smiles and for some unknown reason announces, "He doesn't look Jewish."

Chase and I stare at her in complete shock until I can manage a chastising, "Nancy Kay Adams!"

Mom gets flustered. "I mean, I just thought Abrams was a Jewish last name."

I turn to Chase. "This is the wildly inappropriate part I was warning you about." I turn back to Mom. "First of all, you've seen pictures of Chase online, so you shouldn't be confused about him not, quote, 'looking Jewish.' I'm not even sure what that means. Secondly, his last name is also a British last name and he is very, very Anglican."

"Oh, now I've embarrassed you!" Mom squeezes Chase's hand. "Now, Chase, you know I wouldn't care either way. I was just being observant."

I'm not letting her get away with this. "Yeah, Mom, that can also read as anti-Semitic. So maybe filter the stuff coming out of your mouth hole a little more?"

Mom looks offended and strangely regal. "Honey, you know I'm not anti-Semitic!"

Of course she isn't. She's just Mom. "I know. You're right."

"I mean, I love bagels!"

Chase laughs at the top of his lungs and pulls Mom into a hug. "Mrs. Adams, your son warned me that I would fall in love with you and whisk you away. He was absolutely right and now I need all of your frequent flyer numbers."

Mom hugs Chase back and demands that he call her Nancy Kay. "Now, let me show you around our very elaborate mansion!"

Since Mom has always been an avid painter, our front room is filled with the numerous family portraits she's created over the years. She's actually not half bad. If you look closely at the portraits, it's easy to chart the increasing realization on my face that I didn't fit in and that I was probably as gay as a Fire Island tambourine. But there's something empowering about walking back into my childhood home with my sturdy, chiseled, and successful boyfriend.

Our house is a pretty typical, run-of-the-mill farmhouse, but Mom's great at putting on airs. I mean, it's clear where I get my flair for the dramatic.

"Now, the first stop on the tour—"

I cut Mom off. "There doesn't need to be a tour. Or if there does need to be a tour, couldn't it just be a self-guided tour?"

Mom scoffs. "Noah, you know we can't afford those little recording thingies they have in museums. Now stop interrupting. The first stop on the tour is this upright piano. Noah's dad bought it from the Presbyterian church and had his buddies help him move it here when Noah was ten."

A rush of guilt washes over me. "Jesus. Dad. How is he? He's kind of like the reason we're here."

"Oh, he's fine. He's got one more night in the hospital to make all the nurses crazy. And he's mad as a pistol that I even told you about it." She turns to Chase and whispers, "Macho."

Chase nods. "I've heard of such people."

"Oh, and thank you both for that very expensive-looking Get Well arrangement! It was as big as my head!"

Chase sent my parents flowers? But of course he did. How he manages to think of every thoughtful little detail is a constant wonder. I silently squeeze his hand in gratitude.

Mom continues her tour. "Now, Noah wrote his first song on this piano."

"Mother, stop it."

"It was called 'The Jealous Pancake.'" I can feel the tips of my ears turning red. "The pancake was jealous because it wanted to be a waffle, you see."

Chase is not even trying to hide his smirk. "Makes sense."

"And Noah rhymed 'blueberry' with 'There never was such a *true berry*.'"

Chase gives a professional nod. "He's very serious about his rhymes, this one."

Mom agrees. "I sometimes think we should get a little velvet rope to put around this thing. I mean, now that he's a Broadway writer and all."

"A failed Broadway writer," I can't stop myself from adding.

Mom is annoyingly dismissive. "Setbacks! You're a writer, you should know that every story has setbacks and twists and turns. So this musical didn't stick? Write another one!"

"It's not that easy, Mom."

"Of course it is. You just have to make up your mind to make up your mind! If you're not already working on something new, then you're just being lazy. And I didn't carry you for nine months in the Southern Illinois humidity just to give birth to a lazy child."

I throw up my hands and say to Chase, "I told you. She is certifiably crazy."

Mom waves her hand to dismiss the idea. "Crazy like a fox. Now did Noah ever tell you how I used to embarrass him by the way I pronounced the word 'theater'? I used to pronounce it 'the-ATE-er.' It drove him nuts. So then he told me to think of pronouncing it the same way I would say 'Theodore.' So now I just call it that. As in, 'What time do we have to be at the *Theodore*, Noah?'"

My phone vibrates and there's a text from Kiara: I need to know that you're all right. I am on a plane if you need me.

I respond back: I'm fine.

Her response: I love you so much I would jump off a building for you.

I respond: I love you so much I would put my balls into a wood chipper for you.

Her response: I love you so much I would have my vagina surgically sealed for you.

I respond: Please stop reminding me that there are vaginas in the world.

I'm about to return to whatever Mom is yammering on about when I catch a glimpse of the bedroom off the living room where Mom does her paintings.

"Mom, what in Satan's unholy playroom is happening in there?"

Mom follows my stare. "Oh, it's my new series. Come look!"

We follow her into the paint-splattered room and come face-to-face with several paintings of eggplants in various sizes.

"Now, I'm no professional, Chase. But I do find painting very therapeutic and soothing."

Chase and I take a couple of seconds to stare at the bulging eggplants in uncomfortable silence.

"But, Mom, why eggplants?"

Mom tilts her head to consider for a second. "You know, I don't know. They just seem to be everywhere these days. Little cartoon eggplants. Isn't that so random? But they're selling like crazy."

"You're selling these?"

"Oh, yes! Luke set up a page for me on something called Etsy. Young people are going crazy for them. I've even got one of those PayPal things. Luke says I'm Michelangelo and these eggplants are my Sistine Chapel. Luke thinks—"

Before she can say another word, I grind the conversation to a halt. "Wait, *Luke*? As in Luke Carter?" The feeling of betrayal makes my jaw clench. "You're joking, right? Why are you chumming it up with Luke Carter, Mom? You know he's officially my nemesis."

"Oh, Noah, I can't keep track of all of your . . . oh, what's the plural of the word nemesis?"

"Nemeses," Chase offers, happy to be of help.

"Nemeses. He started working for your father last year and he's an angel sent from heaven."

"But—"

Mom digs her heels in. "But what?"

I'm pacing back and forth in front of the eggplants, shaking my head in disbelief. "After everything he put me through, he works here now? As in on our farm? You're joking, right? And why am I just learning about this now?"

Chase, sensing drama, gamely asks, "What's the problem with this Luke character?"

"Well, for one, he and his friends made high school a waking nightmare for me."

Mom has to burst in. "Oh, I'm sure he's very sorry for all that."

"Well, he's not forgiven. Two, he's basically the son my dad never had. Whenever he'd see Dad in town, they'd end up talking for hours about butch shit like carburetors and football and hay balers."

"He's a very nice boy, Noah."

Anger boils up from my stomach. Hot, acidic anger. Where is my mother's loyalty, damn it? "He is not nice! Stop saying that Luke Carter is nice! He's an asshole. And he has no right to take my . . . my . . . my filial place!"

This elicits a very loud laugh from Chase. "Filial? We're using the word 'filial' now?"

My mother gives Chase a world-weary look. "I rue the day I bought that boy a thesaurus."

I give a loud huff and say, "You're both being fulsomely vexatious."

# three

# "Shakespeare Returns"

The minute the hospital elevator door opens, I can see straight into Dad's room. The floral arrangement Chase sent is the size of a crosstown bus and dwarfs all the other bouquets on the windowsill. Sportscasters yammer away on the television, competing with the beeping sounds from the hospital machines. And sitting there like some self-appointed prince is Luke Carter.

"Not this fucking guy," I grumble and Mom immediately hisses for me to be nice.

As we're walking toward the room, Chase asks, "Is that the notorious Luke? You didn't mention that he was hot."

I stop. Chase stops. Mom continues on.

I speak with as much calm as I can muster. "I will admit that the animators over at Disney might have used Luke Carter as their model when they were creating the animated film *Hercules*, but you do not get to consider him hot. He is an idiot. He is a bully. And he's wearing a baseball cap. Backward. Which is a look that screams douchebag. Which he is."

We continue on into the room and there's Dad looking disgruntled in his hospital bed and Mom annoyingly hugging Luke. I choose to completely ignore the guy and hope that he'll take the hint and just go away.

I turn to Dad and consider whether or not to hug him. It would probably just make everyone uncomfortable, so I pass. "How are you feeling, Dad?"

"Annoyed as hell. They're just keeping me here to make money off the insurance company. I'm as healthy as a horse." Dad's face is tan and leathery from years of working in the sun. It's also baked into a permanent scowl. He used to have a tragic comb-over, but his hair eventually got so sparse that he just gave up and shaved his head. I think Mom was secretly relieved. Thankfully, I was born with Nancy Kay's thick dark hair and eyelashes that she calls "long enough to make a showgirl spit nails."

Dad fiddles with his IV. "I told your mother that you didn't need to fly all the way down here for this, son."

Mom rushes to make nice. "Oh, you're just as excited to see him as I am, Bill. And this is his boyfriend, Chase. He's not Jewish after all. Not that it would matter if he were."

Dad and Chase shake hands awkwardly. Chase is as smooth as they come, but Dad's gruffness makes everything prickly. "So sorry you're feeling under the weather, sir."

"Well, I appreciate you boys making the effort, but you didn't have to bother."

Chase switches into diplomat mode. "No bother at all. It's been a great bit of fun to see where Noah grew up."

Luke actually clears his throat and when I don't acknowledge him everyone starts looking at me like *I'm* somehow the bad guy. It finally gets so uncomfortable that I turn on my heel and give Luke an unenthusiastic, "Hey."

Luke bursts into a smile and shouts out, "Shakespeare returns!" His hand is up in the air and I'm astonished to realize that he's trying to high-five me.

"First of all, I'm an adult and adults don't high-five. Secondly, don't call me that." Unsure what to do with his hand, he thrusts it toward Chase. "I'm Luke."

Chase smiles a little too much for my liking. "Cheers. Chase Abrams."

They do a manly handshake. "We used to call Noah Shakespeare all the time in high school. He was always writing stuff."

"Well, Luke, I prefer Noah. Mainly because it's my name, but also because calling me Shakespeare makes absolutely no sense. Shakespeare wrote plays. I write musicals. It might make sense if you would have called me Sondheim or Richard Rodgers . . ."

Luke blinks. "I don't know who either of those people are."

"Of course you don't."

Luke has the gall to sit on the edge of Dad's bed. "Well, I know your dad is sure glad you made the trip." Luke pats Dad's knee like they're frat buddies. "You gave us all a scare there, Mr. A."

Mr. A? *This fucking guy.*

Chase does his best to keep the conversation going. "So, Luke, you work at the farm now?"

Dad proudly responds for Luke. "Oh, he's great with animals. A real natural."

I remind myself to breathe. In with the good air, out with the resentment over the fact that your father and Luke Carter are apparently BFFs.

It takes me a second to realize that Luke is studying Chase and me like we're some kind of puzzle he can't quite put together. "So, Noah, you got yourself a British guy!"

"Wow, you can detect accents?" I reply with mock surprise. "Did you take a course at the local community college or something?"

Luke actually looks confused. Or hurt. Mom gives me a disapproving scowl, then soldiers on, adjusting Dad's pillow to his great dismay. "Now, Bill, honey, they're going to let you out tomorrow and we can put this whole thing behind us." She turns to me. "So, Noah, we all want to hear about your play!"

"Musical," I mutter.

"Musical. You know, Chase, he forbid us from coming to opening night. Said we'd just make him nervous. We figured we'd fly up and catch it when all the dust settled."

Do we have to have this conversation in front of the ever-present Luke Carter? Is he always going to be around now? Driving our tractors? Patching the roof of our barn? Standing around with his hypnotizing greenish-hazel eyes and his very distracting biceps? Wait, is he flexing them? This is a hospital, not a gym.

I return my attention to Mom.

"Well, you can't see it now. It's closed. Big old flop." I cast my dead eyes out the window to stare at the parking lot as Chase consolingly rubs my back. Having another man rub my back in front of Dad is odd, but I'm too depressed to care.

"Well, surely somebody videotaped it, right?"

"Mom, that's not . . . there are issues with the unions, so they can't tape it. They'd have to pay everyone. The Lincoln Center library would usually record the show for their archives, but we didn't even run long enough to warrant that."

At this revelation, the entire room looks a little sad for me, even Dad. Which I hate. To my complete surprise, Luke's the one to change the topic.

"So, Shakespeare. Sorry. Noah. You excited for tonight?"

I pause. "What's tonight?"

Mom, Dad, and Luke share a round-robin of furtive looks.

"Dang it! Was it supposed to be a surprise? Oh, man, nobody told me!" Luke tugs guiltily at his stupid backward baseball cap.

And Mom consoles him right on cue. "Don't worry, Luke. It's no big deal."

"What's tonight?" I repeat.

Mom's all smiles. "The Plainview Players are having a little reception for you."

"They're the local community theater," Luke explains to Chase, seemingly committed to staying in the conversation.

Mom launches into full brag mode. "That's right! And they are just busting their buttons about Noah. He's been doing plays there since the fifth grade. People still talk about how he stole the show when he played an enchanted boulder in *Robin Hood*."

Chase gives me a confused look. "There's an enchanted boulder in *Robin Hood*?"

I give a tired shrug and say, "Apparently."

"Anyway . . ." Mom chatters away. "They also let him put on all of his little shows. All the other moms in town had to worry where their kids were at night, but I didn't. I knew exactly where Noah was. He was at the Plainview Players, teaching them his songs and generally ordering everyone around."

Chase nods. "He can be very bossy."

Mom seems elated. "But they loved it! And him! Noah made them all feel like stars! Like professional Broadway stars! Noah can really cast a spell when he wants to. Anyway, they're throwing him a little to-do tonight."

I have to put a stop to this. "And I am not going."

Mom looks like I've just slapped her in the face and says, "You most certainly are, young man."

"I'm not going to stand there and have them celebrate the worst professional disaster of my life."

Mom glares at me impatiently. "Now, Noah, they don't think of it as a disaster. They're thrilled about it. You got a show to Broadway, honey. They're all impressed beyond words!"

"That's because they don't know how real theater works. There is nothing to celebrate."

Luke stands up and leans casually against the wall, crossing his arms to make his biceps bulge in an even more annoyingly distracting way. "From what I hear, they've really pulled out all the stops, Shakespeare. Noah, I mean."

"They brought in toasted ravioli from St. Louis!" Mom adds,

as if that somehow seals the deal. When I don't react, she repeats, "From St. Louis!"

"I don't care if they've flown in a naked Lady Gaga on a Goodyear blimp. I'm not going."

"There'll be booze," Luke adds.

"It *is* sounding better," Chase offers, like the traitor he is.

"Why can't you guys understand how colossally embarrassing this whole thing is for me?" Oh, God, I'm flat out whining now.

And then Dad weighs in. "Stop being a prick, Noah." That silences the room.

I stare at him incredulously. "I'm not being . . . you can't call me a prick, Dad."

"I can if you're acting like one." I try, but can't find any reasonable response to that. Dad elaborates. "These people took time out of their busy lives and money out of their pockets to put together a celebration in your honor. They made an effort, son. And you're not gonna spit in their faces. I'm sorry your show closed. I'm sorry it wasn't the next *Hamilson*—"

"He means *Hamilton*," I whisper to Chase, who nods.

"But you need to quit the bellyaching and pull yourself up by the bootstraps and show those nice people a little gratitude."

The room grows still and Dad gives me the coldest stare he has in his arsenal. And I reflect it right back.

Sensing an impasse, Mom decides to step in. "Well, Chase, Luke, I'm sorry you boys have to see this, but I'm going to have to go with the nuclear option."

My face fills with dread as I turn to her. "Don't. You. Dare."

But before I can stop her she's wrapped her arms around me

and is shaking me back and forth in a hug, using her squeakiest baby voice to chant, "Where's my little sweet potato at? Where's my sweet potato at? I know he's under that tough New York exterior, I wanna know WHERE'S MY LITTLE SWEET POTATO AT?!?"

I wriggle out from her embrace and give her a lethal look. "All right, I'll go! Just stop that!"

Both Chase and Luke are staring at me with bemused expressions. Only Dad has the common decency to avert his eyes.

Mom, of course, looks very proud of herself. "I know to everyone else he looks like a grown man, but deep down inside he's just my little sweet potato. I just have to summon him sometimes. Sort of like a reverse exorcism kind of a deal."

Chase slowly shakes his head. "If only I had known that to get my way with your son, I simply had to talk to him as if he were a very small poodle."

I give Chase a sideways glance. "You get your way enough."

Dad coughs and says, "Can someone ask one of those nurses for a bedpan? I gotta shit."

And that was our cue to leave.

Luke rides the elevator down with us. Because, of course.

And though most people look wilted from the relentless August heat, Luke looks fresh enough to shoot a shampoo commercial. He's removed his cap and his perfect blond curls somehow aren't matted down. Instead they look as if they've been carefully zhuzhed by one of Beyoncé's stylists. Whatever.

Luke tries to make small talk with Chase and me, I guess to show us that he's no longer a complete asshole.

"So, how did you guys meet? What's your origin story?" Origin story? Who talks like that? Clearly someone's read too many comic books.

I ignore him, so Chase answers. "I was on a panel at the Dramatists Guild and couldn't take my eyes off this guy. So when it was over, I accidentally on purpose stole his umbrella, a trick I learned from *Howards End* . . . I knew he'd come running down the hallway after me."

"It was a very expensive umbrella. It was from Paul Smith and I was poor," I add, half-heartedly.

"Wow, that's like the beginning of a movie or something."

And without warning, somewhere inside of me a switch is flipped and I'm furious.

"You know, Luke, it's nice of you to pretend you're not a raging homophobe, but no one in the elevator is buying it."

Luke looks hurt and, even more irritatingly, so does Mom. We reach the ground floor and Luke walks off without another word. Mom hisses my name as she exits the elevator.

Chase hangs back to answer his phone, but I'm right behind Mom, chasing her across the hospital lobby.

"Why are you mad at *me*? You know what Luke and his friends started calling me freshman year? It wasn't just Shakespeare, no, it quickly morphed into Shakes-*queer*! Every day in the hallways, in the cafeteria, in the parking lot. And they knew I was too scrawny and too afraid to fight back. Four years of 'Hey, Shakes-queer! How many dicks did you suck last night?' And the whole school laughing along while I pretended to have gone spontaneously deaf. And you want me to just forget all that?"

Mom stops short and turns to me, her eyes unable to meet mine for a moment. I continue on. "He scarred me, Mom. And you're suddenly his biggest fan? I just don't get it!"

Our eyes lock and she grabs my arm and squeezes desperately. "But people can change, Noah. I'm sorry if he did all that, but he's different now or your dad never would have hired him. And maybe I believe in . . . in . . . I don't know, in redemption."

And with that she crumbles into tears. And Mom doesn't crumble. So it's particularly terrible. I gather her up into my arms and immediately realize that she's also talking about Dad. If I don't think Luke can change, how can I think Dad can change? Not that I think Dad's homophobic, but I certainly don't think he'll be starting a PFLAG chapter any time soon.

But the important thing now is to comfort Mom, so I squeeze her tighter.

"Redemption?" I hazard. "That's a pretty fancy word. Have you been digging around in my thesaurus?"

Mom chuckles into my shoulder. "I figured it would impress you, being three syllables and all." She pulls a Kleenex from her purse and blows her nose in an unnecessarily loud way. Apparently pulled back together, she comes up with a plan. "I know what I'm going to do. I'm going to ask Luke to apologize for whatever he said to you in high school and we can all start over with a clean slate."

"That is the exact *opposite* of what you're going to do. I'll just let it go. I'll just figure out a way to let it go. Or push it down into my dark subconscious like I did back then. We're only here for a couple of nights. It doesn't matter. I'll just tell myself it doesn't matter."

Mom puts the used Kleenex back in her purse instead of throwing it away because she's Mom. "And he's not taking your 'filial place,' he's working for your father and they just happen to like each other. They can yak about cars together."

"I don't get the big deal. Aren't cars just metal boxes with wheels?"

We're in the hospital entranceway when Mom stops in her tracks. "Oh, wait! I told your Aunt Sandy I'd get her some See's candy from the gift shop."

"Why are you buying food from a hospital, Mom?"

"It's the only place that sells See's candy and Sandy likes See's candy." She rushes off as Chase approaches.

"Everything okay?" he asks as Luke pulls out of the parking lot in his rusty pickup truck. If Luke notices Chase and me watching him drive past, he pretends not to.

"Of course he drives a beat-up pickup." I huff. "He's like every country music video I never wanted to sit through."

# four

# "Isn't This a Great Idea?"

The Plainview Players building was once an abandoned movie theater until the late 1980s when the group refurbished it in a pretty spectacular fashion. The art deco structure always stood out in our humble little town. It's overly grand and gaudy and I love it for that very reason. The place always smells like fresh paint because someone is constantly building sets in the back of the building. My heart leaps a little when we pull into the parking lot. The building was my second home when I was growing up. A refuge of colored lights and adorably homespun costumes. A place that encouraged singing and tap dancing and ridiculously outsized dreams of grandeur. Where the topic was *never* LeBron James and was *always* Patti LuPone.

Mom stops the car and turns to lecture me. She's dressed up but still has paint under her fingernails. And her tangle of gray and black hair is in its usual disordered state.

"So, honey, everyone put a lot of effort into this little celebration. So you can't offend these nice people. This might not be one of your New York City parties, but they did their best. So act grateful. Don't forget your manners. You can't be like a bull in a china shop right now."

Clearly, she thinks I'm some sort of monster.

"I'm not gonna be a bull in a china shop, Mom. I'm gonna be like . . ." I consider. "Like *china* in a china shop. Although, I've never actually been in a china shop."

Chase is sitting next to Mom in the front seat. He puts a consoling hand on her shoulder. "Don't worry. If he gets even the slightest bit flinty, you have my permission to publicly launch your sweet potato reverse exorcism."

I narrow my eyes at Chase. "Your betrayal has been duly noted."

Mom gives an exasperated look. "I don't understand why you can't just enjoy tonight."

I stare out the car window at the theater marquee. It reads, "Congratulations, Noah!" Congratulations on what? Trying and failing? Thinking I was more talented that I actually was?

And out of the blue, the truth appears in the car like a fourth passenger.

"I can't just enjoy tonight because . . ." And I try not to choke up. "Because I let them down. I let them all down." Both Mom and Chase look at me with such pity that I dissolve into tears on the spot. "I was supposed to come back here the conquering hero, you know? I wanted to make these people proud of me. I wanted to show them that all of the years they let me put on shows here paid off. And now I have to walk in there like the towering disappointment that I am."

Mom's voice is warm in a way that only Mom's voice can be. "You didn't let them down, Noah. You didn't let anyone down."

Chase reaches back to put a hand on my knee. "From what I can tell, you're the Plainview Players' favorite son. All they understand is that you made it to Broadway. They want to celebrate that fact with you. So let them. Pull yourself together and let them."

I nod. Marching orders received. I dry my face and stoically climb out of the car. I can do this. Everything is fine. When we walk into the theater lobby it seems smaller than I remember, but just as heartbreakingly lovable. The lobby's makeshift ticket booth that was repurposed from Lucy's psychiatrist office from a production of *You're a Good Man, Charlie Brown*. The crystal chandelier that some rich doctor's wife had donated to the theater and was previously seen onstage in *Hello, Dolly!* The concession stand has the aroma of stale popcorn that takes me back to when I was performing in their children's shows. And then there are the Plainview Players themselves, who give a hilariously large cheer as we enter the room. It immediately seems impossible that I ever considered not coming tonight.

"Oh, stop!" I shout over the cheering, with mock embarrassment.

The first person to approach us is my high school literature teacher and cheerleader of all things me, Marilyn Henson. She's dressed to the Plainview nines and smiling like a lunatic, and I love her for it. She's pleasantly plump and a giver of enthusiastic hugs. And unlike me, she would never say an unkind word about anyone.

"Noah, we are just pleased as punch that you came! I mean, Broadway! To have a show on Broadway, that is just such a feather in your cap!"

Chase looks on as Mrs. Henson gushes, charmed by it all. Mom has already abandoned us for a glass of wine and a couple of toasted raviolis.

"This is my boyfriend, Chase. Chase, this is Mrs. Henson."

"Oh, Noah, you're an adult now. You can call me Marilyn."

"You will always be Mrs. Henson to me."

She gives my right cheek three quick pats and we share a giggle.

Mrs. Henson turns her attention to Chase. "Now, Chase, I know we must look like a bunch of hayseeds to you, but we just love Noah so much we could eat him for breakfast."

Chase chuckles. "Yes, well, he does go quite nicely with an English muffin."

I interrupt before things get even weirder. "Mrs. Henson inspired my love for theater when she cast me as Moonface Martin in *Anything Goes*."

Mrs. Henson giggles. "The part required a New York accent and Noah was the only one who could even come close to pulling it off."

"I did it up an octave for some reason. So think New York accent crossed with a very gay Jerry Lewis on cocaine."

"Oh, look! There's Melissa! She's been dying to see you! Melissa, come say hi to Noah and his friend, Chase!"

Thank God for Melissa Fazio. She's the only person from high school I even attempted to stay in touch with. We were always honest with one another to a fault. Like junior year when I had to tell her that her hair extensions made her look like a Bratz doll. Or the night before prom when she let me know that Day-Glo animal prints were not my friend. The only glitch in our relationship was when I tried to convince myself I was straight and I felt her up in the band room closet. After a few weeks of radio silence we decided to never speak of it again and fell right back into our old friendship. It isn't until Melissa turns around that I realize she is very, very pregnant.

"Hi, Noah. Congratulations on everything!"

"Holy crap! How did I not know you were pregnant?"

"Um, maybe because I only see you at Christmas and you haven't been home for three years?"

I hang my head in shame. "I suck at keeping in touch. Tell me everything. Are you married now or are you carrying someone's bastard child?" I ask.

Mrs. Henson gives out a shocked, "Noah!"

Melissa laughs it off. "It's okay, Marilyn. This is how we talk to one another. I'm glad we got our old rhythm back so quickly. So, Noah, if you must know, I got married three years ago. I didn't invite you because I knew you were too busy to come. I'm magnanimous like that. I'm not one of those people who sends a nonvitation just to rack up wedding gifts."

I shake my head and smile. "You always were a class act. What's your husband like?"

"I just so happen to be married to a very bald and very loving pharmacist. He gives me a lady boner every time I look at him."

Mrs. Henson titters nervously. "Oh, you kids. Let's watch the language."

Melissa is clearly annoyed at being chastised. "Jesus, Marilyn, lighten up. Go grab a merlot."

"That sounds like a very good idea."

She disappears into the crowd and Melissa turns to Chase. "I'm Melissa, one of Noah's friends that he discarded when he moved to the big city. But he once talked me out of getting a Flo Rida tattoo, so he's forgiven for abandoning me."

I take the opportunity to look at Chase through Melissa's eyes. The Clooney eyebrows, the thick black hair slicked back to perfection, the shoulder muscles giving his shirt seams a run for their money. I stand a little taller. How is all of that mine?

Chase shakes Melissa's hand, all smiles. "It's wonderful to meet you. This little trip has given me a much clearer picture of Noah's childhood. It's been very enlightening, to say the least."

"Have you met anyone else from his Plainview High days?"

"Only the controversial Luke Carter."

Melissa breaks into a knowing smile. "Oh, yes. Good old Luke. He's here somewhere."

"Whoa, wait, what? Luke is here? What the hell is he doing here?"

Unbelievable. He's like a six-foot-something piece of gum that I can't unstick from my shoe.

Mom's back and handing Chase a plate of toasted ravioli. "They're from St. Louis!"

"We know, Mom!"

"Well, I think it's a very thoughtful touch. And if you're not going to introduce Chase around to everyone, then I will." She grabs Chase's arm and whisks him away.

Melissa watches them go. "So, you snagged yourself a hot piece of ass."

I smile, satisfied with myself. "He gives me all kinds of lady boners."

"Not to be rude, but what's with your mom's hair?"

I shrug. "It's never known a friendly chemical."

Melissa's eyes light up. "Well look who's here! Speak of the devil and the devil pops up."

I turn to see Luke lingering behind me. We stare at one another like a couple of idiots. He's wearing a tragic sports jacket that happens to be more misguided than a Frank Wildhorn musical. Is he actually making an effort?

Luke gestures to the room. "So, this is pretty cool, right? I mean, look at all of these people. Quite a turnout."

I remember my vow to play nice. "I guess so. So, what . . . what are you doing here?"

"Your dad always helps the Players build their sets. He started because of you, obviously, but now it's just kind of a hobby of his. He asked me if I'd help out, since he's getting older and moving slower."

Melissa launches into brag mode. "Luke built an actual turntable for our production of *Fiddler on the Roof*. I mean, it was *automated*. The people over at the Irvington Community Theater were green with envy."

Luke gets humble and shrugs. "It was just a wooden disk and a bunch of casters."

Melissa refuses to back down. "It was more than that. Believe me, Noah, you've never sung 'Anatevka' until you've sung it on a revolving floor. There wasn't a dry eye in the house."

And with that, big, macho Luke actually starts to blush. "Just a wooden disk and a bunch of casters," he repeats.

Melissa gives Luke a playful shove. "It was magic. And the set he built for Chekhov's *Four Sisters*!"

I stop her. "*FOUR Sisters*?"

"Well, so many women auditioned that we had to add a sister. We had two Mashas."

Bite your tongue, Noah. Just bite it until it bleeds.

Melissa pauses and eyes me up. "So, it's got to feel strange to be back here. But we all knew you'd make it someday. You always knew exactly what you wanted back in high school. You were always busy writing your plays—"

"Musicals." I can't help but correct her.

"Musicals and directing them and putting them on here and carrying a briefcase . . ."

And now it's my turn to blush. "Oh God, I *did* carry a briefcase. What the hell was that all about?"

Melissa laughs. "Oh, you were all business. You were way more evolved than the rest of us backpack carriers. It was like the rest of us were kids, but you were already a grown-up, hyper-focused on the career you wanted to have. And look at you now. You've made it all happen. You're a Broadway writer. It's just crazy, you know?"

I can't help myself and blurt out, "A failed Broadway writer. My career is officially a garbage fire with extra tires."

Melissa's smile turns slightly strained, and it becomes clear to me that the demise of *Stage of Fools* has been fodder for gossip amongst the Plainview Players.

And then Luke butts in. "But you did have a show on Broadway, right?"

"For one night."

"Doesn't that still count?" Luke asks.

Melissa's curious, too. "Yeah, Noah, doesn't that still count?"

They're both staring at me as if I'm withholding information about a very secretive club. I try my best not to look like a petulant toddler. "I don't know . . . I guess."

I turn to catch Chase staring at me from across the room. Wait—no, not me. He's staring at Luke and I'm instantly flooded with adolescent jealousy. And I remember the reason Luke Carter is here in the first place. Because of Dad. And now my boyfriend of almost two years is staring at him like a hungry wolf that's stumbled upon a buffet of human babies. Fucking Luke Carter. Is there no relationship of mine he can't steal?

Blatant disdain must be clearly written all over my face, because Luke asks carefully, "Everything okay, Shakespeare?" He catches himself. "Noah, I mean."

Before I can answer, someone starts clinking a glass. Oh God, please don't let anyone make a speech.

It's Mrs. Henson, her teeth stained with red wine. "Can I have everyone's attention? We'd like you all to move into the theater now."

People slowly drift into the auditorium and start taking seats. I quickly find Chase and Mom. As we sit, I can't stop myself from whispering to Chase, "Were you checking out Luke Carter or am I seeing things?"

Chase is immediately dismissive. "You're hallucinating."

Far from mollified, I shift my attention to the old stage and let nostalgia wash over me. The dusty red velvet curtains with gold fringe frame the proscenium like an outrageous wig. A new silver drop that I've never seen before covers the rest of the stage as if it's concealing some kind of mystery prize on *The Price Is Right*.

"Looks like they've got some big presentation prepared," Chase says.

"Yikes. I hope they don't want me to reprise my role as the enchanted boulder in *Robin Hood*. I don't remember my lines."

Mom overhears and says, "You didn't have any lines. Just pure stage presence and very expressive eyes. You stole the show."

Once everyone is seated, Mrs. Henson takes the stage, working a microphone like a small-town politician running for office.

"Thank you all for coming here tonight. What a crowd! I've never seen the parking lot so full. Now, we all know why we're here. We're here to celebrate the Broadway debut of our native son and pride and joy, Noah Adams!"

Thunderous applause.

Chase looks completely touched by the enthusiasm.

I whisper into his ear, "I'm going to need approximately forty-six blow jobs tonight to help me forget this."

Chase chuckles. "I'll put a reminder in my iPhone."

I scan the auditorium and catch Luke's eyes. He's sitting several rows away and has removed his hideous sports jacket. He gives me a smile and a nod as if we're best friends. Does he think I've forgiven him for how he used to treat me? Or doesn't he even remember torturing me at all? I'm not sure what's more upsetting. Anger flashes over me and I refuse to smile back at him. In honor of scrawny teenage Noah, there will be no smiles for Luke Carter this evening. It must be obvious how I feel, because Luke's grin evaporates into thin air.

Mrs. Henson continues on. "Now, Noah, you're gonna hate me, but I'm gonna need you to join me onstage if this whole thing is gonna work here."

I should have known I'd have to say something. I also should have listened more carefully to the phrase "this whole thing." But I doggedly get up and climb the steps to the stage. Mrs. Henson gives my arm a squeeze as everyone giggles like the munchkins from *The Wizard of Oz*.

"So we've been a little sneaky here at the Plainview Players. Brace yourself, Noah, because you're in for a surprise!"

The fake smile plastered across my face is so tight it hurts. Surprise? I don't do surprises. I'm terrible with surprises. They throw off what little balance I have.

"So I'm just going to ask our fabulous volunteer stage crew to go ahead and raise the drop so we can end all this suspense."

A bunch of clapping and hooting from the crowd and I feel a whoosh of air as the stage drop ascends into the rafters behind me. The proscenium is immediately bathed in colored light and it takes my eyes a couple of seconds to focus. When they do, I'm gobsmacked to see a set that is an exact replica of the Broadway version of *Stage of Fools*.

I look at Mrs. Henson with what I can only assume is an expression of abject terror. "What is happening?"

Mrs. Henson looks practically giddy. "Well, we've spoken with your agent, Chase, and he's given us the rights to do the first amateur production of *Stage of Fools*! So the million-dollar question is: Will you direct it for us? Will you direct our production, Noah?"

I look into the audience in complete confusion. I can't see Chase because of the lights. I can't see anyone, but I can feel their hopeful looks rushing toward me in an avalanche that might as well be labeled "Isn't This a Great Idea?"

And then I say with a little too much force, "Oh, God, no!"

I'd like to say I imagined it, but I'm pretty sure there was a communal gasp. So, I give a painfully awkward chuckle and add, "You guys are kidding, right?" And it quickly becomes horribly apparent that they aren't.

"Oh. Huh." The room is so frozen we might as well have been packed inside an enormous gelatin mold. "I'm . . . I'm gonna have to get back to you on that."

# five

# "But, Great Gal."

Minutes later, I sit shell-shocked on the car ride home. Mom's driving her janky Toyota and I'm riding shotgun.

"They want Louis Jenkins to play Lear?" I ask, trying to wrap my mind around things. "I mean, isn't he a manager at a barbecue sauce factory?"

Mom gives a dismissive huff. "A damn good barbecue sauce and mostly because of Louis. He's in quality control. So obviously he knows a thing or two about subtlety and finesse of flavor."

"Subtlety and finesse of flavor? You've been watching too many Food Network shows."

"Oh, Noah, he has a beautiful singing voice! And now that his dreadlocks have gone gray, his look is perfect!"

Hmmm. The gray dreadlocks are pretty impressive. But I can't lose focus.

"And they want the McNew twins to play Goneril and Regan?

Those two do know that they don't have to dress alike anymore, right? I mean, they're in their forties. They remind me of the twins from *The Shining*, except for the fact that they've clearly gone through menopause."

Mom shrugs. "What do you expect? This town is full of kooks. They found a human skull in the reservoir last year and nobody even blinked an eye."

"Sounds like the twins might fit their roles perfectly," Chase says. I turn to glare at him.

Chase gives me an exhausted look. "Listen, Noah. They told me it would only be a month-long commitment and they wanted it to be a surprise. They've already assigned all the roles and memorized the songs and dialogue. You basically just have to tell them where to stand and give encouraging notes. And now with your dad's health issues, wouldn't it make sense to be here for a bit? Your mother was very keen on the idea."

I turn to focus my wrath on Mom. "So you two have been in cahoots this whole time?"

"I emailed Chase the day after your show opened and closed, if that counts as being in cahoots. I told him that these are very sweet and caring people. You won't have to do much, just make them feel like stars, just like you used to back in high school. Be nice to them and don't expect too much, they're not professional performers."

"You don't say," I mumble.

"Mrs. Henson said she'd be your assistant, so she'll probably end up doing most of the work. It'll be easier than falling off a log."

Chase continues on. "And it might be good to take the time you need to lick your wounds after everything that's happened with the show. I'll change your return ticket. Just indulge the Plainview Players for four little weeks, then fly back to New York and start considering what's next writing-wise."

"Why are you so gung ho about this?"

"Because I know you, Noah. You dwell. You're the sensei master of dwelling. This will take your mind off things for a few weeks."

"And you'll get to be home tomorrow when your dad gets out of the hospital," Mom adds. "It'll mean a lot to him. He helped them build that set, you know. He volunteered himself. Well, him and Luke. They put a lot of hard work into it. So we can pick your father up tomorrow and the three of us can take him out to a nice dinner at Bumpkins."

"Bumpkins?" Chase asks, probably happy to change the subject.

"Country Bumpkins is the most offensively named restaurant in America. Well, right after Sambo's, I guess."

Chase asks incredulously, "There are restaurants named Sambo's? As in the very racist 'Little Black Sambo'?"

"I think they're all closed now. Although I'm not sure. But if you ask me, the name Country Bumpkins is offensive to their very unsuspecting clientele. And they serve nothing but deep-fried atrocities."

Mom scoffs. "Oh, stop it, you two. They have great soups. It's no Cracker Barrel, but it does the trick."

"If the trick is offering food poisoning and sadness, then technically you're right, Mom."

"Noah prides himself on being finicky. He refuses to eat casseroles," Mom informs Chase.

"That's because casseroles are made out of whatever you find left over in the kitchen garbage disposal."

"Don't listen to him, Chase. I make a lovely casserole."

"The only things you make are deluded conclusions about your casserole-making capabilities."

"Jeepers McCreepers, someone's in a mood." She pauses, and then asks, "Where's my little sweet potato at?"

"He died in a fire." I sigh. "Back to the Plainview Players."

Mom pulls into the driveway as she makes one more pitch, "Have a heart, Noah! Honestly, you're so frosty sometimes it's like you were raised by Chechen wolves."

I consider asking her why these imaginary wolves have to be Chechen, but decide it's probably best not to pull at that thread.

Besides, I have bigger things to consider.

Like am I really going to stay in Plainview and direct a community theater production of my flop Broadway show? Couldn't I find something more pleasant to do? Maybe eat a box of X-Acto knives?

But then it all comes rushing back to me. The way they all looked so crushed when I said no. And I loved every last one of them when I was a kid. I also knew I had to fulfill a silent deal I had made with God back then. I had prayed every night, "Let me get to Broadway and I swear I will pay it back. Or pay it forward. I will contribute somehow." And God in all Her wisdom had finally sent me the bill for managing to get three professional shows produced in Manhattan.

So, maybe I was going to direct the Plainview Players production of *Stage of Fools* after all.

As we enter the house, Mom threatens to cook. "If you boys are hungry, I thought I could make us some Crock-Pot pizza."

I sigh and close my eyes. "What the hell is that?"

"Oh Noah, it's delicious. You just take some tomato sauce, some cheese and some biscuit dough and throw it in the Crock-Pot and serve it with a ladle and eat it."

"You know I love you, Mom, but I would rather be locked in a room with those Chechen wolves you speak of."

Mom brushes me off.

"You see, Chase? You see what I'm dealing with here?"

Chase concurs. "He's a terror."

"I've also got some cottage cheese you could eat with saltine crackers. And there's a Jell-O casserole."

"A Jell-O casserole?" I scoff. "Why do you only have nursing home food?"

"Don't be a snob, Noah. It's delicious and brightly colored."

I turn to Chase in defeat. "If you eat anything that this crazy crone offers you, you only have yourself to blame."

"I'm full of toasted ravioli," Chase answers.

"They were from St. Louis!" Mom enthuses.

I glare at her. "When did your brain break?"

Mom gives Chase a shrug. "He teases because he loves."

"Guilty as charged." I wrap Mom in a hug, and then grab a tub of ice cream from the freezer, settling at the dining table as she rattles on.

"Oh, get this! It turns out that Leila Loomis has been faking her diabetes. I mean, full-on faking it for attention, I guess. She had everyone at Bible study completely convinced that she was going to have her foot partially amputated and that she was going to have to wear a specially made shoe. And we believed her the whole time while she was lying right to our faces." And then Mom adds her standard guilty deflection. "But, great gal. Great gal. Bless her heart."

"Yes, Mom, bless her fake diabetic heart." Chase joins me at the table and I offer him a spoonful of ice cream. He immediately declines, because, you know, abs.

"And I don't mean to be blunt, and Chase, I am not a gossip, because everybody knows it. But our mail delivery guy's wife is a floozy. Her jean shorts leave nothing to the imagination. But, great gal. Great gal."

"Mom calls people 'great gals' when she feels guilty about gossiping about them. As in, 'Well, you know Dawn Fairchild and her family? She comes from a long line of whores dating back to Christopher Columbus times. I mean, she's the product of a long string of sweaty, toothless prostitutes. But, great gal!'"

Mom swats the back of my head with a dish towel. "I should wash your mouth out with soap. And apparently you don't want anything to eat besides ice cream, so I'm going to bed." She stops in her tracks. "Make sure to lock the front door before you come up."

"Yes, Mom, this town is full of marauders."

"But it *is*! Marauders and kooks!"

And with that, she's gone. I return the ice cream to the freezer and turn to Chase. He gets up from the table and slowly pulls me into a hug. It kills me every time how perfectly my chin fits on top of his sculpted shoulder. We softly click together like two human puzzle pieces. The heat from his neck makes my eyelids flutter and my muscles go slack.

"You looked adorable up on that stage. All cheekbones and confusion."

According to Chase, my cheekbones have Timothée Chalamet's beat. I highly doubt it, but Chase gets an A-plus for flattery. He exhales softly into my hair and I feel the last of my resolve draining into the hardwood floor. One of his hands slips under my shirt and over to my lower back. His fingers lightly trace up and down my spine. It's Chase's standard move when he wants something from me and it works like gangbusters.

I frantically start to fiddle with his belt and whisper, "We've got to get you out of those stupid pants immediately."

Chase grabs my wrists and tries to get me back on topic.

"Just say you'll do the show, Noah."

"Okay. But I'm going to miss you like crazy."

Chase takes my face in his hands and gazes into my eyes.

"It's just a month. And it's August. You know how nothing gets done in August. Everyone decamps to the Hamptons until the first Tuesday after Memorial Day. Manhattan is a ghost town until then. But sleep on it, if you like."

I give Chase a half-hearted nod and we climb the stairs and walk into my bedroom. I'm embarrassed at how stuck in time it is. And by the psychotic amount of *Evita* merchandise that's on display. Chase gives the room a once-over. "Hmm. Some little boy appears to have had a thing for singing, bloodthirsty Argentinian dictators."

"I'll never know if I really loved the show or just fantasized about getting to try on the 'Don't Cry for Me Argentina' dress."

And like a quick-change artist, Chase is rapidly stripped of all of his clothes except for his magnificently tight boxer briefs. Does he know how my pulse skyrockets at the sight of his muscular thighs fighting against the fabric? He must, because I'm looking at him with unapologetic lust.

I start to reach for his bare, ridiculously toned chest, but he's too busy pulling on sweatpants to notice. I'm disgruntled and I let it be known. "Hey, why are you putting on sleepy time clothes?"

Chase looks confused. "Because it's time for sleep?"

"But I just thought . . ."

Chase looks around my childhood bedroom as if it's a backed-up sewer. "It's kind of creepy, isn't it? The thought of having sex in your parents' house? And with so many Eva Peróns watching us? I'm also just knackered, to be honest."

I nod, resigned.

I go to the bathroom to brush my teeth and call Kiara. I explain how I've been cajoled into mounting an amateur version of my show starring a barbecue factory worker and a pair of possibly deranged adult twins. To my surprise, she's not appalled.

"They sound like a sweet group of people. And Chase is right about getting your mind off things. So, you know, maybe don't look a gift horse in the mouth."

"I've never understood that phrase. Why is someone gifting

me a horse? Are they assuming I have a place to keep the horse? Like I have that kind of storage space? Also, the last thing I would think to do when being gifted a horse is to check its teeth. I mean, with everything going on in my life, I now have to worry about horse dentistry?"

Kiara exhales. "Baby boy, I could explain it to you with historical references and all, but I think we'd both be bored to death, so we should just move on."

After hanging up with Kiara, I go back into the now dimly lit bedroom and see Chase lying on one side of the bed. He looks beyond irresistible. I snake my hand up his T-shirt and lightly graze his amazing collection of abs. I immediately get a raging hard-on and press it into his lower back. Chase answers me with a snore.

six

# "First Rehearsal Jitters"

Morning comes and I shamelessly beg Chase to stay. While we're hugging goodbye, he whispers into my ear, "Be a very good boy and I will send you many inappropriate texts when I get to New York."

Since this is community theater and everyone has real jobs, rehearsals are at night and on weekends. The day drags on slowly and the only real news is that the hospital wants to keep Dad one more day and he's hopping mad about it.

I dig through my bedroom closet and almost burst out laughing when I find the dated fake leather briefcase I carried around to rehearsals in high school. I pop it open and find a yellowed copy of a musical I wrote my junior year.

It was an adaptation of *Pinocchio*, which I chose because it was no longer under copyright. It was complete and utter trash. But I wrote it, directed it, and put it up with the enthusiastic help of the Plainview Players. Mrs. Henson led the charge and served as musical director.

I hesitantly open the script to a random page to see just how awful it really was. My eyes scan the lyrics for a song I wrote for Pinocchio and his father, Geppetto, just after Pinocchio had been brought to life.

> It gives me such a kick
> To see this little stick
> Is now my son!
> He once was dripping sap
> But now I am his pap
> I have a son!

Oh my fucking God. I turn red and chuck the script back into the closet. What was I thinking? And why didn't anyone stop me?

After that humiliating little stroll down memory lane, I head back into the kitchen to find Mom in a very cheery mood. "I'm having a breakfast burrito. Want one?"

I look down at Mom's plate, which contains a glob of scrambled eggs that manage to look both gelatinous and runny at the same time.

"No. I just want a cappuccino and maybe some toast."

"Well, I don't know where you're going to get yourself any fancy cappuccino around here."

"Mom, I sent you a very expensive cappuccino maker for your birthday."

"And I exchanged it for a very expensive Crock-Pot."

It's too early and I am too un-caffeinated for this malarkey. "Why would you do that?"

"Oh, Noah. I'm not going to sit around this kitchen drinking cappuccinos. I'm not French."

"Cappuccinos are Italian."

"Well, I'm not from Europe, then."

"So what am I supposed to do now? Make a cappuccino with your Crock-Pot?"

"You probably could. Crock-Pots are very versatile."

I fume and pour myself a depressingly plain cup of coffee. "It's fine, I'll just have to make do with an Americano for now."

Mom clucks. "Americano? What is that, Spanish?"

"It's also Italian. It's a cappuccino without foam."

"You know, with all of your cappuccino and Americano talk, you should probably just bite the bullet and move to Italy."

As I climb the stairs, I call back to her, "If I had a bullet it would be lodged squarely between my eyes."

Mom guffaws, which is probably the best sound in the world.

The day passes painfully slow as I flip sluggishly through the script of *Stage of Fools* and try to pinpoint where I went so catastrophically wrong. I also peruse the cast list that someone must have shoved in my fist as I staggered off the stage last night.

Louis Jenkins as King Lear. Well, at least he looks the part, with his weatherworn face and chronically sad eyes. And, of course, those majestic dreadlocks. It might work. And besides, beggars can't be choosers.

Melissa as Cordelia. Good call. I was home for Thanksgiving one year and caught her Cinderella in *Into the Woods*. I cried so hard when she sang "No One Is Alone" that I actually swallowed a contact lens. It somehow slid down my teary cheek and into my mouth. It's probably lodged in my lower intestine to this day.

And maybe Chase was right about the McNew twins. Maybe they were just the right amount of creepy for Goneril and Regan.

I then spot a name that makes me smile in spite of my resolve to find this whole little enterprise ludicrous. Abby Gupta. My grade school bus driver. When I was in seventh grade I got cast as Randolph MacAfee in the Plainview Players' production of *Bye Bye Birdie* and Abby played my mom. On the first day of rehearsal, she confided in me that she was originally hoping to be cast in the Chita Rivera role.

"I mean, my skin and hair combination alone should have made it a lock. But now I get to play your mom and we get to sing 'Ed Sullivan' together and that's just as good!"

Whenever it would rain that year, she'd sing to me as I climbed the steps of the bus, *"Gray skies are gonna clear up!"*

And together we'd belt, *"Put on a happy face!"*

Invariably someone would whisper "freak" as I took my seat on the bus. But I didn't care. I had an inside joke with an actual adult. Top that, you jealous grade school bullies! Abby was listed as playing Gloucester, most likely because not enough men had auditioned. This was typical of most community theaters. If you think you're going to do *Seven Brides for Seven Brothers*, you can think again. You're actually going to be doing *Seven Brides for Three Brothers and Four Cross-Dressing Middle-Aged Women with Badly Painted-On Beard Stubble.*

I scan the rest of the cast list and only a few other names seem vaguely familiar. Someone had stapled a rehearsal schedule to the cast list. Four weeks until the opening night performance on September 1st. Well, the opening night performance and the only performance. Should I be offended that they think my musical can only fill the theater once? Oh, why do I care? Only four weeks to go. Four weeks to pull off the impossible. And it all starts with tonight's first rehearsal.

Before I head over to the theater, my phone vibrates. It's a text from Chase: Landed safely. Wishing you were here so I could do things to your mouth.

I consider for a moment and then respond with a very Victorian: Upon my return, I should very much like to eat your ass like an apple.

To which he responds: Thanks for giving me a semi in the Uber. Sending good thoughts for the old man. Talk later. Xx.

The witching hour arrives and when I get to the theater, it's pretty much empty.

Even though it's just a community theater production, I realize that I have to perform my pencil ritual.

When you're the author of a musical, you have to be ready to make changes on the fly. Tweaks to the script and score come fast and furious. There's no time for computers or iPads. You've got to go old-school. Graphite on paper. So I find a sharpened Ticonderoga #2 pencil in my briefcase and prepare to put it behind my ear. It's a symbol to myself and to everyone in the room that I'm here to work. Let's get down to business. Daddy is in the house.

I melodramatically position the pencil with eyes closed. When

I look up, Luke is staring at me from the stage. "Luke? What are you doing here?"

"Finishing up the set. I sort of got put in charge after your dad's health scare. You're looking at your one-man stage crew."

"Terrific," I say flatly.

"What was that you were doing with your pencil? Is that how you get in the zone?"

"Just pretend you didn't see it. So who's the stage manager?"

Luke looks perplexed. "Um, I don't think we have one of those."

The beginnings of a headache start to percolate at the base of my skull. "Then who calls the show? The lighting cues? The sound cues?"

"Whoever's in the booth just follows along with the script and wings it. We're a little short on volunteers."

"Well, that is as cuckoo bananas as it is unacceptable," I grumble. "Who is going to call 'places'?"

"What does 'places' mean?"

The headache climbs the back of my skull and does a starburst over my entire cranium as I rub my eyes in agony. "'Places' means that everyone should get in their places because the show or rehearsal or what-have-you is about to start."

Luke rocks back on his heels in relief. "Oh, that's nothing! I can do that!"

I can only offer another flat, "Terrific."

Thankfully, I had the presence of mind to toss a bottle of Tylenol into my briefcase. I choke down two capsules and then stop to really examine the set. I have to admit, I'm impressed. It's rough around the edges, but it does look very similar to the Broadway spaceship interior. It's only fair to give credit where credit is due.

"So, the set looks great."

Luke bursts into a huge grin and it's so endearing that I almost smile myself. "Your dad and I wanted to get it right."

It's then that I realize he's wearing what people around these parts call a 'wife beater' and while I'm generally against any garment that's named after spousal abuse, when it's on a body like Luke Carter's, I'll allow it. Wait, what am I thinking? Even admiring Luke's impressive muscles is disrespectful to teenage Noah. The helpless kid Luke terrorized with his friends. Luke was the one who coined the phrase Shakes-queer. Screw that guy.

"There's the old briefcase!" Luke grins, possibly trying to erase the growing scowl on my face. "Did you ever think of naming it? Because I was thinking, you should call it 'The Executive.'" Luke laughs. I don't. I simply stare at him and quietly will him to leave the premises.

Out of nowhere, Mrs. Henson's voice rings through the auditorium. "This is so exciting!!!"

The cast starts to wander in as Luke dutifully sets up folding chairs and several long tables on the stage. No one is talking, except for a few whispers as they take their seats. Only Mrs. Henson is rambling on about what an honor it is to be part of an original show. Other than that, the vibe is odd. Are they actually nervous?

Thankfully, I spot Melissa grabbing a coffee from the kitchenette. She seems like a safe enough port in the storm, so I walk over to her and pat her pregnant stomach. "Hey, fatty."

Melissa turns to me, clearly surprised that I'm actually here. "Well, spill the beans. What made you say yes to all this?"

I put on a glib face. "Because these crazy people gave me my first chance. I told Mrs. Henson when I was fourteen that I wanted to write musicals and she had such faith in me that I actually started writing musicals. Of course, all of my professional ones have been soul-crushing failures. Which has made me start to wonder if flop shows are all I'm capable of. What if I'm just a one-trick pony?"

"Better than a no-trick pony."

"Look at us, pretending we know about livestock. Between you and me, I always get confused. Is it the unicorns that are fictional or is it the zebras?"

"Speak for yourself. I'm no stranger to animals. I had a gerbil in junior high."

"How did that go?"

"It died. I guess I should have cared more. Or at least considered naming it at some point."

"Okay, now your mothering instincts are starting to worry me. Maybe it's best if the minute you give birth you just drive straight to the nearest orphanage and deposit it on the front stoop. Or maybe you could raffle it off."

Melissa says brightly, "These are such helpful suggestions. I finally feel like I have the start of a plan!"

We sip our horrible coffee in silence until Melissa decides it's time to goad me. "You know, you have to start this rehearsal at some point, right? We can't just stand here all night awkwardly trading bon mots."

"Pretty women shouldn't use complicated words like 'bon mots.' It scares off the menfolk."

Melissa shoots me a jaded look. "Noah, just get this over with. I have a tiny human lodged inside of me feasting off what's left of my energy."

I nod my head and project my voice into the theater, WWE announcer–style. "Let's do this thing, bitches!"

Everyone looks back at me, clearly offended.

I pause and remind myself that calling people "bitches" is frowned upon in small-town America. "That's a term of endearment, obviously." Melissa's expression is one of brazen pity.

I try again: "Why don't we form a circle?"

From out of nowhere, Luke yells out, "Places!"

I give him an aggravated grimace and say, "That's not how that works. We're not taking our places, we're just circling up right now."

Luke nods solemnly. "My bad. I'll get it."

I suddenly can't ignore the strange vibe in the air as everyone joins the circle.

"Is everything okay, everybody?"

Mrs. Henson giggles. "We're all just kind of anxious. I guess we have those classic first rehearsal jitters. I mean, we just can't believe this is actually happening."

"I feel the same way!" I grin, probably a little too broadly. "So, Mrs. Henson is going to run through the songs. Let's just start at the top of the show."

Louis Jenkins raises his hand.

"Louis, you don't have to raise your hand. This isn't grade school."

He lowers it awkwardly. "Oh, okay. Well, I was just wondering. Aren't we going to do some kind of improv game to warm up? That's what we usually do. I mean, don't Broadway actors do that?"

"Uh . . . no." Broadway actors are professionals and time is money. There is no time for games.

One of the McNew twins, Jackie to be exact, raises her hand.

I remind them, "Everyone stop raising your hands. We're all adults here."

Although the fact that the twins are dressed in matching Hello Kitty t-shirts makes me wonder.

"The last show we did was *Mame* and to warm up, we would do that mirror exercise. Show him, Julia."

I watch slack-jawed as Julia and Jackie stand and start to pretend to be one another's reflection. They slowly form different poses and the fact that they're identical twins makes it especially disconcerting.

I scan the room and lock eyes with Melissa, who fights not to laugh as she pulls the collar of her shirt over her mouth.

"No, no, no. Let's just skedaddle along and get to singing through Act One."

People look genuinely disappointed.

Louis asks, "Any words of encouragement, then?"

I scan my brain for a second and realize that I'm probably not very good at being encouraging. "Well, um . . . every time you come into this theater, you have to put your egos aside. The show comes first. We're all in the same boat. Not everybody gets a star turn. We won't always agree with one another on things. But when you get hung up on something or feel lost, just ask yourself, 'What is best for the show?'"

Mrs. Henson bursts into a fevered smattering of applause and then realizes she's the only one. She looks around and then at me. "Sorry, that was just so very well said."

"Uh, thanks, I guess. Do you want to take the reins now?"

"Of course. Let's sing through the score." She sits down at a beaten-up piano and begins to play the opening number. As they warble through the songs, I find my eyes drifting back to the stage where Luke is bending over to paint the deck. He's wearing a ridiculously tight pair of jeans. I fight the urge to become completely hypnotized by his ass and lose. It's spectacular. And I'm looking away in five, four, three, two . . .

Mrs. Henson snaps me out of my trance. "Noah, is it okay if we take a break here? We've sung through all of Act One."

We have? How long was I staring at Luke?

I clear my throat and say with as much butch authority as I can muster, "Take ten."

"Coffee's in the kitchenette!" Mrs. Henson announces.

I wander over to Melissa, who has clearly been trying not to crack up this entire time.

"Don't look so worried, Noah. It's just the first day. We'll get there. Eventually."

"I'm not worried. You guys sounded great."

"We sounded nervous. We can tell you're comparing us to the

Broadway cast. Which is understandable, but completely unfair, mister."

"I'm doing no such thing."

I smile and try to surreptitiously check my phone. Not a word from Chase in hours. What's that all about?

Melissa notices and gives me a sympathetic look. "Missing your boyfriend already?"

"He's probably out doing something exciting and glamorous. An opening at an art gallery or maybe a jazz club in the village. Sipping martinis with big-time directors and producers and muckety-mucks."

"And you're here with Plainview's finest amateurs."

"He's not even been gone twelve hours and I'm already home-sick for him. And our friends. Our life together. You're never bored when Chase Abrams is around."

Melissa folds her arms and asks accusatorily, "So now we're boring you?"

I quickly shake my head. "No, not at all! I mean, this is fun and all, it's just . . ."

"It's just not New York City."

"It sure ain't," I reply wistfully. In a funny way, I know who I am in New York. I'm surrounded by risk-taking artists. And thankfully I get to be one of them. I'm also constantly drunk on the fast pace of the city, the exciting hum of a million things happening at once. The pace in Plainview is practically nonexis-tent. Which leaves plenty of time for memories of me as a kid, just dreaming of a way to escape it all.

Melissa mercifully snaps me back to life. "You'll be back with your hot British guy soon enough. But for now, we've got *Magic to Do!*"

Because I'm legally obligated, I respond, "*Let's go on with the show!*"

Once everyone is back from break, we start singing through Act Two. When it comes time for Louis Jenkins to sing Lear's big number, "Terrors of the Earth," something shocking happens. Louis stands up, opens his mouth, and this room-shaking baritone comes pouring out. The hairs on my arms start to rise. Everyone leans forward, savoring each note. And Louis actually has tears in his eyes by the time he hits the first chorus. When the song ends, everyone is silent and then bursts into applause. The whole cast has been transported by his performance. Once the room settles down, I take a moment to collect myself. It occurs to me that I've never been more moved by a performance of one of my songs. "That was amazing, Louis! Have you always been able to sing like that?"

Louis brushes it off. "Church choir."

"Well, it's very impressive." I pause for a second and remember Melissa's remark about how nervous I'm making everyone. So I add, "You know what, guys? You're actually very good! I mean, I know it's just the first rehearsal, but I'm honestly really encouraged by tonight! You guys are crazy talented. You should pat yourselves on the back!" A happy murmur bubbles up from the group and a warm feeling washes over me. Is this what encouraging people feels like? The sensation seems vaguely familiar. Maybe this is what Mom meant when she said I used to cast a spell when I directed shows back in high school. I make a mental note to try this encouraging thing more often. "So with that, I think we should call it a night." Everyone looks genuinely disappointed and it's palpable.

"Is something wrong?"

Abby Gupta starts to raise her hand and then remembers she can just speak. "Well, some of us were talking over the break. And we have some questions. Louis, maybe it's better if you ask. You're the lead, after all."

Louis clears his throat, "Now, I know this is only the first practice—"

"Rehearsal," I correct him, probably too quickly.

"Rehearsal. Right. But what is the play—"

"Musical."

"Musical. Got it. What is the musical about?"

I try to arrange my face in an understanding mask. I doubt it's working. I ask very slowly, "You don't know what *King Lear* is about?"

"Well, no, not really. It just seems like it's a bunch of mean people being mean to one another."

Abby nods her head in agreement. "Yes, they're not very nice people. In fact, they're downright nasty. I mean, they're nothing like the characters in *Bye Bye Birdie*, now are they?" She winks, as if I might have forgotten our glory days as the MacAfees.

I take a calming breath. Easy, Noah. You can do this.

"Well, you could almost say that the characters are archetypes—"

Abby looks confused. "What's an archetype? Is that like a font on a computer?"

Melissa lets a laugh escape and Mrs. Henson gives her a chastising look. Melissa turns guilty and averts her eyes.

"An archetype is sort of a . . . symbol . . . of a type of person. Does that help?"

"Oh, so we're not playing real people?" Julia McNew wants to know.

Jackie McNew quickly corrects her. "Of course not. You and me are cyborgs!"

"Well, um." How is this derailing so fast? "You two are just half cyborgs."

Julia looks confused. "Which half? Like the top half or the bottom half?"

"Okay, I kind of feel like some of you are rowing against the boat right now," I say carefully.

Louis Jenkins continues on. "About the cyborg thing. I'm sure it's obvious to everybody but me, but why are my two daughters robots?"

I try to swallow my very condescending sigh and look open-minded and patient. "Well, first off, Goneril and Regan are not robots, they're cyborgs."

"What's the difference?" Louis wonders. Patience, Noah.

"Well, a robot is a complete machine and a cyborg has some parts that are human. A cyborg has the presence of human life. I made the two daughters cyborgs as a metaphor for how they appear human and appear to love their father, but in fact, they don't. Their scheming nature is represented by the part of them that is mechanical."

Longest silence in recorded history.

"Oh, I think I get it. So that's what makes my character, Captain Lear, kind of forgive them," Louis says.

Whoa, wait, what?

"Um . . . you lost me, Louis."

"Well, if these gals are half machine, they can't have full human feelings. So I can sort of forgive them for betraying me. I mean, if they were full-on humans and betrayed me, that would be ten times more devastating, wouldn't it?"

And much to my chagrin, they're all staring at me.

The awkwardness is a thick fog filling the room and my jaw tenses just slightly in thought. A stunning revelation steals over me. Could Louis Jenkins be right? Could this community theater amateur who works in a barbecue sauce factory actually have a point? Could this guy, who has surely never taken a class in dramatic analysis, be smarter than all of the highly trained professionals that worked on the Broadway production? And am I too much of a narcissist to admit that he's right?

This was not what I was expecting. I had assumed I would be explaining the basics of musical theater until my face turned blue. That I'd be gently talking to them like they were five-year-olds. Explaining lingo like "upstage" and "hold for applause." All the things I had to learn when I made the jump from community theater to professional shows. The last thing I expected was to be getting invaluable dramaturgical advice in the middle of Plainview, Illinois.

So what do I do now?

Come on, Mr. Broadway, what's your move?

Sensing I might be quietly fuming, Mrs. Henson tries to intervene. "Look, Noah clearly knows what he's doing. Maybe we should just say the lines and concentrate on the blocking. We're the amateurs here."

I take a deep breath and with my stomach full of freshly swallowed pride, I say, "No, wait. Louis has a point. Lear would be much more devastated if Goneril and Regan were just human and flawed. So let's change that. We'll need to go through and cut all the cyborg references and also rethink the costumes."

The McNew twins, always late to the game, look up from their scripts. Julia blinkingly asks "Wait, we're not robots anymore? Because we've been working on our robot voices."

"No, I think Louis is right."

Louis blushes and does a kind of "Aw, shucks" face. "I didn't mean to screw up your play, Noah."

"Musical," I correct again, a little too eagerly. "And no, you're not screwing it up. You actually just improved it. And with that, why don't we call it a night?"

A cheer comes up from the group and someone screams, "Bumpkins!"

In the melee that ensues, I apparently agree to join the cast for drinks at the most disgusting restaurant in town. Thankfully, I end up drinking at a booth with Melissa, who primly nurses a lemonade. She gives me a cozy grin. "The cast is so excited about this. You're being a trouper."

"I can't believe that Louis Jenkins can sing like that. He actually made one song in my shitty musical sound halfway good."

82 CHAD BEGUELIN

"It's not a shitty musical. It has some really great moments. You're too hard on yourself."

"Not harder on myself than *The New York Times*."

"Come on, Noah."

"I know. Ugh. Look, clearly the show wasn't perfect, but there were parts of it that I was really proud of and now . . . I'm not so sure. Maybe I was just kidding myself the whole time."

Melissa and I sit in silence for a minute. I decide to usher the conversation away from my questionable talent. "So, is it me or was Louis Jenkins's point about Goneril and Regan totally spot-on? I mean, where did that insight come from?"

Melissa shrugs. "It's that old 'don't judge a book by its cover' thing, I guess."

Out of the blue, Lady Gaga's "Born This Way" comes on and Melissa's eyes go electric with joy. And without hesitation, we're singing at the top of our lungs. It's amazing how just a few notes can transform us both into screeching teenagers. Eyes closed in ecstasy, we bellow along.

Luke appears with a frosty mug of beer. He slides into the booth next to Melissa. We both look embarrassed at being caught belting our brains out. Melissa apologizes to Luke. "Sorry, we both really love that song."

Luke smiles broadly. "Don't apologize to me! You guys sounded great. How's everybody holding up?"

Melissa gives a snort. "Noah is going to need a year of therapy after listening to a bunch of hicks massacring his script and score."

I pull a "no comment" face.

Luke is downright enthusiastic. "I thought it went *great*! I mean, clearly I'm no expert, but it is going *great*, isn't it?"

Melissa turns to me and raises her eyebrows with exaggerated expectation.

I smile tightly. "We are exactly where we're supposed to be at this stage of the process." Melissa cheers and showers my cheek with kisses while Luke announces that he's buying us shots.

Well, him and me shots, since Melissa has a tiny human festering in her uterus.

I protest, but before I know it we're three shots in and Melissa is nowhere to be found. Our hands keep touching every time Luke passes me another shot. His hands are so large and rugged, but his touch is so gentle somehow. It's surprising and confusing. Why is he being so nice to me? And why am I letting him? Somehow Luke winds up on my side of the booth and maybe it's because of the booze, but his muscle-riddled thigh is swaying dangerously close to mine.

"I think what you're doing is really cool." His words are slurry and his lips look so warm and wet with beer that I force myself to look away.

"Well, I've got a lot of free time on my hands now, so—"

"You want another shot?"

I shake my head so hard I risk giving myself a concussion. "No thanks. Are you trying to kill me, Luke? Are you trying to give me alcohol poisoning?"

"I was just offering. Although I'm not sure why *I'm* the one buying. You're the rich guy from New York. You should be buying *me* a round."

I force myself to look into his eyes and try my best not to get lost in them. "I'm not rich."

"Well, you sure as hell look rich. How much do those shoes cost, man?"

"I don't remember."

I do, obviously, but I'm not playing this game.

"Then your haircut. You've got to remember how much your haircut costs, right?"

And then he starts begging and between the booze and the green of his eyes I feel my defenses lowering against my will.

Luke turns into a pouty man-baby. "Please, Noah! Please tell me how much a fancy New York haircut sets you back! Please! Come on, man!"

And just to get him to stop I blurt out, "Two hundred and fifty dollars."

"Ah-ha!" Luke slams his manly hand on the table in triumph. "I knew it! Rich!"

I instantly start to backtrack. "Well, now wait a second. To be honest, Chase is the one who really pays for it. I mean, it's his Amex."

Luke's eyes grow wide with wonder and he pokes his finger into my solar plexus. "You're a kept man!"

"No!"

He's drunkenly teasing me now. "You are!"

I can feel my cheeks and the back of my neck start to heat up. "This is getting ridiculous!"

More poking from Luke.

Wait, is it strange that he's poking me like this? Why aren't I stopping him? I should be stopping him.

"You are, Noah! Hell, you know what you are?"

"Go ahead. Enlighten me, you asshole."

"You're . . . you're his sexy little boy toy!"

Luke and I freeze.

I can tell by the instant panic on his face that he's worried he's crossed an invisible line. And he has, the fucker. I'm about to bite his head off, when suddenly I burst out into uncontrollable laughter. Luke lets out a relieved howl and it takes us several minutes to come back down to earth and the laughter to unspool.

And in the ebbing of the hilarity, I try to get my drunken mind to concentrate. Did he just call me sexy? No, that would be downright crazy.

Shit, I'm drunk. No, no, no. That didn't happen. Pull it together, Noah, you colossal idiot.

But his impressive thigh has definitely gone slack and is resting snugly against mine. Huh.

There's a lull and then Luke turns serious and ruins everything by bringing up Dad. "You know, I gotta confess, I was so worried about Mr. A. Since he's getting released tomorrow, I thought I could pick him up. I've got my truck and he might have some medical equipment."

My mood immediately darkens. Talking about Dad and Luke's relationship puts me on edge once again. Why is he always gunning for Dad's attention? And why was Dad always so willing to give it to him? Even back in high school Dad just loved to rhapsodize about Plainview High's famous Luke Carter. How many Saturday mornings did I have to listen to Dad waxing lyrical about Luke's moves on the football field? Or how Luke had a smile for everyone in town? And the time sophomore year when Dad asked me if I would mind if he gave Luke his old fishing gear, because I clearly wasn't ever going to use it. And, yeah, I wasn't, but still. Come on! It's just weird.

All the shitty memories race through my head and I'm just drunk enough to finally let it all out. "I don't know how this big friendship thing happened between you and Dad, but you win, Luke."

Luke looks leery for a second. "I win what?"

"You win. Dad loves you more than his own son!"

I blurt this out just as Melissa returns and lowers herself carefully into the booth. "What's going on?" she asks, worried.

"I guess Noah's pissed that I'm working for his dad or something."

I let out a long, drunken groan. "It's like you're his fucking BFF. The way you kiss his ass, it's embarrassing. So you never had a dad growing up, does that mean you have to steal mine?"

Melissa gives me a shocked look. "Noah!"

Luke's face goes pale, and I instantly know I've gone too far, but I somehow don't feel any guilt. "What the hell did I ever do to you, Noah?"

I laugh in his stupid, gorgeous face. "Think, Luke. Think real hard. And do that thinking someplace far from me."

Luke jumps up from the table so quickly that I wonder if he

is going to punch my lights out. But he just shakes his head and leaves.

Melissa and I sit in horrible silence for a couple of seconds until I muster up a very frail, "That was mean."

"Yes, that was mean, Noah. You're drunk. Let me drive you home."

Once we're in the car there are approximately three seconds of quiet before Melissa begins to lecture me. "That was a low blow."

"I know, but . . ." My mind swims around in boozy circles for a couple of seconds. "It's just . . . he and his friends treated me like shit growing up. And the theater was the only place I felt safe. And now, he's constantly at my safe place and he's probably like a Trojan horse filled with homophobia just waiting to get out and attack me again."

Melissa sighs. "Maybe he's changed. And maybe he's doing all this stuff for your musical as a kind of penance. Maybe on some level he's trying to make up for who he used to be."

"I just fucking hate him and in honor of my teenage self, I'm going to hold on to that hate and carry it around like a very expensive purse." Blinking lights catch my drunken eyes. "Oh, look, Dairy Queen!"

Melissa proves she will make a very strict mommy. "No Dairy Queen for you. You're too drunk and I'm not cleaning ice cream puke out of my upholstery."

And then my drunken mind circles back on itself. "Or, I don't know, maybe I do owe him an apology."

"Well, that song from *Oklahoma!* does say that the farmer and the cowhand should be friends."

"First of all, I'm not a farmer. Secondly, I'm not taking relationship advice from a musical that ignores the killing of millions of Native Americans."

"Fair enough."

"Fuck. Do I really have to say I'm sorry?"

"Your mom will know." And right on cue we pull up to my house and Mom is waiting on the porch because she's a part-time clairvoyant. I stumble out of Melissa's car and she carefully helps me walk. "He's drunk and needs water," Melissa announces.

Mom shakes her head and replies, "Gatorade is better."

Once inside the kitchen, I'm slowly sipping Gatorade as Mom and Melissa watch. "You have to apologize to that poor young man, Noah. I didn't raise you to hit below the belt like that."

I say nothing, only stare drunkenly at the candy-colored bottle in my hand and then take another swig of artificially flavored awfulness. "He started it. Years ago, in fact."

Melissa decides to double-team me with Mom. "You know, Nancy Kay, even though the musical we're doing is based on *King Lear*, I keep thinking about that line from *Hamlet* about the queen and how she 'doth protest too much.'"

Mom nods like she's hosting a talk show and Melissa is her favorite guest. "You are so smart, Melissa. Sometimes strong emotions are used to hide other strong emotions."

"I'm too drunk to follow this nonsense . . ." I say, slurring my words like the professional alcoholic I might be becoming. "But if you're insurpulating, no . . . insimpulating?"

"Insinuating? Is that what you're trying to say, son?" Mom asks, ever so patiently.

"If you're *inferring* that I actually like Luke and I'm covering it up with anger, you both need to be fitted for straitjackets."

Mom and Melissa exchange very staged looks of skepticism. Booze or not, I find myself on a roll.

"First of all, you've both seen my hot British boyfriend. So there's that. Secondly, I don't get crushes on straight guys."

Melissa looks floored. "You can do that? Control who you have crushes on?"

"Absolutely! It's called self-respect," I reply proudly, tapping my finger on the kitchen table for emphasis. "I refuse, outright *refuse* to be one of those . . . one of those . . . idiots pining over someone they can never have. I developed that self-preserving skill years ago. And it's been tested so many times, it's, uh, what's the word? . . . mullet proof! No, I mean, bulletproof!" I tip my head back and finish the Gatorade like a champ.

Mom considers this for a quick moment and then adds. "Of course we don't know if Luke is straight. He might be gay. Or bi." Something about her words make my stomach give a little lurch that's completely unrelated to alcohol. "He doesn't really talk about dating, but why would he bring up romance with a wizened old crow like me?"

"I don't want to talk about that guy anymore!"

Melissa sighs. "Well, I hate to talk about anyone behind their back, but I did fool around with Luke a couple of years after graduation and he was, shall we say, less than enthusiastic."

Laser focused, I sit straight up in my chair. "How could you not tell me about that?!"

"I thought you didn't want to talk about Luke Carter anymore."

Busted. I collapse back into my seat.

"Pfft! I don't. Forget I asked."

Melissa stands and grabs her purse. "Okay, I'll see you at rehearsal tomorrow, Gertrude!"

And before she's even halfway out the door, I'm yelling after her, "I'm not Queen Gertrude! I don't doth protest too much, not now, not never!"

seven

# "Déjà Vu"

must have immediately passed out on top of my bed from all of the booze, but toward morning I groan and begin to regain consciousness. A nearby conclave of cardinals screeches out an endless fugue that threatens to make my eardrums bleed. And if that isn't enough to split my brain in two, an aggressively perky truck horn blasts repeatedly through the air. As the sun slowly starts to burn geometric patterns through my bedroom curtains, I find myself unable to ignore what happened last night. And the realization hits me right between my bloodshot eyes. I'm going to have to apologize to the person I hate the most.

I look out the window to see Luke's truck pulling into the driveway. Dad's riding shotgun and there is some medical equipment in the back. More perky horn blasts. Mom steps off the porch and goes to greet them. Great. Luke's proving once again what a saint he is. Infallible as scripture. I fight the urge to hide in my room like a coward. Time to man up. I drag myself out of bed and down the stairs.

Mom walks Dad toward the house as I run up to him, trying to think of some way to be helpful. "Sorry I didn't come pick you up."

Dad stops just long enough to say, "Your mom told me you were too drunk."

Mom shoots me a guilty look as she and Dad climb the porch steps. I walk as slowly as humanly possible up to Luke, who's standing on the bed of the truck organizing supplies. I catch my reflection in the truck's back window and realize I'm sporting a gravity-defying case of bedhead. Great. Nothing beats looking like an idiot while you stumble through an apology.

"Hey, Luke."

Luke doesn't look up and only offers me a frosty "Hey" in return.

He's clearly not going to make this easy and maybe I deserve that. I take a deep breath and get down to business.

"So, listen, I'm sorry about what I said last night. I was drunk and I'm a dickhead and . . ." I promptly fizzle out, realizing I have no real excuses to offer.

Luke sighs and climbs down from the truck with a cardboard box in his hands. "I'm not gonna lie. That was a pretty shitty thing to say. But I get it now. You don't like me. That's okay, not everybody is gonna like me."

"But it kind of seems like everybody does," I admit, begrudgingly. "My parents do. Everyone in town does."

"Just not Noah Adams. That's cool. I wish that wasn't the way things were, but . . ."

"It's not that I don't like you. I guess I just can't let go of some things from the past." I take the cardboard box from Luke and he sits on the tailgate, massive arms crossed and staring at the ground. "And I think it's great that you're close with my dad, but it rubs me the wrong way sometimes."

Luke simply stares at me, as if I'm supposed to elaborate or my apology won't stick. I set down the cardboard box and continue.

"Look, things have always been complicated with Dad and me. Like when I was thirteen, he asked me to help him deliver a calf. I mean, what was he thinking? Can you imagine a thirteen-year-old me being forced to look at a cow's vagina? And when yellow liquid exploded out of the cow's vag and then two little sticky hooves followed, well, I immediately threw up all over my brand-new Capezios."

Luke stops me. "Capezios?"

"They're dance shoes. Jazz shoes. Anyway, after I threw up, Dad and I just stared at one another and it was obvious right then that I was never going to be the kind of son he wanted. And, of course, we love one another. But something shattered into a million pieces that day. I kept trying to feign interest in the farm, in the cows and the hay and the tractors, but the incompetent cat was out of the bag. And after a while I got tired of suffering through Dad's disappointing looks so I just, I don't know, gave up."

Luke seems unmoved and reaches back to grab a small oxygen tank. He starts to head toward the house. I quickly grab the cardboard box and follow him. I decide to keep the apology going. "In for a penny, in for a pound," as Chase would say.

"And then you show up here and you don't mind pulling smaller cows out of larger cows. For all I know, you're actually good at it. And Dad's face lights up when he sees you in a way that I can never expect him to light up when he sees me. So I guess all of that fucks with my head and maybe that's why I said something really terrible last night and for that I am truly, truly sorry."

Luke stops in his tracks and appears to be processing this for a moment, invisible wheels turning inside his manly skull. He sets the oxygen tank on the front steps and turns to me. I think about bringing up the years of shit he put me through as a teenager, but I figure that would dilute the apology. And for some inexplicable reason, I need him to absolve me of being a prick.

And then Luke can't look me in the eyes as he says, "I know your dad isn't perfect, Noah. But at least he stayed. Which is more than I can say for mine."

A wave of nausea hits me when I realize just how cruel my words were. Never in a million years did I think I would actually feel sorry for Luke Carter. When I would complain about him to Mrs. Henson during free period in high school, she used to say, "Well, Noah, hurt people hurt people." Maybe she had a point, but I tend to tune people out when they start speaking in bumper stickers.

Luke and I stare at one another, clearly at an impasse. I go to set the box on the front steps and when I turn back to Luke he unexpectedly reaches up and, for a second, it almost seems like he's going to touch my hair. His hand just lingers cautiously in the air.

"What . . . what are you doing?"

Luke hesitates. "Just . . . helping you tamp down that bed-head. Is that okay?"

I find myself nodding. His fingers go through my hair and every nerve ending in my body instantly burns like fire. Something unspoken passes between our eyes. And then Luke's hand is gone and he's heading back to his truck.

"See you at practice." Luke catches himself. "Rehearsal, I mean."

Luke climbs into his pickup and pulls away in a cloud of dust and I stand there in total and utter confusion. What was that all about? I find myself trembling slightly and I realize that I'm holding my breath. All because Luke's rugged fingers ran through my hair? I shouldn't be reacting this way. I force myself to take a breath and regroup. What the hell does it matter if Luke tried to wrangle my bedhead? I have a gorgeous boyfriend back in New York and I'm out of here in four weeks and counting. I'm here to put on a show, not get sidetracked with sexually ambiguous former high school acquaintances.

To my surprise, I find Dad at the kitchen table, drinking coffee with an oxygen tube under his nose.

"What's this?" I ask.

"Stupid doctors are worried about my breathing now. I told them I had a heart attack. What does that have to do with my lungs?"

Mom gives me a conspiratorial look. "Your father is just being a first-class grump because he can't go for a ride at the Balloon Faire this year."

"Are they still doing that?" I ask.

Mom shoots me a scandalized look. "Are they still doing the Balloon Faire? Honey, it's what this town has become famous for.

People drive all the way down from Chicago for the Balloon Faire. It's been a huge economic boon for every business in a thirty-mile radius. Are they still doing the Balloon Faire? How could they not? That'd be like canceling Christmas."

I don't even try to hide my eye roll. The Plainview Balloon Faire. At some point in the 1990s, some local got the idea to sabotage a perfectly good weekend with a parade of hot air balloons. Apparently it started out with just a few balloon enthusiasts meeting in a nearby park and flying their colorful contraptions in tandem over rinky-dink little Plainview. Then it somehow ballooned (pun intended) into a whole three-day celebration that included local bands, craft booths, and costume characters for kids. Though I've never been, it seems to be a study in kitsch and tacky as hell.

But for some reason Dad is on board with the whole thing and now if you don't know what to get him for his birthday, just find him something with a hot air balloon stamped on it and you'll have made his day.

Mom gazes at Dad with unabashed pity. "Your father looks forward to that tethered ride every year."

Since I'm clearly being prompted, I ask, "Tethered ride?"

"You know, they put you in a balloon, but they keep it tied to the ground. You get to go straight up, float for a little bit and then come right back down. It is just heaven."

"If the weather's good, you can see all the way to Salem," Dad adds.

"Sound intoxicating," I say, my voice dripping with sarcasm.

Mom gives me a knowing look. She's the only one who's aware

that I'm not the biggest fan of heights. When I was in the fifth grade a carnival came to town and Mom and I went on the Ferris wheel together. She wanted to treat me to a picturesque view of Plainview from above. Instead, I treated her to the sight of me throwing up into her purse.

"Well, your father can't take his oxygen tank in a hot air balloon. That's just the way it is. The doctor was adamant about it."

"Which doctor? Dr. Dunbar?"

Dad gives a grim nod as Mom brings him over a plate of goop. Mom is a retired nurse, so she gets a little prickly when Dad trash-talks her former colleagues.

"Now you both be nice to Dr. Dunbar. He's got a lot on his plate with that poor wife of his. Joanie Marie Dunbar has lost her mind and insists that her dog has body dysmorphia. How can a dog have body dysmorphia? It's a dachshund. It isn't even big enough to look at itself in a mirror. But, great gal! Great gal!"

Dad chews his food, looking depressed.

I swallow my pride and say slowly, "So the set for the musical. It's pretty impressive, Dad. I mean, everybody thinks so."

"Do you think so? Up to your standards?"

Don't take the bait, Noah. The man has health issues. "It exceeded my expectations, Dad."

I can tell what he's thinking. His face moves as he contemplates exactly how to be unkind. Maybe he'll say something like, "Nothing could exceed your expectations, son." But to my surprise, he simply says, "Glad you liked it."

My phone vibrates. It's Chase. Finally. I run out onto the porch and answer. "You promised inappropriate texts!"

Chase laughs and is instantly contrite. "I've been swamped, but I haven't stopped thinking about you for a moment. Our bed is a very depressing setting without you in it. How's your dad?"

"Fine. I think he might even be mellowing. We were actually cordial just now. Oh, but get this: I'm removing the whole cyborg thing from the musical. It turns out I don't even have to change the dialogue, it's only referred to in the stage directions."

"What made you do that?"

I stretch out on the creaky porch swing. Chase's voice is so sexy that I quickly have the need to be horizontal. The humidity turns me into a puddle of sweat within seconds. "Oh, one of the actors brought it up and I guess I realized the whole idea was way too Star Trek-y and ridiculous in the first place. What was I even thinking?"

"I blame Danielle Vincent."

"No, it was my boneheaded idea. I can't blame her for that one. Although she could have stopped me, maybe. What did you do last night without me? And your answer had better be 'nothing fun.'"

"Nothing fun. I ate all by my lonesome at the bar at Gramercy Tavern. And suffered my way through Aleister Murphy's latest play and resisted the urge to gouge my eyes out when I was through reading it. God, it was absolute rubbish. Then I had a glass of port, thought of you, and wanked off, then went to bed."

"You're so romantic. God, I hope this month speeds by so I can get back home and back to being the one who wanks you off. Or more."

"You're so cute when you try to use British words with your sexy little American accent. I'll call you tomorrow."

A lawn sprinkler snaps on and pathetically tries to urge the sparse grass in the backyard to grow. I put one foot on the porch and give it a shove. I'm hoping that if I swing, I'll magically cool down. But it doesn't work and I give up. "God, I can't stand being away from you, Chase. It sucks! You don't have to send me inappropriate texts, but I do need to know what you're up to. I feel so stranded here."

"I'll do better. And after this is all over, 'we shan't be parted no more.'"

"Good." And then I try a cockney accent just like the character of Scudder in *Maurice*. "I don't wan' 'a be par'ed no more, guv'ner!"

Chase groans. "Please never speak like that again. Love to the family."

"Love you!" And the line goes dead. I sit up on the porch swing and wonder if I should have told Chase about the bedhead incident with Luke. No. That would be ridiculous.

Nothing really happened anyway. Besides, it's not my fault that my hair is so luxurious that even straight guys want to run their fingers through it.

I arrive at the theater that night and find Luke busy threading white Christmas lights through a black backdrop. I make a big show of shuffling papers. Shuffle, shuffle, shuffle. He finally looks up and waves the fabric in his hand. "It's, well, I think it's called a star drop. For the final scene. I sourced the lights from the Methodist church. They don't have any use for Christmas lights in the middle of summer."

"Smart thinking."

More superfluous paper shuffling from me. Busy, busy, busy. Why are we both acting so weird all of the sudden?

"Man, your mom seemed relieved to have your dad back home."

"Thanks for picking him up. And helping with the equipment."

"Oh, it's no problem. She tips me in eggplant paintings."

I laugh. "She told me about her Etsy page. She has no idea what she's actually selling."

Luke drops the Christmas lights and gives the biggest, richest laugh known to mankind. "She told you that? What a liar! She had a booth at a fair over in Fairview Heights and all these hipster wannabes were buying them. She asked me what people saw in them and I explained that they were basically emojis that meant boners. She got all excited and asked if I thought more people would buy them. She's definitely in on the whole thing. Only she calls them 'emotions' instead of 'emojis.'"

There's a pause and Luke jumps off the stage and starts toward me. He gets close enough that I smell him. What is that smell? I noticed it earlier when we were standing by his pickup. It's earthy, kind of. Is it an orchard? Does Luke Carter smell like a fucking orchard?

He stops very close to me, then reconsiders and takes a few steps back.

"So, I just want to say . . . um, I get what you were saying earlier about you and your dad. Just so we're clear, I don't want to try to take your place or anything like that."

"Of course. I mean, I don't really think that . . . because that would make me a crazy person. And I'm not. A crazy person. Well, mostly I'm not."

"Right." Luke hesitates for a moment, then adds, "Hey, so . . . was it weird that I touched your hair this morning? Because I kind of felt weird about it afterward."

I become overly dismissive. "What? No! I actually forgot that even happened."

And then we just stand blinking at one another in complete confusion. We remain like this for an eternity until I decide to ask, "So, random question. What cologne are you wearing?"

Luke screws his face up in a surprised smile. "Do I look like a guy who wears cologne?"

He just smells like that naturally? So not helpful.

The cast starts to arrive and Luke goes back to his star drop as rehearsal begins. I announce that the costumes for the now non-cyborg Goneril and Regan will be the only change. Thankfully no one will have to relearn any dialogue. I'll just have to keep reminding Jackie and Julia not to speak in their so-called robot voices.

I suggest we start blocking some of the easier scenes and out of nowhere Luke yells, "Places!"

He leans out of the wings and gives me a questioning look. "Did I get it right?"

"You did," I say, smiling in spite of myself.

And as we work through the scenes, I can't stop thinking

about the orchard smell. I'm not surprised I confused it for cologne. Chase tends to go a little overboard with the stuff. It's one of Chase's very few flaws. Everywhere he goes he leaves a trail of expensive Gucci cologne mixed with an air of cool superiority.

I realize that everyone is watching me daydream and snap back to reality.

"I think we need to shift Captain Lear's command station module a little more stage left."

Luke comes bounding out of the wings, a cross between an overeager puppy and a Viking, and grabs the set piece. "Got it!"

"I know this is only the second night, but I guess we should start staging the opening number next. Time is of the essence."

Abby asks, "Who's going to teach us the dance moves?"

"What?"

"You know, the dance moves. For when we're singing."

"Oh, it's not really a dance show. There's no choreography, per se."

Abby looks disappointed. "Oh, well I took three years of modern dance in junior high, so just keep that in mind if we get into a pinch."

"I'll keep that in mind. Let's start staging."

Mrs. Henson starts to put the cast through their paces as they belt out the opening number, "Who Doth Love Him Most?" An hour later we've managed to stage the entire opening and we're all sweaty and out of breath.

"Let's call it a night before we melt into the floor from exhaustion."

The cast starts sharing a bunch of furtive looks.

"Is something wrong?" I ask, hoping to God we don't have another cyborg situation on our hands.

Finally, Abby steps forward. "Well, you see, there's a scene in the show that we're all a little concerned about."

"Why am I having a major déjà vu right now?"

She giggles nervously and adds, "It's not your writing, God, no, I blame the source material."

"Okay."

"Well, we're all a little squeamish about the scene where Drew is supposed to pull my eyeball out and stomp on it."

Drew Parees, who teaches economics at the local community college and also happens to be playing Cornwall, steps forward. "How am I even supposed to do that? How is that even going to work?"

"Well, on Broadway we used a lot of stage blood. There are small gel packs that get rigged—"

"I don't mean to interrupt," Abby says, interrupting. "But it just seems like a real nasty thing to do to a person."

"Sure, they're nasty people."

"Oh, I understand that. But it's so gory. It's like a Freddy Krueger movie or something."

"Shakespeare is notoriously gory. Famously so."

Finally, it's Louis's turn to step forward. "What I think these two are trying to say is that there will be children coming to see the show."

"And?"

"Well, what are Abby's grandkids going to think when they see their grandma getting her eyes ripped out of her head?"

"Well, could they just not see the show?"

Abby begins to panic. "Oh, no! They're dying to see it. Everyone in town is. And what about all the children I drive to school every day? Now they can't come either? Their little hearts will be broken!"

I take a very long inhale and Melissa shoots me a "tread lightly" look. I turn to Abby and do my best to put on a strained yet happy face.

"First, you guys didn't like the way I wrote Goneril and Regan. And maybe you had a point. Hence the costume changes. Now you want me to cut a famous and important scene out of my musical?"

Abby is quick to backtrack. "Oh, no, no, no. We wouldn't dream of it. We were just wondering if there was a way to rethink it slightly."

Drew jumps in. "Yeah, like we were just tossing around ideas. Like, instead of gouging her eyes out, maybe I just shove her really hard."

"Or slap me. He could slap me," Abby says quickly. "I think the little children could understand a slap much better. They see it on the playground all the time."

I try to hold in my exasperation. "But for the rest of the plot to work, Gloucester has to be blind. That's the whole point."

"Well . . ." Abby's mind seems to be going a mile a minute. "What if I get hysterical blindness?"

Drew quickly nods. "Yeah, what if I slap her really hard and she gets hysterical blindness?"

I can feel my patience fraying. "First of all, hysterical blindness isn't a thing."

"Oh, yes, it is," Jackie McNew starts in. "Our aunt got it for two weeks when they canceled her favorite soap opera."

"Then your aunt is psychotic," I snap before I can stop myself.

Sensing that I'm about to lose it, Mrs. Henson steps in. "I think we should just table this for now and we'll come back to it later when we all have cooler heads."

"Yes, thank you, Mrs. Henson. My head could definitely use some cooling. See you guys tomorrow night."

Everyone slowly starts to gather their belongings and Luke approaches me cautiously. He tousles his floppy hair and it makes that perfect curl over his left eye and I silently weaken a little from the sight. Then I think of Chase back in New York sleeping alone in our bed and feel a small surge of guilt. Luke shoves his hands in his pockets and rocks back and forth on his heels a little, as if he's trying to figure out what to say.

"Luke?"

"Um . . . I know what they're asking you to do sounds crazy. You shouldn't have to bend your show just for a bunch of kids."

"I agree."

"But . . ."

"Really, Luke? You're going to pile on, too?"

"I'm just saying, if there was a different way to skin that cat, you'd be the man to do it."

"Maybe that's our answer. Instead of Drew gouging out Abby's eyes onstage, he could just skin her cat."

"I get it. None of my business." He changes the topic. "You going to Bumpkins tonight?"

"Oh, no. My liver would crawl out of my body and slither away in protest."

Luke looks crestfallen. "But I like drunk Noah! He tells me all about his pricey New York haircuts!"

"I'm sure you have better things to think about than my hair."

Luke pauses and then says cryptically, "Oh, I wouldn't be so sure about that."

Wait a second. What's with all this ambiguous flirting? Is this guy queerbaiting me? Not cool.

"Well, you know. Rain check."

Luke nods, almost as if he's accepting defeat. "Okay, well. You'll be missed."

Then he gives me a soft punch in the stomach like I'm a five-year-old and saunters away, joining the rest of the cast as they head out the door.

I'll be missed? And what's with the good ole boy punch in the stomach? And the poking me in my chest at Bumpkins? I hate all that frat boy bro shit. Don't I? Yes, I definitely do.

What kind of game is Luke Carter playing?

Whatever. It doesn't matter. I've got to figure out a version of *Stage of Fools* where hysterical blindness is an actual thing. Mom's earlier advice comes back to me. "Just make up your mind to make up your mind."

Sigh.

That sounds like a problem for tomorrow Noah to figure out.

# eight

# "Mutiny"

wake up the following morning to my phone buzzing. I don't recognize the number but it's a St. Louis area code, so maybe I've won some free toasted ravioli. A guy can dream.

"Hello?"

"Is this Noah Adams?" It's a twangy female voice.

"It is."

"Noah, it is so great to meet you, even just over the phone. My name is Audra Bogner and I'm the entertainment critic over here at *The St. Louis Post-Dispatch*. I wondered if I could maybe just ask you a few questions. I know this is probably not how it's done in New York, but I just wanted to be as up to speed as possible before I review the show on September first. Is now a good time?"

I jolt up in bed, wide awake. My arteries turn to ice. "Excuse me? You're reviewing the show? You can't review the show!"

"It's such a great story, you coming back home and working with your town's community theater. I mean, when your mother called me about it, I just couldn't resist!"

I. Am. Going. To. Kill. That. Woman.

I almost drop the phone, but fumble to keep it next to my ear. "Um, Audra, is it? I'm gonna have to call you back. I have an old woman to murder."

I hang up and run downstairs wearing nothing but my boxer briefs and a seething expression of rage. I round the corner at the bottom of the stairs and there's Mom, serenely painting away in the guest bedroom.

"What have you done?!?"

I startle her so completely that she almost drops her paintbrush. "I haven't done anything, Noah. I'm just standing here painting my eggplant emotions like usual."

"You called *The St. Louis Post-Dispatch* and now they're going to review the show? Is my career not enough of a tragedy for you?"

"Oh, so that nice Bogner lady called you? I figured you wouldn't mind if I gave her your cell. I'm sure you're used to dealing with press all the time. Now, more importantly, do you think this eggplant emotion is too curved?"

"Focus, woman! You have doomed me! DOOMED ME!"

"Oh, your mother didn't doom you. Mrs. Bogner was very understanding. I told her it was a community theater show, that there were no professionals involved. Well, except you, of course. She's not going to pan a bunch of amateurs. Besides, she seemed very nice to me. Truth be told, we spent most of our time talking about zinnias."

I fall to my knees and call to the heavens. "If there is a God, please prove your existence by smiting my mother right now!"

"Honey, if she rakes a community theater production over the coals, she will look like Satan himself. And there's no such thing as bad publicity, right?"

I continue to stare at her, my eyes narrowing.

Mom stops in her tracks. "Why are you looking at me like that?"

"I'm trying to figure how big of a frying pan I'll need when I sneak up behind you and whack you over the head with it."

"Well, that's a waste of time. Everyone in our family has extremely thick skulls." Clearly.

I try Audra Bogner back and get her voicemail. I very politely beg her not to review the show. I consider threatening legal action, but I figure I'll go with the "more flies with honey" route. For now.

On my way to rehearsal, I get a text from Chase: Don't be mad, but I'm going to see Odette without you.

I text back: Betrayal! You Judas Iscariot, you!

Chase was the one who introduced me to the American Ballet Theatre and their repertoire of classics. I went kicking and screaming. I mean, I'm gay, but I'm not *that* gay.

But by the time Odette flung herself into the water at the end of *Swan Lake*, tears were shooting out of my eyes like tiny projectiles. I was converted on the spot. Now it doesn't feel like summer without a stage full of twirling ballerinas and a little Tchaikovsky. And not to cheapen the experience, but the perfect asses on the male dancers don't hurt the proceedings any. Now Chase is going without me. Probably wearing the Brunello Cucinelli linen shirt that makes his blue eyes pop. Damn it.

I hastily text: Have fun. Missing you like hell.

When I finally walk into the theater, the cast is huddled around the piano and I hear Mrs. Henson saying, "I don't think we should be doing this."

"Doing what?" I ask cautiously.

Everyone is silent, as if they've been caught in some nefarious act. Abby Gupta starts, "Well—"

"Is this about the eye gouging? Because if it is—"

"Just hear us out," Abby pleads.

I tilt my head and sigh. "Go nuts."

"Now some musicals have these things called dream ballets."

"I know what a dream ballet is, guys."

My mind flashes to Chase sitting alone through *Swan Lake* for a quick second, but there's no time to get homesick.

"Oh, good." Abby continues, "Well, you know, I took three years of modern dance in junior high."

I do not like where this is going. I do not like it one bit.

"So I asked Marilyn if she could sort of weave some of your melodies together as a kind of a soundtrack."

I glare at Mrs. Henson and she mouths the words "I'm sorry" and looks like she's about to cry.

"And then Drew and I put together, well, not a ballet, because I took modern dance, so it's not ballet. So it's sort of like, oh, what did you call it, Drew?"

"A movement piece," Drew offers.

"Right! I like that! A movement piece! All of the dialogue is there, but the eye gouging is merely sort of suggested and kid-friendly." She stops and I feel the entire room staring at me.

"And let me guess. You would like to audition this non-gouging movement piece for me right now."

Abby winces slightly. "If you'll let us?"

I find Melissa, who has become the camera lens I look into when I want to do asides to an imaginary studio audience. She holds both of her hands up as if to say, "Don't look at me."

Finally, I can't take all the Kewpie doll eyes and I give in. "Sure, why not."

"Oh, thank you!" Abby gushes. "Now, this is just a first draft."

Abby and Drew run up onto the stage in excitement. The rest of the cast takes their places slightly upstage of them. Mrs. Henson reluctantly sits at the piano. Abby gets into position and nods to Mrs. Henson to begin. The opening chords of Lear's song "Spit Fire, Spout Rain" fill the theater. But at a much slower tempo, which gives it an eerie quality.

"Pluck out his poor old eyes!" Drew says, pointing at Abby. They then begin to dance the scene in a stylized manner and I warn myself not to laugh.

Then something completely insane happens.

Maybe it's just because the cast is taking it so seriously, or maybe it just . . . works? Drew moves in a sort of hypnotic slow motion toward Abby as she's being held on the floor. Abby says very slowly, "Give me some help! O cruel! O you gods!"

Drew is on top of her in a flash and pulling a red, flowing

ribbon out of Abby's fist, which she holds over her eye. Mrs. Henson segues into the fiery melody of "The Prince of Darkness." Drew pulls another red ribbon from Abby's face and grinds it into the floor. Abby writhes on the ground in pain as Drew stands above her body, raising his fists to the heavens, the ribbons dangling from his fingers and billowing in the air. The music ends and they freeze in a tableau.

Abby breaks out of her pose and comes to the edge of the stage. Everyone is silent for a moment.

"You hated it."

I walk slowly toward her and the rest of the cast looks on nervously. "Abby, you drive a school bus, right? That's your job, am I right?"

Her expression goes from worried to defeated. "Oh, I get it. I know what you're going to say . . . keep my day job, right?"

"Nope. What I'm going to say is that I hope you don't mind moonlighting, because you are now the official choreographer of *Stage of Fools!*"

Abby's eyes widen. "What? You mean, you liked it?"

"Liked it? You're Agnes fucking de Mille!"

"Oh, my God! Oh, my God!"

She starts jumping up and down and tearing up. The entire cast applauds for her, cheering loudly. Drew and Abby share a victorious hug.

"Now, let's get back to work, you talented people!" I shout. "And by the way, Abby, I know you stole that ribbon shit from *The Lion King.*"

She holds up her hands and shrugs. "If you're going to steal, steal from the best, right?"

Strangely invigorated, I start to plan out the rest of the week. "Now, look, I've been thinking this through and I figure if we all really work like crazy, we can have the entire first act up on its feet by the end of rehearsal on Saturday."

I look up to realize a scandalized hush has gone through the cast.

"Is there a problem?" I ask.

Louis, clearly comfortable in his role as group spokesperson, clears his throat. "Well, Noah. We're not really going to rehearse this weekend, are we?"

I give him a baffled look. "And why wouldn't we?"

"You're kidding right? This weekend is the Plainview Balloon Faire."

My eyes go dead. "And?"

"And?" Louis asks incredulously. "You just expect us to miss it?"

"That's exactly what I expect you to do. We've got a truckload of staging to do. And . . ." Out of nowhere Mrs. Bogner pops into my head and I use the poor woman as a weapon. "And, get this, it turns out a critic from *The St. Louis Post-Dispatch* is going to review this little dog and pony show. What do you think about that?"

Everyone is suddenly looking at anything but me. And a light bulb pops on above my head. "Wait, you knew? You all knew that the show was going to be reviewed? How could you not say anything?"

Jackie speaks up. "We figured you knew. I mean, it was your own mother that called the damn paper."

"Fine. The point is we're now going to be judged in print. In black and white. So we have to be perfect. We all have to suck it up and skip the fair this year."

The silence is tense and grim.

To my surprise, it's Melissa who speaks next. "Noah, I know you don't get it, but the Balloon Faire is sacred to this town. It's like a national holiday or something. You can't rehearse during the Balloon Faire. It's just a fact of life in Plainview that everything stops for two days while everyone enjoys the fair."

My eyes remain dead.

"Wait, you've been to the fair before, right?"

"Why would I go to the fair? Standing around looking at hot air balloons and eating funnel cake is not my idea of a good time. I'd rather undergo a colonoscopy performed by a drunken orangutan."

Melissa gives me a very admonishing, Melissa-y look. "You have to give us the weekend off. This show is so important to all of us, maybe even more important to us than it is to you, if that's even possible. But nothing trumps the Plainview Balloon Faire."

A little dial in my brain switches from disbelief to flabbergasted. "So we're going to lose two precious, precious days of rehearsal for some stupid hot air balloons?"

I realize we're clearly in the middle of a standoff that I can't win, even with reason on my side. The cast is teetering toward a full-out mutiny. If I don't give in they'll probably parade my head around town on a pike. And while having your head on a pike can be very slimming, it's never a good look.

I have no choice but to give in. "Okay, go look at your beloved balloons. But today's already Wednesday. So you have to promise that you'll work extra hard tomorrow and that you'll show up here with the new blocking embossed on your brains."

They actually applaud in appreciation. Thankfully, my phone vibrates right on cue and distracts me from this madness. It's a text from Kiara. She's attached an article from *Variety* that says Chase has just signed Aleister Murphy. Kiara adds a "WTF?"

What the fuck indeed. I thought Chase hated Aleister's latest play. I text Kiara back: Will investigate posthaste.

I put down my phone and realize that Luke is sitting next to me. And he's changed into paint-splattered overalls. Very tight paint-splattered overalls. *Without a shirt.*

I actively command my brain cells to continue functioning. Come on, guys. Pull it together.

Luke finally speaks. "You're kidding, right? You've never been to the Balloon Faire?"

This topic just refuses to die. "Oh, come on. Not you, too."

"What do you have against hot air balloons? What did they ever do to you?"

"Maybe I was traumatized as a kid, because a hot air balloon screwed Dorothy Gale over pretty hard. That was supposed to be her ticket out of Oz."

Luke laughs. "That was Toto's fault for jumping out at the last second and you know it. Besides, your dad loves the fair."

"Not anymore. Dr. Dunbar won't let him go up in a tethered

ride because of his oxygen tank. So there are officially two Adams men who are being raw dogged by your pointless balloon fair."

Luke thinks for a second. "Well, he can still go to the Glow. Your mom and dad wouldn't miss the Glow for a million bucks."

And now I have to ask, "The Glow?"

Luke's eyes light up like a pinball machine. "The Glow! You've never been to the Glow? Well, that's just downright criminal."

"Elaborate," I say, my voice as dry as the desert.

"Well, everybody brings blankets or lawn chairs and then just as the sun is going down, hundreds of balloons bunch up in a group on the Francis Park main grounds and then they take turns lighting up against the night sky. It's freakin' beautiful, man. You've got to go. You've got to let me take you and your parents. It's kind of like watching fireworks, only without all the noise. Trust me, you'll love it."

He's got that eager, puppy dog look in his eyes and it melts my jaded heart on the spot. "Fine. I'll go look at idiotic balloons with you."

"Great! I think you're gonna be surprised by how much fun it is."

The boyish enthusiasm written across his face takes my breath away for a second. And I find I can't stop myself from asking, "But seriously, Luke. Overalls?"

His smile morphs into a smirk and he says, "I knew you'd hate them. So I wore them just to fuck with you. Do you really think I'm that big of a hick? Oh, wait, I forgot something . . ." He pulls an actual piece of hay out of his bib pocket and sticks it in his mouth and lets it dangle nonchalantly. "Nature's toothpick."

I cross my arms and study him academically for a second before I announce, "Well, it definitely completes the look."

The crazy thing is, it actually does.

The denim is practically laminated to his powerful thighs. Luke starts posing like a dork with his thumbs hooked casually over the straps. I notice the almost imperceptible trace of tiny blond hairs traveling across his buff chest. And that his button fly is . . . *straining*.

Overalls have never looked so mouthwateringly good.

Fuuucckk!

I quickly snap my attention away and bury my head in my script until Luke's gone. I feel a strange sense of accomplishment that I was able to resist checking out his ass when he turned around to go.

When Chase calls later that night I skip any niceties and get right to the point. "You're signing Aleister Murphy? I thought you hated his latest play."

Chase sighs. "I do hate it. I *loathe* it! But the Shubert Organization happens to be completely chuffed about it. It's a business decision, Noah."

"The Shubert Organization? Is his play going to Broadway?"

"I'm no fortune teller, but possibly."

I can never let sleeping dogs lie. I always have to kick them in the teeth until they're awake and biting. So, of course, I pry further. "What's Aleister's latest play called, anyway?"

Chase hesitates, clearly embarrassed. "It's, um . . . it's called *Pattycakes*."

"You're lying!" I scream in disbelief. "What's it about?"

"Nuremberg."

"Oh, fuck off!" I sit in a dumbfounded silence for a moment. "It'll probably win the Tony for best new play. Or the Pulitzer."

"Jealousy is not a good look on someone as handsome as you, Noah."

"I'm sorry. I guess this isn't exactly the sexy late-night call you were hoping for."

"You'll be back home in three little weeks. And then 'we shan't be parted no more.' How's the musical going?"

"We added a dream ballet."

Chase tries to stifle a chuckle and fails. "You did what?"

"It's a child-friendly, eye-gouging movement piece with ribbons and it's strangely moving."

"Well, all right, then. By the way, I sent Danielle Vincent a bottle of champagne on your behalf."

"Thanks, but why?"

"She's directing the new Michael John LaChiusa musical at the Public."

"Oh," I say. Then add somewhat petulantly, "Glad to hear she's landed on her feet."

Chase gives me a chastising, "Noah."

"No, you're right. I'm happy for her. And you're so sweet to always think of these things. How are you so perfect?"

"I do what I can. Right, well, we both sound knackered. I'm

going to nod off to sleep and dream about riding on top of you in what the kids are calling the 'reverse cowgirl' position."

"No spurs, please. I have delicate skin."

And the line goes dead before we can exchange the words "I love you." Or even say goodbye. I assume he was just hoping to make his joke about performing the reverse cowgirl land. Or he's just tired. That's probably it. "Knackered."

# nine

# "The Balloon Faire"

Thursday night rehearsal comes and like a bunch of middle-aged teacher's pets, the entire cast shows up with yesterday's staging down cold. I remind myself to do the encouraging thing.

"You guys are nailing it! I mean, not one single missed line or flubbed bit of blocking. You've more than earned your balloon thingy!"

The cast shares a few self-congratulatory smiles as they begin to pack up for the night. As they do, I surreptitiously cross a line through week one of the rehearsal schedule. I've already put big Xs through the last four days, but who's counting?

With Friday's rehearsal canceled I have nothing to do, so I opt to tag along with Mom as she grocery shops.

Mom drives as I text Chase: What are your plans for the weekend? Let me live vicariously.

Chase texts: Going to an industry thing in the Bronx. (It's a borough, apparently.) Then Netflix is having a tasting of artisanal honey from an actual hive on a rooftop followed by a screening of the latest Sofia Coppola film. E tu?

I groan and text: Currently hoping that I'm on the guest list at the Plainview Piggly Wiggly. The doorman can be a real prick. If Mom and I get in (she's wearing crocs) I plan on heading straight to check out their artisanal honey section.

I get a "HA HA" Tapback for my efforts.

Soon Mom and I are negotiating the aisles of the grocery store when we bump into Kristy Kim Eldridge, the Presbyterian pastor's wife. She sees me and squeals, "There's our fancy New Yorker!"

I give Kristy Kim a hug and mutter, "I don't know about fancy."

Kristy Kim shakes her head and nods toward her cart. "Would you look at this overpopulated grocery cart of mine? The grandkids are eating us out of house and home. We went through three boxes of Lucky Charms in half an hour flat! And now they're all hopped up on sugar. I caught one of them trying to put baby doll clothes on the cat!"

Mom laughs. "Well, they can blow off some steam at the fair."

"Amen to that. That's all those kids talk about. They just love the Balloon Faire. But what's not to love, right? Say, did you two see in the newspaper that they've got two new balloons this year? One that's shaped like Elvis and one that's shaped like one of those little yellow guys from the Minions movies, I forgot what they're called."

"Minions," I say, helpfully.

"It gets bigger every year!" Mom enthuses. "What time does the face painting start on Saturday? I hear you've got new costumes!"

"Nine a.m. sharp! And yes, Luke and I can't wait to unveil our new look! Anywho. I'd better get back with these provisions. I'll see you all tonight."

And then Kristy Kim disappears in a cloud of floral perfume.

So Luke, the guy who called me a Shakes-queer in the hallways of Plainview High School now volunteers to paint children's faces? I guess it makes sense. It's called image rebranding and I'm not falling for it.

"You don't have to be such a snob about the fair, Noah. The disdain written on your face is more than obvious."

I shrug and examine boxes of pancake batter. "I just don't get it, that's all."

"Well, your father doesn't really get theater, but he still pitches in the only way he knows how. Hot air balloons are his thing. If you can't be enthusiastic, you could at least turn the sarcasm down to a low roar."

"I have to say, I'm glad the Quaker Oats people finally took Aunt Jemima off all their breakfast products. But replacing her with the Pearl Milling Company? Is milling for pearls even ethical?"

Mom snatches the pancake mix I'm holding and slams it back onto the shelf. "Stop deflecting."

"No, no, I heard you," I grumble. "Ease up on the attitude. Got it. I'll try."

Later that night as the sun is setting and I'm pretending to eat Mom's ambrosia salad, a horrifying combination of canned pineapple, miniature marshmallows, and coconut flakes, there's a knock on the door. I get up to open it only to find Luke wearing a t-shirt with the words "Plainview Balloon Faire" scrawled across it in rainbow colors. The expression on my face must be crystal clear because he immediately says, "What? You don't like the shirt?"

"That's an understatement."

Luke seems pleased with himself. "I knew you'd hate it."

"Let me guess. You wore it just to fuck with me, you fucker."

To my complete and abject horror, Luke holds up a plastic bag. "And I got you one!"

I immediately freeze. "No. Absolutely not."

Luke's enthusiasm isn't dimmed in the slightest by my refusal. "Arms up above your head!"

I stand as still as a statue with a look of disdain on my face, but Luke doesn't give up.

"Come on, Noah! Arms up! Up! Up! Up! Just like Superman!"

And for reasons that will forever remain unknown, I begrudgingly obey. Luke slides the t-shirt over my polo and lingers for a second when he gets to my waist. If I lowered my hands to his shoulders, we'd be in the perfect position for slow dancing. But Luke steps back and smiles triumphantly at me in the tacky t-shirt. Unsure what to do, I lower my arms and call for Mom and Dad to get a move on.

After some griping from Dad about not getting to do his

tethered ride thing, we finally pile into Mom's Toyota. It doesn't take long for Dad's foul mood to fill the air.

When we get to Francis Park, it is teeming with people. Mom parks the car and we make our way through the crowd slowly so that Dad can keep up. Festive music is already blaring and the air is warm and smells like popcorn and cotton candy. We finally get to the center of the park where it seems like an infinite amount of hot air balloons wait majestically against the sky. We walk through them in awe as they flicker almost in time to the music, glowing like enormous stained glass windows in the growing darkness of night.

Mom and Dad wander ahead, but Luke catches the look on my face and turns smug. He leans over and whispers in my ear, "Did I tell you or did I tell you?"

"It's like walking through a kaleidoscope," I say. "You were right. You did, in fact, tell me, and I refused to be told."

Luke stares up at the balloons and I allow myself to take in his face under the fluctuating haze of the Glow. His cheekbones light up in shifting waves of orange and red, the gold in his hair goes from purple to blue. He notices me staring and he stops and stares right back, while more flashes of color rhythmically wash over us. There's something so innocent in his eyes that I begin to wonder if Mom was right about people changing. Maybe Luke volunteered to paint children's faces not because he was trying to rehabilitate his image. Maybe he volunteered because he likes . . . oh, what is that word again?

Oh, right.

*Helping.*

Chase pops up in my head and I make a mental note to call him later. Yes, focus, Noah. Concentrate on your boyfriend. The dreamy one whom you're committed to.

Luke must notice a change in my expression, because he snaps out of our shared trance. "Oh, I almost forgot. We don't want to be late."

"Be late for what?" I ask.

"You'll see." Luke jogs a few steps ahead toward Mom and Dad. "Mr. and Mrs. A., I've got a surprise for you, if you'll follow me."

Confused, we follow Luke through a crowded maze of people and down a small dirt pathway. We end up in a hidden clearing off to the side of the park. Waiting there like enormous fireflies are two impressive hot air balloons. One burns a neon green and yellow checkerboard pattern into the night sky and the other one has an art deco design of red and silver diamonds. A two-person crew stands waiting patiently beside each basket.

Dad looks perplexed. "What's going on, Luke?"

Luke folds his arms and strikes an authoritative pose. Clearly he's got some sort of plan and none of us should even think of questioning it.

"Well, me and Dr. Dunbar had a little chat. He agreed that it'd be okay for you to go without your oxygen for about an hour. But that's the absolute limit. *So*, then, I figured if that's the case, why waste the time on just some boring tethered ride? The four of us are going to take a little tour of Plainview from the sky."

Dad is speechless. We all are.

I finally ask, "How did you arrange all this?"

Luke goes smug. "I know a guy."

Before any of us can think twice, people are loading Mom and Dad into one balloon and Luke and me into another. As we start to lift up into the air it feels as if gravity is evaporating all around us. The ascent is quicker than I expected and the smell of the propane heater powering the balloon makes me slightly dizzy. The trees around us appear to shrink as we rise up into the night sky. It's all happening so fast that I forget to be afraid of being up so high. I look over and see Dad's eyes go wide with wonder as he takes it all in. Without thinking, I grab Luke's tree trunk of an arm and shout, "Look at Dad!"

Dad catches us staring at him and a goofy smile spreads across his face almost against his will. The burner shoots a loud blast of air up into their balloon, startling Dad. He laughs at getting caught off guard and then gives Luke and me an enthusiastic thumbs-up. Mom, on the other hand, is too busy taking a million pictures with her phone to notice anything else.

As we climb farther into the night sky, everything goes blissfully silent. Only the occasional whoosh from the balloon's burner breaks the spell. A tinge of fear runs through me as the ground gets farther away and I'm suddenly full of a million questions.

"How high does this thing go?"

Luke shrugs. "Pretty high. Three thousand feet or so." Luke must read the smallest bit of trepidation in my expression. "You're not scared of heights, are you? I guess I should have asked that first."

I try my best to play it cool and put on a brave face. "I'm fine. Just, um, where exactly are we going?"

Another shrug from Luke. "Wherever the wind takes us."

Below us, the Glow continues and the distant glimmering balloons make the park grounds look like some kind of vintage Lite-Brite toy.

And on we float.

As we climb higher, my nerves seem to dissipate. Something about the serene look on Luke's face makes me feel strangely safe soaring through the air. Am I really getting used to being up this high? Or is his confidence simply that contagious?

The geometric patchwork fields below us look like something a scenic artist from an old MGM film has dreamed up. Rows of grain silos seem like little bullets pointing skyward. Here and there, tiny creeks spread across the ground like glistening arteries. Soon, Mom lets out a giddy squeal and I look down to realize we're hovering just above our farm. Dad and Mom's place looks like a meticulously detailed dollhouse that some toymaker wired with electricity to make the windows light up.

It almost becomes too much to bear. I turn to Luke, brimming with so much gratitude that I can't even form the words to thank him. I mean, how did he even plan all of this? And how much is this costing him? It's just all so unlike the Luke I used to know that it's mind-boggling. And yet here I am, marveling at the view as well as Luke's thoughtfulness. Before I can say anything, the guy piloting the balloon suddenly turns informative.

"There are basically three parts to this little beauty. There's the envelope, that's what most people just call the balloon. Then there's the burner, which runs on propane and keeps us afloat. Some envelopes are big enough to need multiple burners, but this one's perfectly good with just one."

I glance at Luke with a quizzical look. Why is this guy lecturing us? But Luke seems to be hanging on his every word. He clearly shares Dad's fascination with how things work. I never care how things work, as long as they do.

"Then there's the basket or the 'gondola' if you want to get fancy about it."

As the pilot goes on, Luke gives me a self-satisfied look. "How do you like the fair now?"

"Okay, it's pretty great," I confess. "But I still think they shouldn't put the ridiculous 'e' on the end of the word 'faire.' Talk about getting superfluous with vowels."

Luke stares at me once again with those lingering eyes.

"So, why didn't we all just go in one balloon?" I ask. "There's plenty of room."

"Um . . . because I wanted to talk to you. In private."

We both avert our gaze for a long moment and I wonder if there's another uncomfortable conversation looming on the horizon. Do we really have to do this right now? Right when everything seems so unreal and perfect?

"So you wanted to have a captive audience for this little chat?"

Luke nods. "I'm assuming you won't jump."

I exhale slowly. "Fine. Fire away."

"So, why did you call me a homophobe that day at the hospital?"

And in a flash, all the old anger is back. "You're joking, right?!"

"No. You told me to go think about what I had done to you, and I have. And honestly, I'm still totally clueless."

"Luke, you and your buddies were fucking horrible to me in high school. I used to dread walking the halls, knowing that you guys were gonna start calling me a faggot or a cocksucker or the ever-popular Shakes-queer. And I'm just supposed to forget all that? Just act like it never happened and pretend we're best friends? I know it was a million years ago, but that shit lingers!"

Luke looks completely stunned for a moment but then starts aggressively shaking his head. "Hey, hold up. I never said anything like that. That might have been true of some of the other guys, but . . ."

"No, Luke. That bullshit is seared on my brain. It was you and Casey Martin, and that exchange student Alek Gunhus, and that kid Jared what's-his-name. And don't even get me started about what your best buddy Eddie did to me."

"What did Eddie do to you?"

"I don't want to talk about it because I don't want to relive it."

"Look, I know those guys were dickheads, but I never said anything mean to you. Not ever. Not in the slightest."

Teenage Noah has possessed my body and he isn't accepting any excuses. "But you let it happen. Which is almost worse."

"But I didn't let it happen."

I pause for a second while my brain stops functioning. The ghost of teenage Noah wavers. "What do you mean?"

"I didn't let it happen. I know you remember all that terrible shit those assholes made you suffer through. But you also have to remember that one day it suddenly stopped, right?"

I take a very long time to concentrate. Is he gaslighting me? No, no, it's vaguely coming back to me. There was a day when the clouds lifted and the hurtful taunting stopped. They just started to ignore me, which was like heaven compared to what daily life had been like when they were constantly tormenting me.

And then the biggest shock of all descends onto my slightly stalled brain. "Wait . . . that was because of . . . you?"

Luke shifts his gaze to the fields below us, seemingly contrite. "I should have said something sooner or right when it happened, but I guess I was scared. But yeah, eventually I told them that they were dicks. And if they were hoping to impress girls or get laid by being assholes to you, it wasn't working. And I told them I'd stop hanging out with them if they didn't cut that shit out."

We're silent as we float over the Plainview train station, which looks like a miniature Christmas display from a store window. Another whoosh of hot air keeps us bobbing along.

Both teenage Noah and adult Noah have questions. "Okay, well, let's say that's true. Then let me ask you this and I honestly want to know: Why?"

"Why what?"

"Why did you stick up for me?"

"Because you didn't deserve any of that bullshit. And I also thought you were, I don't know." He throws his head back and gives an embarrassed moan. "I thought you were cool, Noah."

I can't stop myself and laugh right in his face. "Cool? I was never cool! And if you had such a high opinion of me back then, why didn't you ever talk to me?"

Luke stares at me, obviously at a total loss. "I don't know." My gaze wanders back down to Earth. Another farm goes by below us. Stacks of hay look like little bars of gold. "I guess I was intimidated by you."

I turn back to Luke as another way-too-loud laugh escapes me.

Luke continues. "Oh, come on, man! Did you completely black out Mrs. Henson's English Lit class? The two of you would carry on for hours about poetry and metaphors and a million other things that I had no clue about. That none of us had any clue about. You wrote one of your term papers in iambic pentameter, Noah! I didn't even know what that was. I had to google it. What was I going to talk to you about, your dad's new cow-milking machine with the graphite pump? The 49ers? You were the guy everybody called Shakespeare."

"And Shakes-queer," I say.

"Hey, I never called you that. I only called you Shakespeare and I'm sorry that turned out the way it did. I sorta meant it as a compliment."

The balloon makes an unexpected dip and my heart shoots up into the back of my throat. I grab the side of the basket without thinking and give Luke a frantic look.

"Are you okay?"

My voice trembles and I hate myself for it. "I lied. I sometimes do have a thing with heights. It comes and goes. It's fine. I'm fine." I roll my eyes at my own stupidity. "Just ignore me."

But he doesn't. Luke reaches up and puts a gentle hand on my shoulder and says, "I'm not going to let anything happen to you, Noah. We're safe."

A nervous laugh escapes me. "You can't possibly know that."

Luke says with complete certainty, "If I say we're safe, we're safe."

And all at once my nerves are gone, but my heart remains in my throat for a very different reason.

I find myself staring so deeply into Luke's eyes that a Sondheim lyric pops into my head: "*I could look at him forever.*"

Okay, Noah. Time to look away. You're not in a Sondheim musical.

I turn my gaze bravely back out toward the sky and it takes me a second to realize that we're already sailing our way back to Francis Park. Before I know it, our basket gently lands on the grass as Mom and Dad's touches down beside us seconds later.

We're all in a kind of lightheaded daze during the car ride home. Mom and Dad seem dizzy from the flight, but I'm dizzy from something else entirely. Have I misjudged Luke for the last fifteen years? After the bullying stopped, I was so focused on getting the hell out of Plainview and making it to Broadway that I never even considered *why* it stopped.

Dad's busy fiddling with his oxygen tube, but manages to say from the front passenger seat, "I don't know how to thank you for that, Luke."

Luke is silent for a minute, and then utters the noblest lie ever. "Noah and I came up with the idea together."

Dad is quiet for a split second and then adds, "Well, thank you, too, son."

In the darkness of the back seat, I silently wonder if the world will ever make sense to me again.

ten

# "Send in the Clowns"

Every time I close my eyes and try to drift off to sleep, the balloon ride with Luke snaps me right back into consciousness. If what he said is true, I've been treating Luke Carter like shit for absolutely no reason. Patti LuPone glares down at me from one of my many framed *Evita* window cards. I whine back at her, "I know, Patti. I *know*!"

Feeling perplexed, I decide it's time for a check-in with Kiara. I shoot her a text and my phone immediately rings. "Hi, baby boy! What's happening over at Green Acres?"

"Confusion is happening."

Kiara squeals. "Ooh, spill! I've got a nice full glass of malbec and as I sip and sink into the couch, you are going to spill every last juicy bean! Go!"

"So it turns out that this guy I thought was a complete prick, isn't. Turns out I had the wrong idea about him for years. And he took me on a private balloon ride tonight."

"Come again?"

"A hot air balloon ride. There's a big fair here. A fair with an 'e' on the end of it. It's a thing."

"Okay."

"It gets worse." I pause, and then confess, "We wore matching t-shirts."

Kiara is silent for a moment and then says very gravely, "I'm going to need a list of all the medications you're currently taking."

"And the other day, he ran his fingers through my hair."

More silence from Kiara, then a very worried, "Uh-oh."

"But he's straight, Kiara. At least, I think."

"He's not straight, baby boy. Straight men do not run their fingers through other men's hair."

"Are you sure?"

"Hold up." I hear her call out to Stephen. "Stephen, do straight men ever run their fingers through other men's hair?"

Stephen shouts out adamantly, "Negative!"

"I rest my case."

"Then what is going on?"

"He's gay. Or he's bi. And you have a boyfriend, so you better make sure his fingers don't end up back in your hair. Or anywhere else."

"I do have a boyfriend. A wonderful, gorgeous boyfriend who is going to negotiate Aleister Murphy's Broadway debut."

"So it's true?"

"His latest play already has producers attached."

"You need to get back here and start working on something new. Forget those balloon-riding yokels and return to the big city where you belong! Now, I've got to go, but promise me you'll not take up with any of those farm people behind Chase's back."

"I love and miss you to the Milky Way and back!"

"Ditto, baby boy! Just three more weeks!"

She hangs up and I'm so homesick for Kiara and Chase and Manhattan that I consider just saying screw it all and hopping on a plane back home. But I couldn't do that to the Plainview Players. They'd be devastated and, who knows, maybe they're starting to grow on me. Plus, there's still a critic coming. I just have to stay focused.

I roll over and finally fall into a fitful sleep, but early in the morning there's a panicky banging on my bedroom door. Without waiting for a response, Mom bursts in and frantically yanks the bed sheet off me so fast that it actually makes a muffled snap.

"Mom, what the hell?"

"It's an emergency, Noah. Get up! Get up now!"

I jump to my feet like a dutiful boy scout and pull on the nearest t-shirt. "What's wrong? Is it Dad? Is he okay?"

Mom wags her head, dismissing the idea. "Your dad's fine. You couldn't kill him with a stick!"

I anxiously scan her face. "Then what? Is something on fire? Is the house on fire? You're scaring me!"

It takes me a quick second to realize that she's sizing up my body for some reason. "No, it's Booboo! You have to be Booboo! Luke's downstairs with your costume."

I command my jumbled brain to get back on track. "What the actual fuckity-fuck are you talking about?"

"Booboo! From Britches and Booboo! You know!"

It's finally happened. Nancy Kay Adams has officially lost whatever tiny shred of sanity she had left.

"Mom, it's too early on a Saturday morning to have you committed, so I'm just going back to bed for a couple more hours until the local insane asylum opens for business."

I start to crawl back toward my rumpled bed, when Luke appears behind Mom dressed in ridiculous baggy clown pants, a tattered derby, and scary white kabuki makeup. I stare at him in confusion. "What the hell is John Wayne Gacy doing in my bedroom at this point in time?!?"

Luke sounds like he's trying to remain calm, but there's an urgency to his voice that makes no sense coming from someone wearing a rainbow fright wig. "Kristy Kim's sick, Noah. You're the only one we can think of who will fit into the costume."

I glower at them both. "What?"

Mom gives me an exasperated look. "Noah, you know that Kristy Kim and Luke dress up as Britches and Booboo every year when they do face painting at the Balloon Faire!"

"Why would I know that?" I ask. "Why would I have any of that information?"

"Well, you have it now. And the kids go crazy for them. But Kristy Kim's sick, so you have to be Booboo!"

Luke holds up a flouncy crinoline-lined dress covered with brightly colored buttons and bows. "You're, what, five foot eight? A hundred and fifty-five pounds? A hundred and sixty?"

"Stop trying to guess my weight like I'm some sort of prize pig!" I self-consciously wrap the bed sheet around my waist, wondering if I've put on a few extra pounds. With nothing but Mom's nursing home food to eat, I'm doubtful.

"Can you both get out of here? I am not dressing up like Bop Bop!"

"Booboo!" they correct me in unison.

"I can't be a clown. Clowns terrify children. And I can't do funny voices!"

Before I can stop them, they're pulling me out of bed and yanking the scratchy dress over my head.

"I'm not doing this. I'm not dressing up like a female clown. As a cis white male, it would be offensive of me to co-opt someone else's gender identity."

"It's for charity, Noah! Just paint some stars and moons on the kids' cheeks and you'll raise a couple of bucks for the hospital."

Mom dusts me from head to toe with glitter spray. As I choke on the fumes, I try one last-ditch effort to stop the madness.

"I am not leaving this bedroom dressed like this! I only have a tiny amount of dignity left and I intend to cling to it!"

And a half an hour later, I'm doing my gay Jerry Lewis voice while painting butterflies on a seemingly endless row of children's faces. I only stop once to whip out my phone with the full intention of sending Chase a selfie of me dressed as the bastard love child of Ronald McDonald and the girl from the Wendy's fast food logo. But when I see myself, I quickly reconsider. The image of me in carrot-colored braids and falsies is a definite boner killer. I return my phone to my dainty clown lady purse.

I start feeling bizarrely jealous of Luke, who's getting a much bigger reaction from the kids. I chalk it up to the fact that he not only has a water-squirting boutonniere, but also a motorized spinning bowtie.

"It's not fair that you get all the fun props. Where's my gimmick?" I complain to Luke as he impressively transforms a twelve-year-old boy's face into a werewolf.

"You wanna borrow my flower? Just don't shoot water at little girls. They don't like it and they'll tell their moms. And you don't want the moms after you. They're relentless."

I consider it, then huff, "No, I've just decided that Booboo isn't that kind of a girl. She relies on her buoyant personality and natural moxie. She doesn't need cheap gags."

Luke laughs. "So Booboo believes in self-reliance?"

"Oh, definitely. She even put herself through clown college."

"Impressive. What was her major?"

"She has a doctorate in balloon animals."

I take a moment to admire Luke's handiwork. "You really know how to transform a face. How did you get roped into this gig?"

"Well, I was on the stage crew for *Godspell* a couple of years ago. They needed someone to paint the cast's faces and they drafted me. Pastor Ed and Kristy Kim came to see the show and that night Britches and Booboo were born."

Pretty soon, Luke and I are pounding out face paintings like we're trying to fill a very ambitious quota. I've just graduated from stars and moons to very rudimentary unicorns when I hear a brassy voice ring out, "Well, look at Mr. Fancy Pants who said he was too good for the Balloon Faire now!"

To my complete humiliation, it's Jackie McNew staring at me

in my clown drag while she chomps on a half-eaten funnel cake.
She elbows her sister in triumph. "See, Julia! I told you he'd come
around!" They share a laugh, both of their faces plastered in
powdered sugar. "Hey, Noah! What would all your fancy Broadway friends think if they saw you dressed up like a lady clown?"

She inspects the cheek of the little girl I'm working on. "You
call that a unicorn? It looks like a horse with a cancerous growth
sticking out of its forehead."

The little girl immediately looks panic-stricken.

"Nice, Jackie. You think you could do better?"

"I know I could." Jackie grabs a washcloth from our worktable
and rubs my handiwork away without a second thought. "Let
Aunt Jackie draw you a real unicorn. A healthy one with rain-
bows and crap!"

I'm about to protest, but I catch Luke out of the corner of my
eye. He's gone white as a ghost, which is saying a lot since he's
wearing clown makeup. He notices me staring. "I've gotta go."

Before I can say anything, Luke yanks off his rainbow wig
and is making a beeline for the park's welcome center. I quickly
turn to the McNew twins. "You two think you could cover
for us?"

Jackie shoos me away. "Julia and I got this. You should stick to
writing anyway, because you sure don't know shit about unicorns."

"Agreed," I say and then head off after Luke.

I quickly search the welcome center, which is crowded with
people hawking a never-ending procession of hot-air balloon–
themed souvenirs. There's everything from refrigerator magnets
to automated baby crib mobiles for sale. But no Luke.

I finally find him behind the building washing his makeup off with a garden hose. Relieved, I yank my Pippi Longstocking wig off and patiently wait my turn. Luke silently hands me the hose and goes to sit on the ground while I finish washing what's left of Booboo from my face. The white clown makeup swirls into the mud at my feet.

I cautiously sit down next to Luke and sense him trembling beside me. He refuses to look at me and seems only interested in the blinding blue sky above us. Every once in a while random people walk by and give us curious looks.

And even though I know that I look like a freak with makeup still smudged around the edges of my face, I feel the need to support Luke. I can't just sit here in silence. The guy who has a smile for everyone in town looks dangerously close to crumbling.

"So . . . are you okay?"

"Yep," Luke answers a little too quickly and then reconsiders. "Well, no, actually. I think . . . I think I saw my dad back there."

"Oh. I . . . here? Does he live around here or something?"

Luke's expression goes grim and I'm not sure if I should push the issue. But I can't stop myself. Like a clumsy doctor trying exploratory surgery, I ask as carefully as possible, "So . . . when did you last see him?"

Silence.

I quickly add, "I mean, you don't have to talk about it if you don't want to."

Luke sighs and continues to stare off into the slowly ambling clouds for a couple of seconds. "You want the whole shebang?"

"I want whatever you want to tell me. The whole shebang.

The half shebang. The travel-sized shebang . . ." My voice trails off as I realize that I sound like a babbling moron.

Surprisingly, words start coming out of Luke like hot lava, picking up steam as he speaks. "I guess I was six, maybe seven when he left. I don't remember much about him really. Just that he was mean as shit. And it got worse as the days would grind on. He'd just be sort of grumpy in the morning, but he was usually too hungover to make much of a stink. But then he'd get to drinking and bit by bit, hour by hour, he'd get more agitated. More mad at the world. By nighttime he was downright fucking terrifying. So I remember just being scared of him. Scared for myself and for Mom. And Mom, man, the shit she put up with. The way she would run around like his freakin' servant, walking on eggshells the whole time. I guess we both were. And the booze turned to drugs and from what I can remember it got really bad. He would just wipe the floor with Mom and there was nothing I could do. I couldn't even cry, because that would make him even angrier. And then one day, he was gone. Took our station wagon, drained the checking account and left. And even though Mom was crushed, it was the happiest day of my life."

Luke pauses, slightly self-conscious. A car backfires somewhere close by, scaring several blue jays from a tree. We watch them beat a wing-flapping retreat.

I try to think of something positive to say.

"I'm sure your mom had to feel a little relieved that he was gone, right?"

"Nope. A few years later, I heard her talking to my grandma and I realized that she was still missing Dad. She asked over the phone, 'How could Luke and me be so easy to leave?' Well, that just destroyed me. I mean, why in hell would she want a guy like that back in her life? Mom was kind of a mess after that. She wasn't really thinking straight. And the whole town has never let her forget any of the bad choices she made. I guess that's made me pretty protective of her. Maybe overprotective."

Luke pauses and I struggle to find something to say. Nothing seems appropriate. "Is this the first time you've seen him? Since he left, I mean."

"Oh, no. When I was a sophomore in high school, I did some digging around on the internet. I found out he was working at a John Deere dealership over in Mt. Vernon. Remarried to some woman named Jillian who had a ten-year-old son, Matt. So I looked up their address and I don't know what possessed me, but I drove to his house. And there he was, clean and sober, playing basketball with little Matty in the driveway. And Jillian is sitting on the porch, watching with a mug of coffee and smiling. And it just struck me, you know? He was able to get clean and sober for them, but not for Mom and me. I guess we just weren't worth the effort. I guess we were easy to leave, after all."

More silence.

"Jesus, Luke. I'm so sorry. That is some fucked-up shit," I finally say.

"I just wasn't prepared to see him again. He's probably here with his shiny new family playing horseshoes or eating corndogs. And Mom and me, well, we're just some faded memory that he doesn't give a fuck about anymore."

Feeling completely incompetent, I reach up to put a consoling hand on Luke's shoulder. But before I can, he quickly jumps to his feet. His voice is strangely cold and all business. "Thanks for helping today. I'm sure the McNew girls have things under control. So you don't have to hang around anymore."

And with that Luke is walking toward the parking lot and all I can do is helplessly watch him go. An unfamiliar urgency comes over me and I quickly stand up and call after him.

"Luke! Wait!"

But he doesn't wait. And for reasons that make absolutely no sense, I feel like I'm losing something with each step he takes.

# eleven

# "The Pickle"

To absolutely no one's surprise, Sunday morning begins with a guilt trip about church services. As soon as I stumble into the kitchen, Mom's face brightens. "Oh, you're just in time! Go change clothes so we can all ride to church together! We can sit with the Glucks!"

"With who?"

"Jerry and Judy Gluck! They said they'd save us a seat in their pew. They always get the good one, right under the air conditioner vent."

"Yeah, no. I'm not going. But feel free to take a cardboard cut-out of me!"

Dad's busy shoveling some grizzled Franken-meat into his mouth. "Leave him alone, Nancy Kay."

"But Pastor Ed and everybody in the choir . . ."

"Listen, Mom. I love Pastor Ed and everybody in the choir. But I'm not up to it. So why don't you and Dad just take your sin-stained souls to church without me?"

Dad noisily clears his throat. "Son, I just wanted to say that it was real nice of you and Luke to arrange that private balloon ride the other night. I still can't get over it. That put all them tethered rides to shame!"

Do I tell him that it was all Luke's idea? But why spoil a rare happy moment with Dad? Luke was the one who lied about us arranging the ride together. And the lie was Luke's gift to me, so why ruin it?

"I'm glad you both enjoyed it."

Mom pretends to be intensely concentrating on wiping down the counter when she is really, in fact, prying. "So, how did the face painting go? Did you and Luke make a good team?"

"Yeah, yeah. I might have . . . um, I don't know. Misjudged the guy."

"Well, that's why you should come with us to church and pray on it."

"Nancy Kay!" Dad bellows. Mom deflates, giving in.

"Have fun!" I yell over my shoulder as I start to climb the stairs.

Mom calls out behind me, "Would you like a couple pieces of fried Spam before I clear the table?"

I yell over my shoulder, "You know I would not!"

I'd like to say that I spent the rest of the day fighting off the urge to google news articles about Aleister Murphy's new play. But that would be a lie. I end up trolling several theater chat sites for any negative reactions I can find. I try to console myself by reasoning that professional jealousy is a perfectly human response. But what seems to console me even more is imagining Carrie Payne's review of a play about Nuremberg called *Pattycakes*.

What? I'm only human.

Later on I decide to scavenge through the fridge for something fit for human consumption. Hanging on the refrigerator door under one of Mom's garish magnets is a picture of Dad and Luke from last year's fair. The old me would have put the photo through the nearest shredder. But now, I shudder when I think about what I said the night after our first rehearsal. I believe the exact phrase was, "So you never had a dad growing up, does that mean you have to steal mine?" I take a scalding shower in an attempt to burn the guilt from my skin, but I just end up blotchy and remorseful.

Thankfully, Monday rolls around and brings with it plenty of diversions.

Local seamstress Allison Egan does all of the costumes for the Plainview Players. Partly because she knows how to sew and partly because she owns a fabric store and that means free notions and zippers. There's also a costume closet full of old clothes from past productions. We start Monday off seeing what Allison's come up with for Cordelia's look. She brings Melissa over in her costume and has her rotate in front of me as if she's standing on an invisible lazy Susan. The costume is a little bit Shakespearean and a little bit futuristic at the same time. And Melissa is unabashedly beaming.

"You look amazing, Melissa. Great work, Allison!"

Melissa curtsies. "I've decided that my character's subtext is that she's secretly pregnant."

"It ain't so secret, sister." I realize that Melissa is wearing a dainty tiara made out of greenery. "What's on her head?"

"Oh, that's a crown of oak leaves," Allison replies.

"Yeah, but, I mean, why is it there?"

"The way I see it, she's kind of the heroine of the musical. Or at least the moral center."

"And she should probably have more stage time," Melissa adds.

I give Melissa a look. "Don't start with me, you attention whore."

Melissa does a mocking pout. Allison continues, "And a crown of oak leaves symbolizes that heroism. And since her character was royalty, until her father disowned her that is, I figured she should still wear a crown. But now, instead of wearing a royal one, she wears one representing honesty and integrity."

I shake my head in awe. "That is really, really smart, Allison."

"Well, I like to research any show we do here."

Amazing. Allison Egan is so much more than just free zippers.

While I'm busy admiring Melissa's costume there seems to be yet another brouhaha brewing. Mrs. Henson is arguing with Jackie McNew over near the piano and from what I can make out, she's begging her not to say anything.

"What's going on, ladies?" I ask, though I'm sure I really don't want to know.

Jackie starts out, "Well, the thing is, Booboo—"

I stop her, nipping the nickname in the bud. "No."

Jackie rolls her eyes. "Fine. The thing is, Noah, I get you probably don't want to hear any more of our thoughts."

"Do I have a choice?"

Julia McNew steps forward wearing a ridiculous t-shirt with a

cartoon mouse clutching an olive that reads, "Olive you." Her sister wears the same thing, naturally. "You're not gonna like this."

"Then why tell me?"

"It's just the dialogue—" Jackie starts and I can feel my blood
pressure soar.

"The dialogue? The *dialogue*?"

Julia corrects her twin. "Well, that's not true, it's also the lyrics, too."

Veins threaten to explode in my forehead as the rest of the cast
gathers around me. "What about the dialogue and the lyrics?"

Julia hesitates. "Now, don't take this the wrong way."

"We're talking about my dialogue and lyrics. Is there a right
way I could take it?"

Jackie, always the alpha twin, takes over. "Look, nobody is
criticizing your writing here. We're just wondering why we're using all this 'ye' and 'thou' talk."

I give a disgruntled look to Melissa, who averts her eyes.
Whose side is she on, anyway? And before I know what's happening, I snap. I snap big time.

"Why are we using 'ye' and 'thou' talk?! Well, let's think about
that, you middle-aged twins who wear identical clothing as if
you were babies! Maybe we're using 'ye' and 'thou' talk because
it's an adaptation of a play written by William Shakespeare.
Which it clearly states on the title page of everyone's script!"

Jackie morphs into a spitfire, jutting her chin out and putting
her fists on her hips. "First of all, don't talk about the way me and
my sister dress. Second of all, we don't speak with all of that

'thee' and 'thy' and 'thyself' nowadays. And we're already a thousand years after when Shakespeare even lived!"

"What was that? A *thousand* years after Shakespeare even lived? A *thousand*? Is that what you think?"

Jackie shouts out, "I'm not good at math and that's not the point!"

"Well, maybe you should get good at math. You know what numbers are, right? Them's the squiggles that ain't letters?!"

Jackie shakes her head like she's convincing herself not to jump me. "Forget it, Mr. Broadway. So sorry we had an idea. I thought you said the best idea wins when you made that big speech the first day!"

The room freezes. No one can actually look at anyone else for a few minutes.

Mrs. Henson pipes up as gently as possible. "That *is* what you said, Noah. About the best idea winning."

I feel my chest deflate slightly. Of course my own words would come back to haunt me. Of course!

"Fine! Explain to me why this is the best idea, then!"

Jackie gives what can only be a smoker's cough and then begins talking to me like I'm an infant. "So, we don't speak Shakespeare talk today and we're only however many years ahead of his time. Why—if your show is set even *further* in the future—do they speak Shakespeare talk when we even don't speak it *now*? I mean, I don't get it! Did everyone in the future suddenly revert back to all this 'my liege' crap?"

"Okay, okay. Let's say I even agreed with you about this, which I don't. But if I did, even if I decided to change the dialogue . . .

what about the so-called 'Shakespeare talk' in the lyrics? If I tried to change that, the lyrics wouldn't sit right. The syllables would be all off and wouldn't fit with the melodies."

Jackie looks at me like I'm a dummy. "But, like, didn't you write the melodies, too? Couldn't you just change them as well?"

"We open in less than three weeks! I mean, come on, people! Or maybe we just shouldn't open. Maybe this was all a terrible, terrible idea. You know what? Maybe we should not be doing this. So let's just not! Everybody go home! Rehearsal is canceled!"

There's a communal gasp and Mrs. Henson quietly bursts into tears. I rush toward the back of the theater, out through the exit and stop only long enough to kick a dumpster waiting in the darkness. I pace back and forth, trying to breathe and get my pulse to slow down. But it doesn't work and my mind keeps racing.

I turn to realize that Melissa has silently emerged from the building and is watching me pace.

"I'm the fucking author of this show, Melissa!"

Melissa's face is blank, but she nods and calmly says, "Yes, you are."

"What was I thinking? I should have known this would happen! I was giving everyone too much creative freedom! I've dedicated my entire life to theater, studied the great composers and librettists and somehow I ended up listening to a bunch of, no offense, amateurs!"

"That's exactly what we are."

"You guys don't know what it takes to craft a melody or come up with innovative rhymes or build a musical number to show character growth or story development!"

Melissa remains still and sphinxlike, her face giving nothing away. "You're right. We haven't the foggiest."

I freeze in my tracks. "What's going on? What are you doing right now?"

Melissa serenely replies, "Agreeing with you. Trying to avoid saying anything that will send you off into another screaming frenzy. Because you were kind of frightening back there."

A horrible realization hits me like a ton of bricks.

And it turns out that even if it's metaphorical, a ton of bricks is not fun to be hit by. Not by a long shot.

"Oh, no, Melissa," I say slowly. "I just screamed at all of those nice people."

"You sure did."

I find a patchy piece of grass and sit down with a thud. At least the stars seem happy, twinkling away and unaware that I just made a senior citizen piano player burst into tears.

Melissa approaches and puts her hand on my shoulder for leverage, lowering her pregnant body down to the ground next to me with a grunt. We are silent for a minute or two.

"So, to be clear I just threw a hissy fit of epic proportions in there, right?"

"Boy howdy."

I moan in shame.

I plop my throbbing head into my hands and squeeze my temples. It doesn't help.

Melissa gently asks, "Are you really going to just take your ball and go home?"

"Of course not. It's just . . . it's just that my mother, who is clearly in need of a lobotomy, invited a critic. And now everyone in there thinks I can just snap my fingers and transform the entire score in time for them to learn new lyrics before opening night."

"So . . . you agree with them? About the, I don't know what to call them, 'Shakespeare-isms?'"

"I don't know, Melissa. No. Maybe. I guess? But it doesn't matter because there is no time."

"We've got . . ." She stops, clearly counting in her head. "Fifteen rehearsals left. That's doable, right?"

"But it's a major undertaking. I'll admit, changing the dialogue would be relatively easy. But lyrics, they scan, you know?"

"I don't know what 'scan' means."

"Okay, take the opening number. The hook is 'Who doth love him most?' If I change that to 'Who loves him most?' then it won't match with the notes in the melody."

"Now, are you all yelled out? Because I want to suggest something, but pregnant ladies shouldn't be yelled at."

I heave a sigh. "Suggest away."

"If you're married to that melody, can't you just stretch the word 'loves' over two notes?"

Huh.

It could work.

It could actually work.

I stare at her, my mind spinning. And before I know what I'm doing, I jump to my feet and offer her a hand.

"Um, Noah? Where are we going?"

"To the Batmobile!"

I help Melissa up and we go inside to the upright piano. Thankfully, everyone has gone home, most likely to avoid being yelled at some more. I pull out the score and grab my trusty Ticonderoga and start making alterations to the opening number. "Does this sound better if I change the modulation here?"

Melissa listens carefully, her head cocked to one side like a Schnauzer. "You know, I think it does. It's kind of more foreboding that way. There's more tension."

I start scribbling like crazy over the sheet music. "It's almost like everyone onstage already knows that Captain Lear is going to make a bad choice. And if the people on the spaceship know anything about Cordelia, they'll know she won't be able to flatter her father."

Melissa and I are on fire now. "Noah, get this! What if after the bridge, it goes even more minor?"

"You crazy genius!!! I mean, it's not technically possible to go 'more minor,' but I think I know what you mean. Like this?"

I play a few bars and Melissa isn't too pregnant to jump up and down. "I'm getting goose bumps!"

"Okay, I can play around with that some more. But, ugh, the Goneril and Regan duet is riddled with period words. How do we even start to hack away at that?"

Melissa gives me a grimace. "Noah, I love that you're on a roll right now. But I'm exhausted and have to get home to my husband before I absolutely collapse."

"Of course you do. Go ahead, I'll figure this out. Daddy is cooking with gas now!"

Once I'm alone in the theater, I have to admit it feels a little creepy. Theaters are notoriously haunted and, though I'm not like my mom who sees ghosts on a daily basis, I'm still a little spooked. But then I look at the sheet music scattered across the top of the piano and the work ahead distracts me. I wonder when I started caring about this little community theater production. At what point did I decide that it mattered to me? I can't really remember when the switch had flipped, but it clearly had. The Plainview Players had definitely grown on me and their roots were starting to furrow somewhere deep inside of me.

I'm slowly starting to work through the score and replace or cut the old timey words when I look up and see a ghost on the stage and gasp like an old lady.

Luke steps into the light. "It's just me."

"You fucker! You scared the shit out of me!"

Luke laughs. He walks over to me with his signature Luke Carter saunter. "I was just doing some adjustments to the set. Your dad gave me a list. An actual list."

I hesitate to even ask, but I have to. "So . . . were you there to witness my epic meltdown?"

"I might have been in the vicinity."

"Great. Now I'm extra mortified."

"Look, man, I think you've been a real sport. What you do is important to you, right? It's personal. And to have a bunch of people knock it so openly. That can't be easy."

"But I yelled at them. I yelled at those poor, sweet, apple-cheeked people who were just excited to do my show. How do I fix that? How do I make this into a safe space for them again? I was an epic asshole."

"Well, then, I guess you just have to make an epic apology. You know, one of those big speeches. You're good at those."

I close my eyes and consider for a second. "Yes, I suppose I *could* do that." I then look at Luke with a better idea. "*Or* I could pray to our Father in heaven and ask him to start the rapture in the next hour or so and then I'll be off the hook."

Luke morphs into a stern but handsome high school principal. "Noah."

"Fine. Epic apology it is." I sit back down at the piano. "You can go home. I'm gonna be here for a while. I can lock up," I say.

"No, I'll just silently keep you company, if that's okay."

"Why would you do that?"

Luke shrugs. "I owe you one. I mean, after dumping that sob story on you Saturday morning. I shouldn't have said all that shit about my dad. I think that's what people on TV call 'oversharing.' Anyway, that's kinda why I left all the sudden. So, you know, sorry about that."

"I'm actually glad you felt comfortable enough to . . . um . . . tell me . . . about . . . all that . . . stuff . . ."

Luke just nods and walks over to a beat-up couch at the side of the auditorium. He slowly stretches and then collapses on the couch, crossing his colossal arms and closing his eyes. I pause long enough to take him in. There's the tiniest smudge of white face paint just below his jawline. All that's left of Britches, the lovable tramp. And though I'm not sure why he's staying, I have to admit I'm relieved. The theater is creepy as hell at night.

Without opening his eyes, Luke says, "And Noah, I think you were just about to figure out that duet between the evil daughters."

He's right. I was. Come on, mighty Ticonderoga. Don't fail me now.

As the hot summer sun comes up over Plainview, I shake Luke awake. I've stuffed all of my sheet music into my briefcase—a.k.a. The Executive—and as Luke locks up, I'm talking like a kid back from his first day of school. He grins crookedly as I breathlessly tell him about all the changes I've made during the night.

"Man, you're actually talking a mile a minute."

"I guess I'm just feeling so . . ." I search for the word I want to use and can't believe what I end up with. "Exhilarated? Strangely, frantically exhilarated? And also completely sleep-deprived, but that's another story. It's like I'm out of town with a new show."

"Explain the phrase 'out of town.'"

Does he really care about theater lingo? And if he doesn't, I have to say that for the record he's a much better actor than I am. I couldn't feign the same level of enthusiasm for his love of football or cars. Not in a million years.

We head out toward the parking lot.

"Well, when you're putting together a brand-new Broadway show, before you hit Manhattan and the snake pit of New York critics, you pack the whole kit and caboodle up and go to a less toxic place. Seattle, Boston, Chicago. Anywhere that isn't New York. And when I say pack up, I mean everything. The cast, the crew, the orchestra, the stagehands, the sets, the costumes, the wigs, the lighting rig . . . I'm sure I'm forgetting something."

"I'm starting to get the picture."

"And then you put the show up 'out of town' to get feedback. Not just from the local reviews, although those come out at some point and can absolutely kill a show's chances of making it to Broadway. But you also feel the vibe of the audience. Are they laughing at the right time? Are they not clapping quite loudly enough after a production number? And as the creative team, you're always surprised. The joke or song that you thought would bring down the house fizzles and dies. Conversely, the thing that you had little faith in while you were in rehearsals kills and people are laughing or jumping to their feet and clapping until their hands bleed. So an 'out of town' is crucial for a show. And now, St. Louis critic aside, I get to work on the show without all that pressure. I guess it's kind of, I don't know . . . creatively freeing?"

I stop myself, embarrassed. "Did I just use the words 'creatively freeing'?"

"You did."

I wince. "God, am I fucking pretentious or what?"

"It's okay." Luke smiles. "In fact, it's kinda hot."

And there it is. Right out in the open.

It happens in the blink of an eye. His big pillowy lips are on mine and I'm backed up against the pickup. And my knees are actually disengaging. My mind is unspooling and it's so gruff and tender that I'm sliding down the side of the truck slightly. Somehow instinctively Luke wraps his arms around me and he's holding me up, both hands snaking around my waist. Without giving it a second thought, I grab his face and pull his mouth so desperately onto mine it borders on painful. When we finally come up for air, we just stare at one another in wonder. And then I ruin it with too many words.

"I, um . . . my knees sometimes . . . my knees have buckles. They don't *have* buckles, that would be weird. They do buckle. It's a funny-sounding word: buckle. It gets funnier the more you say it. Buckle, buckle, buckle—"

"Would you shut up?" And we're kissing again. And I'm buckling and sliding down the truck all over again. Then suddenly I think of Chase. What the fuck am I doing?

Guilt rushes through my arteries and I shove Luke away. The world stops spinning and the expression on my face must not be good because Luke looks contrite, regret filling his eyes.

"Shit! Shit, I'm so sorry," he says, panicked.

"I have to go." I quickly head for Mom's beat-up Toyota as the gravel parking lot and the surrounding hackberry trees whirligig as if I'm drunk.

Luke is right behind me and now he's the one talking a mile a minute. "I shouldn't have done that. I'm . . . Noah, I'm really sorry. Please, just let me explain!"

I'm fumbling with the keys to the car when, like out of a bad farce, my briefcase pops open and millions of pages of sheet music fall out onto the ground. "Fuck!"

I scramble to gather the sheet music up and Luke bends down to help. "Listen, you have to know something. I've had feelings for you for years. I mean, I couldn't admit that to myself when we were in school. I kept wondering why I was constantly thinking about Shakesp—Noah freakin' Adams—and all this time, I didn't know how to tell you, because I didn't know how to tell myself! And then you're back in town and getting all passionate about your job and standing there just now in front of me with that pretty boy face of yours—"

"Well, it's attached to my skull, so—" I grab the sheet music from him and shove it inside my stupid briefcase. "This isn't funny, Luke."

Luke gives a frustrated groan and a vein pumps in his thick, gorgeous neck. "None of this is funny to me! Confusing as hell, but not funny! My feelings aren't a joke, Noah!"

I finally unlock the car and toss the briefcase inside. "I have a boyfriend. Of almost two years. I'm in a committed relationship!"

Luke's eyes are clamped shut as he chants, "I know, I know, I know . . ." He's practically davening. "I just fucked everything up. Please say you forgive me, Noah."

"Sure! No problem!" I say and then I hop into the Toyota and peel out of the parking lot as fast as I can. What just happened? And why am I still shaking like crazy? Nothing, not one thing makes any sense. I burn rubber all the way home and barrel my way into the kitchen just as Mom is getting off the phone.

Mom halts, noticing me slumped in the kitchen chair with a look of horror on my face. "What's wrong? Did something happen?"

I slowly try to piece it together. "Luke kissed me. Just now. In the parking lot of the Plainview Players."

"Well, I'm not surprised, honey," Mom says, unfazed. "You are very good-looking. It's genetic. You're welcome."

"I also have a boyfriend, Mom. A serious, live-in boyfriend."

Mom considers this for a second. "Oh, that is a pickle."

"Chase and I are in a monogamous relationship. Kissing high school friends or anyone else on planet Earth is against the rules."

"Oh, that is a *dill* pickle."

"Would you please stop talking about condiments and concentrate on whether or not I tell Chase?"

Mom takes another well-considered pause, then offers, "Well, I guess you have to decide what Luke's kiss meant to you."

And that's Mom in a nutshell.

A fucking Yoda in a JCPenney pajama set.

I have to decide what Luke's kiss meant to me? Easier said than done.

On the one hand, it's actually completely inconceivable that big, hunky Luke Carter had his lips anywhere near my mine. And while it was happening, aliens could have invaded and I wouldn't have noticed. It was that intense. On the other hand, I love Chase. Chase who introduced me to jazz clubs and the ABT and art galleries. Who believed in my scripts and championed them when no one else cared. The man who patiently walked me through every professional disappointment and never once complained because he loved me.

Oh God. The guilt is all over me like hot sticky goo. I have to tell him.

After all, it wasn't my fault. Luke was the one who kissed me and pressed me into the side of his rusty pickup truck. True, I could have stopped it sooner, but I was in a state of shock. And Chase would understand. With my Broadway show closing and Dad's heart attack, I wasn't exactly in the right mind space to fight off advances.

"It's just such a surprise to find out that Luke Carter is actually gay. Or bi?"

"Well, one thing is clear. He's certainly a little gay for you, Noah." Mom sighs and shakes her head knowingly. "And I can't say I didn't see this whole thing coming."

I stare at her in total disbelief. "What do you mean you saw it coming?"

"Oh, Noah, that boy looks at you like you not only walk on water, but invented the stuff."

"If you actually thought that, then why for the love of God wouldn't you tell me?"

Mom shrugs. "People have to come around to these things naturally. And besides, I'm no gossip."

The guilt is wearing me down so much that I can't even contradict her. Mom can sense it and puts her hand on mine. "Chase will understand. After all, it was Luke who kissed you."

I ignore her and grab my cell. "I have to call Melissa."

Melissa answers and I don't even bother with small talk. "Luke Carter kissed me in the parking lot. Hard. And twice. And I kind of let him. But then I stopped him."

The line is silent for a moment. "No wonder Luke was such a bad lay back in the day. He was a total closet case." She pauses again. "Wait, do I turn people gay? Is every gay guy in this town gay because of me?"

"Probably, but let's stay on topic here. I have a boyfriend, Melissa! A loyal, well-dressed, hot boyfriend who is going to be furious to learn that I've been out kissing strapping cowhands!"

"But as Oscar Hammerstein said, 'The farmer and the cow-hand should be friends.'"

"Stop saying that. And he said 'friends,' not parking lot kissers."

My cell beeps and I look at it only to realize that it's Chase calling. I throw the phone on the kitchen table like it's a hot potato. Mom glares at me. "What's wrong?"

"It's Chase."

Mom shakes her head in resignation. "Time to face the music, Noah."

I reluctantly walk over to the kitchen table and slowly pick up my cell phone like it's a stick of dynamite with the wick already lit. I softly tell Melissa that I'll have to call her back. The minute I switch over to Chase's call I break out into a cold sweat.

"Hi, Chase . . . um . . ."

"Noah? Is something wrong?"

He can hear it in my voice. This is why I could never be an actor. I was never good at inner monologues. Subtext bleeds through my voice when I try to lie.

"I have something to tell you and it's really not a big deal, so please don't get upset."

Chase gives a leery, "Okaaaaay."

I step out onto the back porch to get some privacy.

"Um, it's just that . . . it's just that . . ." And then I take the coward's way out. "It's just that we're changing lots of stuff in the show, and it's going to take a lot of work, so I might not be able to talk as much. Because of all the work, I mean."

There's a patina of relief in Chase's voice. "Oh. Is that all? Well, I'm delighted to hear that you're so invested in this little production."

"It's crazy. I don't know why, but I am."

After I hang up, I walk back into the kitchen and Mom's curious glare.

She finally asks, "Well?"

"Um."

Before I can even lie about not telling Chase the truth, Mom gives me a scandalized, "Noah!" All I can do in response is give a slight shrug and stare at the refrigerator. Mom promptly goes as quiet and judgmental as a Franciscan nun. Trying to avoid her disapproving glare, I announce that I have a few more songs to tweak before tonight's rehearsal.

I start toward the stairs and Mom can't help herself. "Noah?"

I hesitate. "I know, Mom. I'll tell Chase soon. But it was just a kiss."

That's all it was. Really.

twelve

# "Baby Mine"

Later that night when I arrive with a flotilla of new score pages it's chilly in the Plainview Players Theater, and not just because of the industrial air-conditioning. As I walk into the room, everyone is sitting quietly onstage in folding chairs and busy either looking at their scripts or at their phones. I heave a guilty sigh and trudge forward to deliver what Luke prescribed for the situation: an epic apology.

"Hey, guys, before we start tonight, I'd like to say something." The silence is deafening. If this were a sitcom there would be a soundtrack of crickets. "Um, I know that I made that great big speech on our first day together. And the basic upshot of it was that every time anyone comes into this theater they have to put their egos aside. That the show comes first. That we're all in the same boat and so on. Blipitty blapitty. Well, guys, I forgot that meant me, too. I know I told you to ask yourself at any point when you were lost, 'What is best for the show?' Turns out that was really good advice. And now I see that I have to take that advice, too. Cyborgs? Eye gouging? 'Ye' talk? I am slowly realizing all of that isn't what's best for the show. I mean, how many things can I be wrong about?"

Luke flashes through my mind. Yet another thing I had totally wrong. But stick to the apology at hand, Noah.

"Look, you guys have been pretty open with me, so I'll return the favor. This musical crashed and burned in New York. And it was a devastating blow to my self-esteem. And it was actually kind of humiliating when you threw that party for me. I was worried you'd all think, 'Oh, look at Noah. Guess he's not as great as he thought he was. But we'll give him a little shindig anyway, even though his show closed and he's a total fraud . . . '"

Melissa shakes her head. "No one thought that, Noah. No one thinks you're a fraud."

"The point is, after everything that's happened, I get extra defensive when people start pointing out all of the musical's obvious flaws. But the truth is, this has become a better show because of you guys. You're not just amazing performers, you're also incredibly insightful. I guess I wasn't prepared for that. But I'm more grateful than any of you know. And I am so sorry that I freaked out yesterday and that I got heated with Jackie and that I made Mrs. Henson cry at her piano. There's a lot of pressure that comes along with this little enterprise, especially since we're apparently going to get reviewed. But that's no excuse. I am not letting myself off the hook. Believe you me. No one can punish *me* more than *me*. I'm kind of an expert at it. But even so, I do know this: I love this place and I love all of you talented people. All I can ask is that you understand that I'm completely stupid and overly sensitive and can be a—I don't know—a *total tool* sometimes. I'm asking if you can forgive me for being a jackass and if we can just move forward in our small, beautiful little boat together."

Dramatic pause. (Which I deserve, for sure.)

But then the cast finally responds.

It's not a hero's welcome, but there is some general head nodding and slightly positive murmuring and I will take what I can get.

Time to start pushing forward. I launch into work mode. "So. Changes! The Shakespeare talk is OUT!"

I hold up a batch of freshly copied pages and everyone actually cheers. "The biggest learning curve is the music. I'm going to let Mrs. Henson take you through the lyric changes first."

Always the faithful trooper, Mrs. Henson graciously takes over and starts leading the cast through the newly fine-tuned songs. I take the opportunity to pull Jackie McNew aside.

"I owe you a personal apology, Jackie. You made the smartest insight of all about our musical and I reacted by being a grade A prick. I'm just hoping that you can find it in your heart to forgive me."

Jackie's eyes narrow for a moment. "You were a grade A prick. But . . ." She smirks and shakes her head slightly. "But the truth is I've had worse things said to me at the Elks Club on dollar margarita night, so I guess I can let it slide."

I heave a pent-up sigh of relief. "Thank you, Jackie. That's very kind of you."

"I made the smartest insight of all, huh?"

She looks triumphant and she deserves to, so I just say, "Yep."

"Don't worry, I won't let it go to my head. As long as you don't mouth off to me ever again."

A second sigh of relief from me. "Jackie, we have a deal."

Just as Jackie joins the others to go over the score, Luke appears, fiddling with a prop lantern. One problem solved, another one to go. I decide it's time to Esther Williams out of the frying pan and into the fire.

But I start with the easy part first.

"So . . . did you hear that apology? Was that epic enough?"

Luke nods, jiggering the battery-operated lantern candle instead of looking at me. "It was better than epic. It was sincere."

It becomes obvious that it's time to address the big gay-or-possibly-bisexual elephant in the room. It's pointless to put it off any longer.

"Um, so that thing that happened in the parking lot? We were both up all night while I was rewriting and clearly that means we weren't thinking straight. So, is it possible that we could just act like it never happened? Are you, like, capable of just sweeping that whole incident under the rug?"

Luke looks at me as if he's trying to hold himself back from asking something, but then goes ahead and asks all the same. "Did you tell your boyfriend about it?"

I answer without thinking. "Oh, God, no. It's not like it meant anything, so why bring it up, right?"

There's a hiccup of a pause and then Luke offers a small shrug and the prop lantern snaps on as if it's hoping to illuminate the situation. But it flickers and dies. Luke and his lantern beat a hasty retreat backstage.

When did I pick up a talent for saying exactly the wrong thing? Was I born with it or is it a learned skill? I wonder why I'm so confident writing dialogue for imaginary characters when my own actual dialogue is so coarse and casually hurtful. "It's not like it meant anything"? Even if it didn't, those are not the words to choose. But something magical happens to interrupt my shame spiral. The freshly tweaked lyrics float over to me from the other side of the stage and they're working. They're actually a huge improvement. The Plainview Players were right once more! As I stand there, I realize that I'm smiling like an idiot. Did I ever smile like this during rehearsals for the Broadway version of the show? I'm not positive, but I'm pretty sure the answer is no.

Rehearsal ends with everyone swearing to commit the rewrites to memory as quickly as possible. I actually feel touched when I think of them sacrificing their free time so willingly. Or going over the new changes as they work. Louis singing through his day as he tests samples at the barbecue sauce factory or Abby reciting her lines as she drives her school bus chock-full of babbling kids. How did we all end up caring so much about this broken little musical?

Back at home I'm greeted with a little pantomime performance from Mom. Instead of sleeping, she's sitting on the front porch swing and picking flecks of paint off her "painting apron" as she calls it. Well, that's what she appears to be doing. In reality, she's busy transmitting little silent radio waves of disapproval in my general direction as I climb the front steps.

I choose the classic dodge and talk about the weather. "It's so unbelievably hot tonight, right?"

"Well, maybe you feel that way because your pants are on fire."

Of course. Here we go.

"I'm not a liar, Mom. I'm not lying to Chase."

Mom's voice goes singsongy. "Lying by omission is still lying."

A humid gust of wind rattles the trees and I realize that when Mom is right, she's right. This is going to suck, but maybe it's best to just pull the Band-Aid off as quickly as possible.

I take out my cell and very theatrically text Chase with a great amount of flourish for Mom's benefit. "There. I just texted Chase to ask if we could chat. I hope you're satisfied. I'm officially about to face the music."

"Good. Take it adagio."

The Executive and I climb the stairs to my bedroom and I try to ignore the bubbles of dread percolating in my chest.

Chase texts back: Just finishing something up. Will call in a few.

In order to distract myself, I open my laptop and begin to go over the latest script changes for the millionth time.

My phone buzzes and I see another text from Chase: Lunch tomorrow at the Intercontinental? I booked us a room for afterwards. Be prepared to eat a big lunch. You're going to need lots of energy. And then a wink emoji.

I stare at my phone, confused for a minute. Chase wants me to have lunch with him at a hotel? And he's booked us a room? What is he talking about?

Then the hand holding my phone begins to tremble. Then outright shake. In an instant I'm shaking all over. My skin is freezing cold and burning hot at the same time.

My phone buzzes. It's Chase.

"Hi, Chase . . ." I start off as slowly and calmly as is humanly possible.

"Hi, there. How's your old man doing?" Unbelievable. He doesn't even realize what he's done. I pretend for a second that everything is fine. If you pretend things are fine, they morph into fine. Isn't that how life works?

"He's good. Annoyed, of course, but what else is new?"

"Well, I'm sure he's relieved to be in his own bed again."

(Speaking of beds, you adulterous man whore.)

I start off breezily. "So, Chase, I'm a little confused by your last text. How am I going to have sex with you tomorrow at the Intercontinental if I'm here in Plainview? Do you have a private jet you're going to send to pick me up? Or is there a hidden enchanted portal that will transport me there?"

The line is deadly silent and I imagine Chase going through a mental card catalog of excuses, wondering if there are any that might actually cover his tracks. Finally, he lets out a very long and low, "Fuuuuuck."

And I find to my complete shock that I want him to lie. I want him to lie, because I don't want it to be true.

Neither of us knows what to say for an eternity. Finally, Chase begins.

"I'm not going to lie to you, because I respect you too much and, God knows, you're too smart to believe a lie anyway. I've been meaning to have a proper talk with you about this for some time now, but you've been going through so much—"

"Oh, so it's out of respect for me that you've been hiding the fact that you've been fucking someone else? You are such a giver, Chase. Such a selfless giver."

"I knew this was how you would react. Maybe I was just . . . I really was just waiting for things to settle down in your life before I told you about Aleister and me."

The floor beneath me evaporates. I'm plunging into darkness.

"ALEISTER!?! You've been fucking Aleister Murphy behind my back?! What the fuck is going on here? So you're into twinks now? None of this makes sense! And by the way, have you noticed the way that guy walks? He doesn't walk, he slinks. So you're into *slinky twinks*, now?"

Chase gets defensive. "Look, I'm sorry if I wanted some, I don't know, variety. He's young and full of energy and enthusiasm. I guess I got caught up in it all."

I'm suddenly, very embarrassingly, choking on tears. "But I was loyal to you, Chase. Loyal."

Chase huffs. "You were the one who wanted a monogamous relationship. You know I had my doubts—"

"But you agreed to it! You agreed to it, Chase, and I trusted you! Don't you understand that was our deal? And I . . . I loved you with all of my fucking heart and now . . ." Another horrible realization washes over me. "This is why you wanted me to stay here. So you could fuck Aleister Murphy in expensive hotels without me getting in the way!"

Feeling lightheaded, I sink to the floor.

I try to get my bearings and say slowly, "I just don't understand. What changed? Did I do something wrong?"

There's a frosty pause and then Chase says coldly, "I knew
you'd make this all about you."

"I think I deserve to know what the fuck happened! There has
to be some reason you're destroying our entire lives together!"

Chase groans. "It's just, I don't know, Noah, you're just so
bloody needy sometimes. You do whinge on about yourself. And
don't blame it on being a writer; I work with many artists that
aren't constantly ME! ME! ME!"

I stifle a shocked sob, but he hears it and mercifully softens. "I
wanted to do this in person. Properly. Once all of the dust had
settled. I'm gutted that it's like this, over the phone, so far away
from each other."

I'm so numb that I just sit there quietly trembling and barely
able to keep the phone up to my ear.

"So—" I can't stop myself. I know it's pathetic and cliché and
devoid of any self-respect, but I just can't stop myself. "Did
you ever actually love me? Because I loved you completely, you
know."

Chase sighs, as if being forced to act out a scene he has been
dreading for weeks, years maybe. "Of course I loved you. I still
do. You're a brilliant guy and your career had real potential."

Holy fucking gut punch. "*Had?*"

"Has. You know what I mean."

Except that I don't.

"But . . . but you said when this was over, that 'we shan't be
parted no more.'"

I sit silently hoping that the quote will work its magic. That it'll bring Chase back to his senses and back to us.

But Chase simply says, "I was merely quoting E. M. Forster."

And as if that wasn't devastating enough, something ten times worse happens. Chase switches to his agent voice.

He uses his agent voice on *me*.

"Look, you're a handsome fellow and God knows you're bloody great in the sack, you'll make out just fine." I can feel myself crumbling. I'm losing him. He's throwing me away. "There will be loads of logistical things for us to figure out now, so I hope we can both act friendly. Like adults."

"Fuck you and fuck friendly!" I scream. "I hope you get attacked by a group of angry bikers and that they . . . they . . . they chop your dick off!"

And then I add for good measure, "If they can find it, that is!"

I disconnect the call and throw my phone across the room like it's somehow to blame. And then I run into the bathroom and throw up. I throw up three times.

I hear Mom quickly climbing the stairs and she finds me covered in tears and clutching the toilet for strength. Her face goes desperate with worry and she runs to me, holding me by the shoulders as I turn around. She frantically searches my face.

"Honey, what happened?"

I shake my head, thinking I'm going to be sick again. I wait to see if it passes. I finally get enough air to blurt out, "He dumped me."

Mom bursts into tears, which makes everything a million times worse somehow. "He didn't! Because of a stupid little kiss?"

I'm hyperventilating now. I try to speak while gulping air.

"No! We didn't even talk about that. He's . . . he's . . . seeing . . . someone new . . ."

Mom's nurse training kicks in. "Okay, don't try to talk, honey. Focus on your breathing. Let's both take long inhales and exhales together."

I try. We both do. And then I lunge for the toilet to throw up again and Mom rubs my back. She wets a washcloth and cleans my face. Mom helps me walk slowly to my room and gently lays me onto the bed. She sits next to me and strokes my hair like she did when I was a kid. I lie there and search her face for answers. "Was it a lie? Was our whole relationship a lie?"

This stumps Mom for a second.

"No. I just can't see how it could be."

"How can he just do that? How can he just take back his love like that?"

I'm crying again and gravity makes my tears trickle backward into my hair. They leave little wet roadways on my scalp. Finally, Mom stands up and announces, "I'm going to get you some broth."

"What?"

"I read this wonderful book by Joan Didion . . ."

Even though I'm weeping, I'm intrigued and sit up on my elbows. "Since when do you read Joan Didion?"

"I have layers, Noah! Anyway, she said that when people are grieving a loss, they'll lose their appetite. But they can usually tolerate a warm broth. You've barely eaten a thing today. And after something like this, you have to eat."

Once she's gone, I stare at the ceiling, utterly lost and shell-shocked.

I call Kiara. It's the only thing I can think of to do. She answers and my voice is noticeably small. "Hi, it's me."

We sometimes share a kind of twin telepathy, especially when things go south for one of us.

"You're scaring me, Noah. Tell me quickly."

"Chase broke up with me. He's been sleeping with Aleister Murphy and it's over, Kiara. It's over and I have no say in the matter."

Kiara sucks in air like she's just been kicked in the stomach. "Are you alone? Are you with your parents?"

"Yeah," I say weakly.

"Okay. Don't go anywhere. I'm getting on a plane."

I immediately protest. "If you get on a plane, I will punch you right in your beautiful face!" She hangs up without another word. Mom comes back with her broth and though I don't feel like it, I choke down a spoonful or two.

"Can you call Mrs. Henson and tell her rehearsal is canceled for tomorrow? I'm just in no shape."

"Of course, honey. You just lie in bed and rest. You've had a nasty shock from a very nasty man."

"Also, can I ask you to do something stupid?"

"Anything you want, honey."

"Remember when I was a kid and I couldn't sleep and you would sing that song 'Baby Mine' from the animated feature *Dumbo*?"

"Yes, and you don't have to say 'animated feature,' honey."

"Actually I do, because they made a really shitty live-action version."

This makes us both laugh half-heartedly. Then I close my eyes. And Mom strokes my hair and sings softly.

> *Baby mine, don't you cry*
> *Baby mine, dry your eyes*
> *Rest your head close to my heart*
> *Never to part, baby of mine . . .*

Mom continues gently and I fall apart with every note. Especially when she gets to the lyrics in the middle, which were my favorite when I was young.

> *If they knew all about you*
> *They'd end up loving you, too*
> *All those same people who scold you*
> *What they'd give just for the right to hold you . . .*

We sit in silence for a little while when she's done.

thirteen

# "A Very Complicated Woman"

wake up in slow motion. As my eyes are beginning to register shapes and I start to replay the phone call from last night in my head, there is an obnoxious pounding on my bedroom door.

"Oh, no . . ." I hear myself whimper.

Kiara tears open the door and tosses her irresponsibly expensive Hermès bag into my room, throws her hands up, and yells, "Punch me, bitch!"

And I'm ugly crying and running toward her as fast as I can. She folds her arms around me and I collapse into her. She smells like safety. Mom pushes her way into the room, right behind her.

"Now, just a second! She blew right past me. I deserve a hug, too!" Mom pulls Kiara in.

Mom first met Kiara at my graduation from college. The two immediately became thick as thieves and I remember feeling excluded and yet completely thrilled.

Kiara breaks out of Mom's hug and goes into crisis management mode. "Noah, shower. Now. Your mom and I will be downstairs in the war room. And don't worry; I'm making breakfast, not your mom. Sorry, Nancy Kay, but we all have our strengths and nobody comes close to my waffles."

I start to protest, but no one dares to argue when Kiara takes control.

Soon the smell of waffles permeates the house as I walk downstairs and find Kiara pounding out fluffy breakfast treats like a one-woman factory. She and Mom are talking in hushed tones and Dad is at his usual place at the kitchen table. Both Mom and Kiara brighten somewhat artificially when they see me.

Mom's voice is an overpopulated birdcage of chirpy encouragement. "There he is! And he even shaved! Doesn't a good, long shower just change your whole perspective on things, honey?!"

"Nope. My career and love life are still over. Nothing the people down at the Garnier Fructis shampoo factory can do about that."

I glumly pull out a chair and sit down with a thud and immediately regret my tone. "Um . . . sorry, Mom. Yes, the shower did feel good, actually."

Kiara serves us all waffles and we eat in a silence that couldn't be more uncomfortable if it were created in a laboratory for that exact purpose. I get half a bite of the cloudlike deliciousness in my mouth and have to stop. Maybe Joan Didion was onto something. I put my head in my hands and can feel everyone's eyes on me.

Out of nowhere, Dad decides to say, "Just get over the guy. He was a jerk."

I slowly level my eyes at Dad. "I was with him for almost two years. We shared a life together. And an apartment. And an entire future. He betrayed and hurt me. Get over it? It hasn't even been twenty-four hours." I hop up from the table, defiant and ready for a throwdown. "I'm sorry if any demonstration of emotion makes you uncomfortable, Dad. Maybe I should just go to a hotel."

Mom snaps into referee mode. "No one's going to a hotel."

Dad turns on her. "You said to say something to him and I did. Sorry if I didn't say the right thing. Jesus Howard Christ!" And we watch him struggle to his feet and haul his oxygen tank behind him on his way up the stairs.

And now I turn on Mom. "You told him to say something to me? Why? Just so he could look like he actually gave a shit?"

"Noah, I just . . ." But then Mom just slowly trails off. More marathon silence.

Kiara gets up and says, "You know, I'm going to give you two some privacy. I've got calls to make anyway. I'll just be right there on the front porch." And she's gone. The screen door stutters, punctuating her exit.

"I don't need your help, Mom. If Dad doesn't care about me, you don't have to give him acting tips on how to fake it."

Mom gives a pained sigh. "That's not . . . I just . . . he doesn't know how to react in these kinds of situations."

"What kinds of situations? Having a big, old homo for a son who gets dumped by another homo?"

"It would be just the same if you were straight. I honestly believe that."

"Oh, please, Mom. You know what Dad's like. He has never said the words 'I love you' to me in my entire life."

A cloud passes over Mom's face. "Well, you know, Noah, not everyone knows how to use words like you do. Who built all the sets for your little skits and plays? That's his 'I love you.' Who sold his beloved 1968 Mustang to pay for you to go to NYU? That's his 'I love you.' Who calls the local papers every time you have a show go up just to make sure this entire town is proud of you? So he doesn't have your *bravery* with words. But he . . . he . . . does what he can."

With an angry slam of the back door, Mom's gone. She's gone and there's nothing but the worst possible silence left in her wake. And to top things off, seconds later she's trying to hide the fact that she's crying on the back porch.

This isn't Mom and me. We don't fight. I don't make her angry and she doesn't storm off. I walk to the back porch and sit next to Mom on the steps. She dries her face with what I've told her a million times is a hideous apron and slowly puts a hand on the back of my neck.

But she's still not looking at me.

"Jesus, Mom. That was some monologue."

"Well, you're not the only one in this family who gets to be a drama queen."

Fact.

"Look, I know that Dad has made sacrifices for me. I know you both have, and I'm very grateful. And I think I say so enough, but if I don't—"

"No, it's not that. It's just . . . I hate the gulf that stands between you two. It's like you speak two different languages. You're speaking French or Greek and he's speaking caveman, I guess.

But he hurts for you, Noah. Those days when you came home from school with those boys teasing you? A man like your father doesn't know what to say, but he hurts for you when he doesn't know how to fix it. And he's also proud of you. But he doesn't know how to say that, either. So he builds a set or he calls a newspaper. So if you're waiting for words, you might not get them. But look at his actions. They don't say, 'I love you.' They shout it."

We sit there for what seems like an hour as I let that sink in.

I take her hand and give it a squeeze. Once I'm sure the tears have stopped, I say, "Mom, on a much more serious note, I really have to put my foot down about that apron you're wearing."

"You don't like it?"

"Oh, it's perfect if you're selling yams out of a truck in a Steinbeck novel."

"What a coincidence! That's exactly the look I was going for!"

After a reasonable amount of time has passed and sensing that the thing with Mom and me is over, Kiara appears and says, "I just came around the side of the house and discovered one of my favorite things in the world! You guys have a trampoline? And you didn't tell me? I love a trampoline!"

I'd actually forgotten all about the thing. "It's still there? The springs are probably rusted all the way through."

"Only one way to find out!"

Kiara and I make fools out of ourselves bouncing around like a couple of clowns, until, exhausted, we lie back on the trampoline and stare blankly at the sky. A scream ricochets off the hickory trees and Kiara startles.

"What was that? Was that human?"

"Nope. Red-tailed hawk."

Kiara shakes her head. "Fucking nature."

More silence until I finally say, "First my Broadway show is destroyed, then my relationship explodes. What did I do to deserve this? Why is Baby Jesus so mad at me?"

Kiara scoffs. "Just to put things in perspective, Baby Jesus is probably too busy trying to remind most Americans that he isn't actually white. So let's assume destroying your career and love life isn't even on his vision board. But I will admit that you've had a run of bad luck. And Chase . . . damn it, he had us all fooled. I thought he was this super great guy. But turns out he is clearly shady as fuck. So what we do now is we do not blame ourselves. We self-soothe. And we realize that we have people who love us and would even fly to a place that has no Michelin-starred restaurants, which is a very serious sacrifice."

I pull myself into a sitting position and when my eyes focus, I see Luke standing outside the barn, talking to . . . Eddie Gregory? What the hell is Eddie fucking Gregory doing here? In a flash, my temples are pounding and white-hot anger floods my brain.

"You see that guy? The trashy one, smoking the cigarette? I've hated that guy since sixth grade. I think . . . I think he's actually working here! At my Goddamn family farm." Before I even know what I'm doing, I'm on my feet and ready to pounce. I hop slightly on the trampoline, growing more agitated with each bounce.

Kiara hops up and grabs my arm, desperate to calm me down. "Forget about it, Noah."

"No fucking way! That guy threw me into the dumpster behind the cafeteria. I sprained my ankle and ruined my favorite Abercrombie & Fitch hoodie."

"You were wearing Abercrombie & Fitch? Sounds like he did you a favor."

Kiara laughs, trying to lighten the mood. When that doesn't work, she attempts the pinky holding thing, but I pull away.

"The whole thing was fucking humiliating, but the worst part was the look of pity on Dad's face when he came to pick me up. I just stood there dripping with garbage hoping Dad wouldn't notice I was covered in creamed corn and sloppy joes. And then I had to suffer through a lecture from Dad about standing up for myself. How can Luke still be friends with an asshole like that?"

"Noah, let's just go inside."

"Not on your life! I'm gonna go read that fucker for filth!"

"Noah, please don't do this. I'm just saying, I don't cosign this decision!"

"Then stay here."

I leap off the trampoline as Kiara collapses back onto it and moans, "No, Noah . . ."

As I start furiously making my way over to them, Luke is the first one to see me and his face fills with worry. I scowl and shake my head, approaching at warp speed. Eddie looks up and I notice he now has a cheap neck tattoo and a scraggly goatee that makes him look like an extra from an episode of *Prison Break*. How very on-brand of him. Plus, he's trying to rock a pathetic man bun. Because what thirty-year-old guy doesn't want to look like a young Mrs. Claus?

"Hey, Noah. You okay?" Luke asks carefully.

But before I know what I'm doing, I shove Eddie in the chest. He staggers backward, but manages not to fall. To my small satisfaction, his cigarette flies out of his mouth and onto the ground where it gets crushed under his boot.

Luke is immediately between us and puts a forceful hand on my chest. "Jesus, Noah! What the hell are you doing?"

I ignore him and yell at a stunned Eddie, "Do you work here? Do you actually work on my family's farm?"

Luke seems to read the situation immediately. "Hey, Noah, calm down. I know what you're thinking, but just calm down and take a second."

I give Luke a furious look. "How can you even hang out with this guy?"

I stare at Eddie for a long moment and then he slowly averts his eyes and says, "I get that. If I were you, I wouldn't want me around, either."

I pause, confused. "What . . . what does that mean?"

"Just that Luke and me, we were talking about some shit a few days ago, and I guess I kind of owe you an apology."

What sorta mind games is this guy playing? I cross my arms defiantly and give my best skeptical look. "So you've been guilted into an apology?"

"I don't know about guilted, but I really am sorry. My buddies and me were pretty much dicks to you until Luke here put a stop to it. So, you know, sorry. Especially for that dumpster nonsense. I was just a stupid kid trying to look cool and failing at it."

And all the angry wind goes out of my sails. Not sure what to do or how to react, my body goes all jangling and awkward. Mom's wind chimes give a twee little jingle from the back porch and add an extra layer of girly frivolity to my tough guy act.

"Well, um . . . thank you for your apology, I guess." Why are my words coming out of me like English is my second language? "And, um, I would like to apologize for pushing you in the chest."

Eddie brushes it off. "I probably had it coming. Actually, why don't you take a swing at me and we'll call it all even."

I blink at Eddie, completely incredulous. "You're not serious."

Eddie holds his arms out as if he's being crucified. "Do your worst."

My shoulders slump and all I can do is let out a sad little laugh and shake my head. "I don't want to hit you, Eddie. I don't want to hit anyone. I'm just—"

Luke stares at me, confused. "You're just what, Noah?"

"Examining old wounds? Having a day? Suffering the slings and arrows of outrageous fortune?"

They both look at me like I'm a word jumble that no one could possibly solve.

And they're probably right.

"And Eddie, uh . . . I'm sorry about ruining your cigarette. Can I buy you another one to replace it?"

They both stifle a laugh. I immediately feel stupid and my skull turns into a life-sized bobblehead, nodding in agreement with how idiotic that sounded.

Eddie punches my arm like we're best buddies who go way back. "We're good, Noah. I've got plenty of cancer sticks. I better get back to work. I've got cow titties to squeeze."

He heads toward the barn. When we're alone, Luke looks at me with concern. "What's going on with you, Noah?"

I heave the world's biggest sigh. "I don't want to talk about it."

Back toward the house, I find Kiara hiding under the trampoline. "What are you doing under there?"

"I couldn't bear to watch you possibly humiliate yourself."

"Well, the crazy thing is, he apologized."

Kiara crawls out from under the trampoline and wrinkles her brow in confusion. "You sound angry. Isn't that a good thing?"

"It further screws up my understanding of the world's order of things. He even offered to let me punch him."

Kiara looks like she doesn't believe me for a second and then wags her head. "This place is fucking weird."

"You're preaching to the choir on that one."

"Well, since it seems like that little bit of drama is over, let's get back to me cheering you up."

I wrap my arms around her and sigh into her shoulder. "Nothing can cheer me up right now. This has been the worst twenty-four hours of my life. I mean, I'm thrilled you're here, but trying to cheer me up is a fool's errand."

Kiara puts her arms around me and squeezes back. "You know I love a challenge. I suggest it is time to pay a visit to . . . THE QUEEN!"

I let go of her and start hopping up and down like a toddler. How does she know me so well?

———

As we sit on one of the benches outside the Dairy Queen devouring Peanut Buster Parfaits, stars begin to pop up in the twilight sky. Just as I'm making a mental note to go for a run to combat the ridiculous amount of calories I'm consuming, a dark thought crosses my mind.

Kiara senses it. "What's wrong?"

"Something Chase said while he was busy ripping my heart from my chest. He said that I *had* a promising career. And I did when we first met. I was getting some buzz. And we met when he was on a panel at the Dramatists Guild. Do you think he was just there trolling for new clients? Do you think our whole relationship was just because I might make a good addition to his roster?"

Her face goes grim with reflection. "If Chase did date you for ulterior motives . . . well, I don't even want to live in a world where that is even a possibility. It's like we're in the Upside Down right now."

"What's that?"

"The Upside Down. From *Stranger Things*."

"Kiara, you know I don't get science fiction references. Know your audience."

"You set your entire musical on a spaceship, Noah."

I shrug. "That was just to be arty."

Kiara changes tactics and obviously tries to get me to look on the bright side. "Look, sorry if it's too soon to say this, but you're free now. You can have anything you want."

"Except the thing that I want. Which is Chase. Horrible, beautiful Chase."

And then I give into the desperate siren song of hope. "Do you think this is all just a strange blip in our relationship or something? Like maybe it was something he had to get out of his system?"

Kiara's eyes flood with disbelief. "After everything you've just been through, why would you even want him back?"

I sigh. "I don't know. I'm just . . . I'm just a very complicated woman."

"Who isn't?" Kiara grumbles. "Get in line."

And even though I know how tragic I'm being, I can't seem to let the sad little glimmer of hope fade into the wind. "Who knows, maybe this thing with Aleister will get stale quickly and Chase will come back to me. To us. To the us we used to be. I mean, things like that happen, right?"

Kiara's face toggles between wanting to comfort me and not wanting to encourage false hope. She turns her gaze toward the plastic parfait cup in her hand and the leftover peanuts sadly bobbing in the small swimming pool of watery fudge.

"Remember your sophomore year in college when you got on your *Ragtime* kick and played the cast album nonstop?"

"What do Ahrens and Flaherty have to do with anything?"

"What soaring ballad did you play on repeat until you cried so much that you got dehydrated and had to go to the student health center where they quickly diagnosed you with a strong case of drama queen-itis?"

"That was a misdiagnosis." I huff.

"What was the soaring ballad, Noah?"

I can barely speak the title of the song. "'Back to Before,' sung by the incomparable Marin Mazzie."

Kiara takes my hand tenderly, almost as if it's made of glass. "I think that's where you are, Noah. Just like the lyric says, 'You can never go back to before.'"

I hear a tiny whimper somewhere and look around searching for a small, wounded animal. It takes a second or two before I realize the whimper came from me.

Kiara's pinky circles mine.

"But just remember that I love you so much that I would crawl on my knees through broken glass for you."

The routine again. Thank God for the familiar. The reliable. The comforting Kiara and Noah catechism.

I laugh and quickly come up with, "I love you so much that I would take a bubble bath with Mario Batali for you."

Kiara counters, "I love you so much that I would come to Plainview, Illinois, for you."

And we're both laughing wildly into the night air. And then, I'm crying. In front of a Dairy Queen in the middle of the Midwest. And she's holding me until it stops.

After I pull myself together, I ask, "How's Stephen?"

"Really, really good. Still seeing that therapist you recommended. They seem to have found the right dosage for his Lexapro. And he's making major real estate deals like a boss."

"And how's work? Is your firm suing anybody juicy or famous?"

Kiara gives me a look. "I'm not here to talk about my boring job. I'm here to cheer up my best friend. Is there any place to get some hardcore liquor around here?"

I sigh, defeated. "There's a place called Bumpkins."

"Isn't that when you give somebody a blowjob while they're sitting on a toilet?"

"What? No! That's a 'blumpkin.' And why do you even know that?"

"I'm a woman of the world. And now I need to shake my Sharons at Bumpkins."

A half an hour later, Kiara and I are doing shots at the bar and she's yelling over the music, "I'm adding an eleventh commandment to the Bible: Thou shalt not take the name of Country Bumpkins in vain! I'm going to change my passport to say I'm a citizen of Country fucking Bumpkins!"

She's drunk. We both are.

And she's raving. "I am going to marry these onion rings! I'm going to build a little man out of them, put a tuxedo on my little onion ring man, and go before a justice of the peace!"

"God, I love it when you get wasted and babble!"

I thought my heart had been broken, when in fact it's sitting right next to me, sloppily shoving onion rings down its throat.

Kiara looks up and her jaw goes slack, displaying a jumble of half-eaten rings. I follow her gaze to see Luke standing before me.

He looks concerned. "Hey. I, uh, wanted to check and make sure everything was okay. I mean, first rehearsal got canceled and then that thing with Eddie."

Before I can even respond, Kiara is enthusiastically pointing at Luke and drunkenly snapping her fingers. "Is this the guy?!? Is this the . . . the . . . the kissing guy?"

The thing is, I don't even remember telling Kiara about the kiss with Luke. Maybe in my miserable rambling it came up? I've been in such a fog of despair, it's possible. But it doesn't matter now, because Luke is looking shocked that I've told anyone. My face turns bright red. I wonder if committing hara-kiri in the middle of the restaurant would turn me into some kind of local urban legend.

I try to apologize. "We've been overserved."

Kiara's eyes almost pop out of her head with realization. "Noah's single now! He and his asshole boyfriend broke up! You two should kiss! The two of you should kiss right now! Put your mouths together, I wanna watch!"

I quickly search the floor, wondering why there isn't a trap door to swallow me whole. "We were just leaving."

"Well, neither of you are in any condition to drive. Pay up and get in my truck."

Kiara is oddly excited. "I've never been in a truck! Can I ride in the back?"

Luke looks leery. "If you promise not to stand."

"Safety first, Aladdin!"

Luke gives me a baffled look. I try to explain. "I might have told her that you look like the title character in Disney's *Hercules*. She's getting her animated features mixed up."

Luke seems actually a little, I don't know, happy that I've been comparing him to cartoons with my friends?

As she climbs into the back of the truck, Kiara announces to the entire parking lot, "I had a dream last night that Queen Elizabeth came back to life, you guys! And she was a zombie! A motherfucking zombie! And she kept a bunch of human brains in her handbag! That's why she's never without the handbag! Mystery solved!"

Thankfully, everyone ignores the drunk, crazy lady.

"No standing in the back," Luke commands in a controlling and strangely hot way. There's something about authoritative Luke that makes me a little lightheaded. It reminds me of our ride in the hot air balloon when he told me we were safe. His words were not to be questioned. His resolve was not to be doubted. It's intimidating and intoxicating as hell at the same time. But the parking lot at Bumpkins is the last place to start getting turned on, so I file the thought away for later.

Once we're in the truck, Luke says, "She really likes those onion rings."

"Well, that's good. Because she'll be able to enjoy them all over again when she barfs them up into my parents' toilet."

Kiara opens the little sliding window thing to blather at us. "Here's what's going to happen. You two are going to hook up and if you, Aladdin, break my best friend's heart, you're going to have to deal with me! And I'm from Queens, Ali Baba! We know how to deal with . . . with . . . yeah . . ."

And thankfully she trails off and falls asleep with her face resting halfway into the cab of the truck.

Luke ventures a look at Kiara dozing off. "Are all of your New York friends drunken supermodels?"

"Pretty much."

Luke revs the engine and we ride self-consciously, a quiet hush filling the front seat like fog from a horror movie. We pause at a stoplight across from Hawkins' Drug Store and watch the lonely manager count the money in the till instead of talking. The stoplight blinks green and we roll onward.

Finally, Luke carefully asks, "So I know it's none of my business, but what happened with your guy?"

Ugh. "Well, he's officially not 'my guy' anymore. He slept with a very promising, very much younger playwright and I found out."

Luke actually pumps the breaks in response, which elicits an unladylike half belch from a dead-to-the-world Kiara.

Luke stares at me, looking perplexed. "He stepped out on you?"

I fight the urge to make fun of the phrase "stepped out on" and simply nod.

"Are you . . . okay?"

"I'm a total disaster, but that tracks with everything that's happening in my life right now. I like to think of it as a theme. And the theme of my life is 'The *Hindenburg*.' I'm considering making t-shirts."

Luke resumes driving, still looking baffled. And fucking gorgeous. His window is down and the night air plays with his blond curls. He clearly didn't shave this morning and the scruff on his face has the tiniest shades of ginger that matches the hair on his forearms. My God, his forearms. How do you even get forearms that muscular? My mind travels back to the day he kissed me and how forcefully those forearms wrapped around my waist and locked me in place.

To my surprise, I snap out of my trance to find Luke talking about the very same day.

"I know that I made a mistake with the whole kissing thing. And, man, I'm not here to make an opportunity out of your breakup or anything. But I'm not afraid to say this: that guy was a phony."

It's now my turn to look baffled. "Chase?"

"Yeah, total dickhead. Walking around like he was better than everybody. Nose in the air. That guy was super hoity-toity."

I will not make fun of him for using that phrase.

I will not make fun of him for using that phrase.

I will not make fun of him for using that phrase.

Luke continues, "He just seemed, I don't know . . . unworthy of you. Like the two of you don't belong together."

"Well, apparently he agrees because he's banging someone else in a very expensive hotel."

"Well, he's a dickhead, then. Here we are."

When we pull up, Kiara does a spectacular nosedive out of the back of the truck.

But she pops up like an Olympic gymnast and starts screaming a hideously off-key rendition of "A Whole New World."

I look at Luke and mutter, "I should probably take care of the beautiful drunk woman."

"I'd be disappointed in your lack of chivalry if you didn't."

I sigh and proceed to extract Kiara out of the shrubbery she's fallen into and haul her toward the house. We take less than three steps before Kiara turns around and shouts to Luke, "Noah saved my husband's life! He's a good person! Don't you hurt him, Aladdin!"

Luke gives me a questioning look from behind the windshield.

"Just ignore her."

Luke nods and pulls out of the driveway just as Mom comes out with a bucket in each hand. I'm presuming they're for Kiara and me to vomit into. If Mom clocks the fact that it's her personal patron saint chauffeuring Kiara and me home, she doesn't let on.

I gesture toward the buckets and ask, "How did you know we'd end up shitfaced?"

"Oh, Noah. Don't you realize how many times I've seen this movie? Spoiler alert, Kiara comes to town and I have to protect my wall-to-wall carpet from the both of you. This is about the sixth sequel."

Then she gets tender and says, "She's a good friend."

I grab both buckets and maneuver Kiara up the stairs while her body sags like a drunken scarecrow.

The next day, I'm hugging a very hungover Kiara in front of her rental car and not wanting to let her go. "I'm going to be lost without you."

"No, you're not, because Stephen and I have already spoken and we have a plan of attack. If you'll let me, I'll handle everything with Chase. I'll arrange to have your things picked up. I'll make sure your name gets taken off the lease. Stephen will find you a new apartment—"

"A cheap new apartment. I have to figure out how to live on my own meager savings now. God, do I have to move into a studio? That is so depressing. What am I going to do for money, Kiara? Am I going to have to go back to bartending and waiting tables? Am I going to have to sell my hair like Fantine from *Les Mis*?

"You'll be fine. Just let me take care of everything so you don't have to even think about it."

"But you can't do that. You have a full-time job. You're going to be too busy helping evil corporations stick it to the little people."

"Um, first off, I do a ton of pro bono work, so I deflect any negative karma. And secondly, I am going to love making Chase squirm like a little bitch. And if he calls or texts you, ghost that fucker!"

And after about fifty-three more tiny hugs, Kiara gets into her rental car and drives off.

As I head back toward the house, Luke pulls up in his truck, ready to start work. And of course he's wearing a t-shirt with no sleeves. I assume they were torn off in a tornado. His impressive biceps are on full display.

For a second the sight of him makes me forget that I'm completely and utterly devastated about Chase. But that second passes.

"Kiara headed back to New York?"

"Yep." I hear the sadness in my own voice. I suspect we both do.

"She's pretty funny when she's drunk. And . . . uh, you told her about the kiss?"

"Apparently. I don't know. My brain is basically just a bunch of cartoon monkeys playing bongos at this point."

Luke nods. I notice he's no longer wearing his baseball cap

backward and I wonder if he can read minds. His hair is doing its usual curly thing over his left eye and I'm a little disappointed when I realize he's shaved. The ever-present babble of cows mooing to each other fills the silence.

"So is practice back on tonight?"

"Rehearsal," I correct him. "And yes, it is."

"You sure you're up to it?"

"I guess we'll find out." I turn and walk away, not able to stand any more of his pity.


Later that evening I find myself sitting on the hood of Mom's Toyota, unable to enter the theater. Minutes tick by until Melissa quietly appears from inside the building and takes her place next to me on the hood.

"Are you coming inside, Noah?"

"They all know I've been dumped, right?"

"Well, it's a small town, so . . ."

"I figured." Melissa gives me a gentle hug and I accept it with a mopey grunt. "They're all going to feel sorry for me. And act like my eyes aren't bloodshot from crying. Do you think it would be okay if I wore a burka?"

Melissa is dubious. "I think that might be considered cultural appropriation."

"Christ! Chase could have given me some kind of warning that he was going to throw our entire relationship down the metaphorical garbage disposal. He could have at least ended things before he started screwing someone else. But no, he played me for a fool."

"That says more about him than it does you."

"I'm officially a cuckold."

"No, you're not."

"It just hurts so . . . I don't even know what the word is. Profoundly, I guess? It just hurts so profoundly. How can I ever trust anyone ever again?"

Melissa offers no counsel.

"The saddest part is that I'm not even sure how to exist without Chase. He was so good at adulting. He planned the vacations and made the restaurant reservations and calculated how many calories we should eat per day if we wanted to maintain some semblance of a waist. It was just so . . ."

"Controlling?" Melissa asks cautiously.

"I was going to say thoughtful. Or comforting. But maybe controlling is right. But I loved him for it. He just always had all the answers when all I ever had were questions. Who's going to have all the answers now? And you want to know the worst part? I was considering proposing to him."

"Oh, Noah . . ." Her voice is saturated with so much pity that I hesitate. But I can't stop myself.

"There's a fancy French place in the city called Ladurée. I was going to put together a little tea hamper full of macarons and other extravagant shit. This was when I allowed myself to dream that *Stage of Fools* would have a somewhat healthy run. My fantasy was that I would lure Chase to Central Park on a perfect

Sunday afternoon. And between the macarons and champagne I would get down on one knee and seal our hearts together for all eternity. The plan was to buy him an obnoxious ring from Tiffany's. The Paloma's Groove Ring in sterling silver, to be specific. But that's all gone now . . . and I'll never fall in love again. Just like Burt Bacharach and Hal David said."

Melissa sits with me in silence.

Finally, she asks, "Do you want to just go back home? The rest of us can run lines or something."

"No. If I give up even for a minute, Chase wins. I'm just going to walk into that building and act like everything is fine. Even though I know I'll be wearing an invisible scarlet letter. But instead of standing for adultery, it'll stand for abandoned."

And I'm up on my feet and heading toward the side door of the theater. Melissa trails me like a pregnant handmaiden of sorrow.

I suddenly feel Melissa's hand on my elbow and she spins me around to face her. Not used to being manhandled, I give her a questioning look and Melissa takes a deep breath and starts to speak.

"Look, Noah, I get things have been rough lately. And I know that you think that the curtain is coming down for you, both professionally and personally. But maybe . . . just maybe, you're only at intermission on both counts. What if this is just time for you to regroup, to take a bathroom break and eat some stale popcorn before Act Two starts?"

I give her a weary look. "Well, that would be horrifying, because new musicals are notorious for having second act problems."

"In that case, we'd better get back to work."

We share a determined nod and head back into rehearsal.

The flurry of sad looks from the cast is just as uncomfortable as I had predicted. I quickly decide to become Momma Rose from *Gypsy* and muster all the chutzpah I can. "Sorry we had to cancel yesterday's rehearsal. My fault completely. So, for good measure, let's run through the entire score just to burn those new lyrics into our brains. And, you know, sing out, Louise!"

Relieved to have something other than the sad, shipwrecked homosexual to focus on, the cast obediently gathers around the piano.

While they get down to work, I turn to see Dad coming through the side door with his oxygen tank and a blueprint tube under his arm.

"Dad, what are you doing here?"

"Dr. Dunbar said I need to get some light exercise in, whatever that means. Anyway, Luke said you were taking out all the old timey talk."

"And?"

"Well, so that means that everybody's just going to talk like normal people. Like we're talking right now, right?"

"Uh-huh."

"Well, it got me to thinking." He hands me the blueprint tube. "Here's my thought. It might be stupid. I don't mind if you think it is or don't agree. But this here is my thought, son."

I walk over to a table and pop the cap off the tube. As I unfurl Dad's blueprint and spread it onto the tabletop, my heart skips a little. "Dad, is this . . . is this a new set?"

"I know this isn't my area of expertise, and I hope this doesn't look like I'm trying to step on your toes or anything. But it just kinda occurred to me that maybe if everyone was talking normal, well, maybe they should have a normal set instead of some spaceship."

I stare at the blueprint spread out before me. It's a farmhouse. Dad's made King Lear a farmer. Just like him. And I immediately remember Mom's little soliloquy about how Dad says "I love you" with his actions. Maybe she was right.

"It's probably stupid, son—"

Dad reaches for the rendering and I stop his wrinkled hand. I assume my hands will look the same someday in the not-so-distant future. "No. I love it, Dad. I totally love it."

"You do?"

"It just makes the whole show seem so much more grounded. It's a major improvement."

And it's then that I wished we had the kind of relationship that included hugs. But instead we turn into department store dummies. Stiff department store dummies unable to close the space between us. But at the very least we're happy to finally nod at one another from across the abyss.

"I do, Dad. I love it. I'm really touched that you put so much thought into it."

I've said too much and we both know it. Thankfully, Dad knows when and how to change the subject. It's his specialty. "There's Luke. We should make a game plan."

I follow Dad's gaze and to my surprise I see Luke talking to Eddie Gregory.

Confused, I wander over with Dad.

"Hi, Eddie," I say cautiously.

Eddie just nods a casual hello. "Hey, Noah."

Luke starts explaining, "I have a lot of set pieces to move around. I realized that when we ran those first few scenes together. So Eddie said he'd being willing to help."

"Do you even like theater?" I ask.

Eddie shrugs. "I don't know. Closest thing I ever saw was a puppet show over at the church. But if Luke needs help and as long as he can show me what to do, I thought, sure. And also . . . well, I think we both know I owe you one."

Eddie Gregory wants to be on the stage crew for my musical. We really are in the Upside Down now. Whatever that is.

"Okay, sure. Great. Welcome aboard."

Dad hands the blueprint to Luke. "Well, I just doubled our workload, so we need all the hands we can get."

I go backstage and try to find Allison Egan to break the news. If we're changing the setting to a farm, all of her work on the costumes will have been in vain. She looks understandably disappointed and I feel terrible. "I'm sorry, Allison. You've put so much amazing effort into this show. So much consideration and care. I'm just really, really sorry to do this to you."

Allison thinks for a minute, her arms crossed. Then she shrugs and says, "The best idea wins. And that's the best idea. I can work with the cast and the clothes they have. And I can pull stuff from the costume closet, too."

"You're a saint," I say. "But with this new direction, do you think it would look strange to keep the crown of oak leaves for

Melissa? I know it might seem out of place, but it's just so cool looking."

Allison smiles. "I think we can take some artistic license with the crown."

By the time we get to our first break, the cast is up in arms when they see Dad, Luke, and Eddie starting to dismantle the set.

I try to smooth their very easily ruffled feathers the best I can. "Calm down, you guys. We decided that the spaceship thing just isn't working anymore. In fact, I'm not sure it ever worked. So we're setting the musical on a farm. And in the present day, instead of the future."

Jackie McNew gives a knowing look. "I've been suggesting that from day one."

Julia turns to the rest of the cast. "She has not."

"It was actually my dad's idea." There's some positive murmuring and then a spontaneous smattering of applause for Dad. Dad shakes his head, clearly embarrassed, and quickly pushes Captain Lear's command station module into the wings.

# fourteen

# "Gay Godzilla"

C hase once called me the sensei master of dwelling and now this master seems to be dwelling almost exclusively on Chase. How long will he wait before he moves Aleister into our apartment? Will he kiss Aleister's nose at opening night parties like he used to kiss mine? When Aleister grows nervous, will Chase offer his bum to be cuddled? Although it's hard to imagine Aleister actually being nervous. The guy walks around like everything is owed to him and free for the taking. My boyfriend included, I guess. The puzzle piece that left me confused was that Chase usually liked to be completely dominated in bed. It was hard to imagine a twink with over-plucked eyebrows being able to accommodate. And every time I did try to envision it, I only succeeded in making myself nauseous or depressed. Or both.

Chase eventually does end up sending me a text that reads simply: Kiara has forbidden you to speak to me? Am I really supposed to go through her and Stephen?

I have to harvest every tiny morsel of self-control I have left in order to stop myself from texting him back. Why is the temptation so strong?

I hastily shoot Kiara a text: Not sure why, but I feel bad ghosting Chase.

Kiara's response: Ghosts don't have feelings so they can't feel bad.

Maybe she's right.

Dad's new set for the show meant some slight alterations to the blocking. The next few rehearsals pass by without much more drama, except for one close call that threatened to turn the theater gods against us.

Over a ten-minute break, Louis Jenkins and I are sipping horrible coffee when he asks out of the blue, "Hey, so, Noah, why did you choose *King Lear* to turn into a musical?"

I shoot him a deflated look. "Well, because I clearly have daddy issues. I mean, isn't that obvious to everyone in a forty-mile radius?"

Louis chuckles and gives a noncommittal shrug. "Well, I don't know about that. But why not *Hamlet* or *Macbeth*?"

Mrs. Henson lets out a bloodcurdling scream from across the auditorium and the entire cast looks up, their faces stricken with panic.

"What did I say? What did I say?" Louis asks, clearly spooked.

I shout at him with possibly a little more fervor than is necessary, "You don't say the *Scottish play* in a theater unless you're performing it, Louis!"

Louis bursts into a relieved laugh. "What? That's crazy!"

Mrs. Henson is quickly at my side and as serious as an undertaker. "It's not crazy in the least. You've cursed us. And now you have to fix it."

The cast starts to gather around a defiant Louis. "I didn't curse anybody, I just said *Macbeth*."

Now everyone screams, including me. I put a solemn hand on his shoulder. "You've got to fix this, Louis. We're not rehearsing for one more minute until you do."

"Come on, guys, this is crazy talk." He scans the room and his grin quickly dissolves. He can see that we all mean business, especially Mrs. Henson and me.

"Fine, what do I do?"

Mrs. Henson speaks at a deliberate pace, hoping to make sure that Louis gets the order right. "First, you go outside. Then you spin around three times and spit on the ground. Then you say a curse word of your choosing. And then, finally, you knock on the door until one of us lets you back inside."

"You guys really expect me to do all that nonsense?"

Louis reads the room and realizes that he has no choice.

"Fine." Louis dutifully walks out of the theater. When he knocks on the side door a few seconds later, I consider not letting him in. But since he's playing by the rules, I open the door and bow theatrically to him as he reenters the building.

"Jeez, is there anything else I need to know?"

The cast stares at me and I quickly oblige. "Well, you're not supposed to whistle backstage. That's a definite jinx. And we've just established that saying the Scottish play is a big no-no. And I'm sure you all know the whole 'break a leg' thing."

Jackie looks confused for a moment. "Break a leg?"

"Yeah, like if I see you before the show, I'll tell you to break a leg."

Jackie smirks. "Yeah, well, then I'll tell you to go fracture a fucking arm!"

"No, it means 'good luck.'"

Jackie shrugs. "Well, I'm not superstitious, except that thing where if you spill salt, you're supposed to throw a pinch of it over your left shoulder."

Confused, I can't help but ask, "Why the left shoulder?"

"That's where the devil stands, ya ding-dong! God, I thought you went to college."

And with that, we return to rehearsal before burning up any more precious time with questionable folklore. The evening goes on without another hitch until Melissa feels a wave of morning sickness and throws up all over her costume. She swears that she's been long over any queasiness and apologizes profusely to everyone. Eddie mops the stage while Allison diligently washes the puke out of Melissa's shirt.

Heigh-ho, the glamorous life!

To everyone's amazement, we manage to get almost all of Act Two sloppily up on its feet by the following night. In fact, the nights here in Plainview have rushed by at a surprisingly speedy pace thanks to the distraction provided by rehearsals.

The days? Not so much.

There's been little for me to do during the daylight hours other than ridiculously pine away for Chase. And feel lost and abandoned. At least he's clearly given up texting me, which somehow feels even worse. Ugh. I put the thought out of my head as I start packing up The Executive and trying to make a mental game plan for tomorrow's rehearsal. Do we dare try to run the whole show? I consult my crumpled rehearsal schedule and quickly count. Thirteen rehearsals left. Better save the run-through for Saturday. I'm busy scribbling notes to myself when Luke approaches pensively.

"Hey, Luke."

"Hey." He just stands there, looking down at his scuffed-up duck boots.

"What's up?"

He shifts his weight from side to side. It sounds stupid to call a grown man adorable, but no other word fits. And then it strikes me all at once. He's nervous. Luke Carter can probably bench-press the Taj Mahal. Why is he nervous?

"Are you doing anything Saturday night after rehearsal?"

"You finally called it rehearsal. See, I knew you could do it!"

He gives a cautious half laugh and then asks, "Well, are you?"

I'm confused for a second, then completely dumbfounded. Is he asking me out on a date? He is! He's asking me out on a date. He's actually standing there in the tightest t-shirt in North America with his chest muscles straining to break free like he's a superhero and asking me on a date.

What do I say?

I mean, I'm obviously single now. Painfully so. But getting dumped still feels pretty fresh. And aren't I supposed to wait until the sadness numbs? Aren't I supposed to avoid rebound dating? And yet, Romeo went out with Juliet just to get over someone else and everything turned out pretty great for those two kids, right?

"If you have to think this long, I get it. You're not ready and that's cool."

Fuck it.

"No, um . . . sure. I'm free."

And now we're both nervous.

"You could come over to my place. You're not too fancy for burgers, are you?"

"I am not."

"So, I know this is probably real soon after the whole breakup thing with Chase, but I just want to be clear. This is a date. Like an official date. And if that's not okay, I totally understand."

Why is my mouth dry? When did my body stop producing saliva? I clear my throat and look as unassuming as possible.

"No, I would love to come over for a very official date."

Luke breaks out into a devastating smile. Then we're both smiling. Like fools. Like a stage of fools.

"Cool," he says, then turns and leaves. When I'm sure he's gone, I do a very melodramatic collapse to the floor, which hurts a little because it's solid concrete. Melodrama has its price, I guess.

The next night after rehearsal, the sky is an inky blue and I'm practically lightheaded when I turn and see Luke running toward me through the parking lot. I've been slightly stunned how forcefully thoughts of Luke have been crowding Chase and Aleister out of my mind. I've given up obsessively following Aleister's career online and deleted almost all of Chase's pictures.

Instead, I find myself trying to remember teenage Luke and wondering how I had gotten the past so wrong. It's almost sad to think we could have been friends all those years ago. Or maybe even more.

Luke asks, slightly out of breath, "Hey, just checking if we're still on for Saturday night."

"Definitely," I say. "You know, I don't even know where you live."

"Oh, I'm on Walnut Street. Twenty-three Walnut Street. It's a little white house with a blue door. You can't miss it."

"Great." And then I add for good measure, "I'm kind of relieved. I was worried you might have lived in a trailer or something and I don't do trailers."

Luke looks like I've just stabbed him in the face. I'm suddenly scared I've done something terrible, but not sure what.

"Uh, Luke? Are you okay?"

"I was raised in a trailer. In fact, my mom still lives in that exact same trailer."

Fuck. Oh, fuck my stupid mouth.

"Oh God, I'm so sorry, Luke. I didn't mean—"

"A lot of people that are a ton better than the both of us live in trailers." Luke is getting pissed now and I'm not sure what to say to fix it.

"I know that. I'm sorry, I was just trying to be funny, I guess. I was trying to be charming and it backfired because I'm an idiot."

Luke starts to walk away.

"You're not just leaving, are you?"

He spins back around and walks back toward me. A pair of inquisitive crows watches us from a telephone pole.

"You know, not everyone was born rich like you, Noah."

I can't help but laugh incredulously. "Rich? Dad's farm has been hanging by a thread for as long as I can remember!"

"Yeah, but you went to college."

"Lots of people go to college."

"Lots of people don't. And let me ask you this, did you have to work when you were in college? Even a part-time job?"

"I was on several scholarships, which I *earned*."

Why am I getting defensive? I'm supposed to be apologizing.

"But did you have to work and go to school at the same time?"

I stare at him, lost and exasperated. "No."

"That's what I figured."

Silence. Why are we fighting about this? Is this our first fight? We haven't even had our first date.

"I don't know what you want me to say. Sorry I didn't have to *personally pay* for my education?"

"I just think you should be a little more careful about going around and looking down on people."

My face flushes and I stare stupidly at the ground. Jesus. He's right. Luke is totally fucking right. When did I become this person? Have I always gone around making jokes at other people's expense? Do I really want to be the kind of guy who punches down like that? For a second I'm tempted to blame New York for turning me cynical and cruel, but I know that's a total cop-out. The remorse is so thick I can taste it in the back of my throat. I force myself to look Luke in the eyes and try to figure out where to even begin.

"Luke, I'm . . . I am so sorry I made a stupid joke about trailers. Oh God, I'm such a dumb man-baby sometimes. I guess all this time I thought you were the bully, but it turns out I'm the bully . . ."

I hang my head, disgusted with myself. "Looks like I'm just some spoiled little prick whose parents paid for his college. And his car. And . . ."

My mind races. I'm a total fraud. So much was handed to me on a silver platter and yet all I do to thank the world is spout an endless stream of snarky commentary. How did I end up becoming such an entitled douchebag? And so blind to my own privilege?

I've ruined everything with one flippant remark. It takes a pretty amazing amount of talent to wreck things so easily. Willy-nilly. I'm like some enormous, gay Godzilla clomping through the tiny cityscape of sweet Luke Carter's heart.

"Please don't be mad at me, Luke. I'm an asshole, I guess. But I can try to be better."

Luke's greenish-hazel eyes soften. "You're not an asshole, Noah. But you sure as hell didn't used to be like this. I guess you sort of live in a bubble now. You have to remember that you've been given a lot more than most people, and you shouldn't just take it all for granted. Not everybody has had it as easy as you have." Luke pauses, searching. "And also I'm really overprotective of my mom. This town hasn't been nice to her."

And then the words just come pouring out of me, without even giving the jaded part of my brain time to edit them.

"Luke, you are by far the nicest fucking person I've ever met. And for some reason I had you pegged wrong for so many years. And you couldn't have just been born that way. Clearly you are the way that you are because of how you were raised. All that credit is obviously due to your mother. I know without a doubt she has to be one of the most amazing people on this side of the Mississippi River if Luke Carter is her son."

Luke smiles a little. Jesus, does talking to people without sarcasm actually work? "Apology accepted."

"Will you still cook burgers for me on Saturday night? I promise I can be a better person. I swear I'm not totally rotten to the core. There's hope for me yet."

Luke glances around the parking lot, I assume to check if we're being watched by anyone other than the crows. I'm not sure what he's worried about. Ninjas, maybe? Then he puts his hand on the back off my neck and pulls me into a warm and gentle kiss. Before my knees can start to do their buckling thing he pulls away.

"We're on for Saturday," he says and climbs into his truck. I have a date with a hot cowhand who drives a truck.

What would teenage me think?

# fifteen

# "A Very Official Date"

S aturdays in community theater have always been a marathon. On weekdays the cast can only rehearse at night and on Sundays we can't rehearse at all because everyone goes to one of the fifty-three thousand churches in town. So Saturday is where everyone buckles down and hopes to make great strides.

Since we're going to attempt to run the whole enchilada, I try to give an inspiring little speech before we begin.

"So, I don't think you guys really understand just how fucking good you're getting. You've actually made me forget about the Broadway cast. And we had three Tony Award winners! The way you're connecting to your characters and to one another is just . . . well, it's kind of breathtaking. Your family and friends are going to be blown away. Get prepared to sign some autographs on opening night."

The cast laughs, but I double down.

"I'm not kidding. You're going to sign so many autographs you're going to get carpal tunnel syndrome. Now, let's keep the good momentum going. Let's work like gangbusters to get as far as we can through the whole show. Let's just plow through like total wildebeests. We can go back and polish up any mistakes later. Let's focus on quantity now and worry about quality another day. Are you with me, people?"

The cast roars and the tempo in the theater goes into overdrive as Luke yells out his now standard, "Places!"

To everyone's amazement, we almost make it through the entire show. We get as far as Lear and Cordelia's duet "The Mystery of Things" before we have to stop. That means we have all next week to polish and fine-tune. I've been so consumed with the run-through that I realize I haven't thought about my date with Luke all day. He comes up to me as I'm going over some musical notes with Mrs. Henson. And in a snap, I'm nervous and clumsy.

"So, is seven o'clock good?"

I force my voice not to go up an octave. "Yep. Twenty-three Walnut Street."

That smile of his again. It's so intense it's probably blinding people as far away as Europe.

"Good. See ya." And with that, he's gone.

Mrs. Henson gives me a sly look. Surprising. She doesn't usually do sly. I glare at her. "What?"

"Oh, nothing. He's just a very fine man, that Luke Carter. He had it pretty rough as a kid, but it's almost impossible to find him without a smile on his face. That says a lot about a person."

"Do you think . . . do you think I should go home and change? I should probably change clothes, right?"

"I don't think it will matter to Luke, but if it'll make you feel better."

So now I'm asking my high school lit teacher what to wear on a first date. And I'm almost thirty years old. Super.

After agonizing over the very few outfits I brought to town, I go with a navy Tom Ford shirt and a pair of jeans looped with my favorite Paul Smith belt. I'm going for "I'm casual, but I still care." My insecurities are like a game of Whac-A-Mole, popping up all over the place. And I'm very bad at whacking moles. Or any carnival games that include skill or hand-eye coordination.

When I knock on Luke's door, he opens it and he's wearing a tie. And not just a tie; he's wearing a plaid collared shirt, khakis, and dress shoes.

I look down at my clothes, immediately self-conscious. "I feel a little underdressed. I thought you said we were having burgers, but you're wearing a tie."

"But it's still a date." Apparently date equals tie in Luke's mind. Not sure why he feels that way, but he does look ridiculously handsome.

"Right. An official date. A very official date. We probably should have signed some paperwork or something." I pause and give his tie a small tug. "I feel kind of bad. I don't have any ties on me. And clearly we're wearing ties. Do you have one I can borrow?"

Luke loosens his tie and puts it around my neck.

Instead of mauling him right there, I simply say, "We are such problem solvers."

I hand him a bottle of shiraz. "I brought a red. Apparently the tannins go with hamburgers. I'll admit, I googled that."

A fluffy mutt of a dog squeezes between Luke's legs and starts trying to climb me like I'm a mountain.

"Bosco, get down!"

I kneel down to pet the dog and he immediately rolls over onto his back for me and I scratch his stomach. His little right leg kicks frantically at something invisible in the air.

Luke seems surprised. "Wow! He likes you."

"He's got good taste. Where'd you get him?"

"He used to belong to Mrs. Holland. I would go over and mow her lawn on weekends and Bosco and me always got along. She gave him to me when she had to go into a nursing home. She said I was the only one she would trust him with. She named him Bosco after the chocolate syrup. I guess because of his coloring. I still take him to see her at the home. She loves it. Well, they both do, I guess."

He takes in stranded dogs and visits old women in nursing homes. This is never going to work.

Luke gives Bosco a hearty pat on the stomach. "All right, Bosco, go make your business."

Bosco rolls to his feet and runs out into the yard.

We stand there awkwardly in the doorway for a second.

I finally can't take it anymore and say, "I'm kind of like a vampire, Luke. You have to invite me in."

Luke laughs. "Sorry. I . . . I'm kinda nervous. Come in."

The first thing I see in Luke's living room are a couple of

football trophies on his fireplace mantel. I go to inspect them and Luke brushes them off, embarrassed. "Those are just—"

"Proof you're a show-off?"

"Uh, I think I remember Mrs. Henson giving out trophies every year for the school musical."

"Yeah, instead of calling them 'Tonys' she called them 'Phonies.' She can be a real wordsmith when she wants to."

Wordsmith? Why am I using words like "wordsmith"?

Nervous, nervous, nervous.

Luke laughs to himself. "Can I show you something really embarrassing?"

"I wish you would."

He leads me to his surprisingly tidy bedroom. Aren't straight-acting guys supposed to be slobs? Not Luke, I guess. Everything's very masculine and very buttoned-up. He reaches into his dresser drawer and pulls out a faded program and hands it to me.

"You have a program from *Anything Goes*?"

He looks sheepishly at the floor. "I told you it was embarrassing. I saved it."

"You were there? You saw me doing gay Jerry Lewis in real time? Luke Carter went to see musicals when he was in high school?"

"Well, I didn't advertise it, because my friends would have been assholes about it. But I wanted to see it. For you. I didn't know you could tap dance. It was very impressive. And kind of sexy."

"Tap dancing is the complete opposite of sexy, Luke."

"Not when you were doing it. I remember you danced with

your hands in your pockets. Like you were too cool for school. And you had a pouty little smirk on your face."

"I could teach you a step or two," I offer. "Maybe a simple 'Shuffle off to Buffalo.'"

Luke explodes into laughter. "There's no way I could ever tap dance! And why is it called that? 'Shuffle off to Buffalo'?"

"I don't know. I guess people used to think that just walking off to Buffalo wasn't fancy enough."

"I liked the show so much I even bought the soundtrack."

"Cast album."

"I liked the show so much I even bought the cast album."

"Do you ever listen to it?"

"Honestly? Not really. I was kind of surprised when I figured out that one song was kind of sexual."

"Which one?"

In a surprisingly good baritone, Luke sings, "*You're the top, you're the coliseum . . .*"

"Hey, wait a second? You can sing?"

Luke blushes, which is endearing and hot at the same time. "No, I can't."

"You can sing better than me. Anytime I have to present a song to producers, I hire vocalists if I can afford it. If I sing, they'll think lesser of the song."

"But all that 'top,' 'coliseum' stuff. He's talking about gay sex stuff, right?"

"Oh, Cole Porter was a big old queen. And I doubt very much he was the coliseum in any relationship, if you know what I mean."

We're lost for words for a minute, so I look around the room

and find something completely unexpected. "You have a copy of
E. E. Cummings poetry?"

"Well, you and Mrs. Henson would talk about him forever
and I figured I had to check him out."

"And?"

"I mean, some of it just seems like gibberish."

"That's because it is. It's gobbledygook."

"But some of it . . . like that one poem that's called 'anyone
lived in a pretty how town.' When the guy dies and the poem
says 'and noone stooped to kiss his face.' That's just kind of
devastating."

Luke quoting poetry is so mind-shatteringly hot that I can't
trust my knees and I actually have to sit down.

Feigning a newfound interest in the dog-eared book, I park
myself on the bed and start to leaf through the pages. Luke
slowly joins me and our thighs collide just like the first night we
got drunk together. He turns his head until his face is so close
to my throat that his breath starts raising the tiny hairs on my neck.

And then he whispers softly into my ear in a voice that immediately makes my bone marrow liquefy, "I know what you're doing."

Holy shit.

I don't know this version of Luke. I only know ambiguously
flirting Luke. But if he wants to play this game he sure as hell
doesn't have to ask me twice.

I consider my next move and then decide to lie back on the
bed, still perusing the book and answer as nonchalantly as possible, "I'm just boning up on my twentieth-century American
poets."

Luke gives a low, suggestive laugh before he reclines next to me. "Is that what you're doing? Boning up?"

I casually toss the book on the floor and turn my face to his. "You have no idea."

It takes every ounce of self-control I have not to devour him right there. Not to "jump his bones" as the saying goes in Plainview. But the yearning in his eyes is so intense that I kind of want it to linger a little more. So we float for a moment in a state of mutual questioning until Luke's head makes the tiniest movement toward mine. It's almost imperceptible. But he nudges slightly closer to me, just within definite kissing range. He's so close that his gorgeous face is blurred and my heart is knocking at my chest cavity.

And then a timer goes off somewhere in the house. Luke rolls off the bed and onto his feet. "Cornbread's done."

I heave a frustrated sigh. "Fucking cornbread."

He grabs my arm and pulls me off the bed. Apparently the boning up will have to wait. Luke heads to the kitchen and I linger in the hallway to reorganize the situation in my jeans. I mean, you can't whisper things into my ear and not expect me to do some stage management in my boxer briefs.

Luke calls out, "So how do you take your burgers?"

"Chef's choice," I reply.

"You sure? Because I like them pretty rare."

"Is it strange to take care of cows all day and then come home and eat them at night?"

Luke sighs. "I'm not going to get a lecture, am I?"

"Oh, no. I charge for lectures and my fees are ambitiously high."

We head out to the backyard where a charcoal grill is already happily smoking away. I make myself stop for a second to take it all in. It's a perfect backyard. The smell of freshly cut grass and a fading magnolia tree. Dog-day cicadas chatter. A couple of hummingbirds do-si-do around a feeder filled with water colored an artificial candy apple red. I notice a table set with metal army green plates that I'm assuming Luke uses for camping. He's extra masculine even down to the flatware.

Luke gets busy grilling, while I open the wine to show that I'm handy. Of course it's a screw top, but even so.

Bosco comes tearing around the side of the house with a tattered tennis ball in his mouth and we play fetch until dinner is served.

Luke and I sit at the table in silence for a second until I say, "This is my favorite song."

Luke gives me a confused look because there's no music playing, then gets it. "Oh, right." He pulls out his iPhone and plops it into a portable speaker. "What kind of music do you like? I'm guessing country is out."

"You're correct, unless it's Patsy Cline."

"It's not."

"How about top forty? Can we agree on that?"

"We can."

Luke's hamburgers are downright amazing. I shake my head and think, "He Can Cook, too!"

Luke gives me a questioning glance and I quickly sing his praises. "These are great. They have a little kick to them."

"Cayenne pepper."

I finally can't take it anymore. "I'm sorry, but I've got to be blunt—"

Luke grins. "Really? That doesn't sound like you."

"So, are you gay? Bi? Don't like labels?"

He chuckles and looks toward the sky. "I knew this would come up. I tried for years to deny it, to push it away, but it was too depressing. I should have known a couple years after high school when I couldn't get it up for Melissa Fazio."

"That poor girl. I tried to finger her once and it apparently felt like she was being poked in her vagina by Edward Scissorhands."

Luke lets out a loud bark of a laugh and Bosco follows suit. "He does that sometimes. He thinks I'm barking and joins in."

"Cute."

"Anyway, you have no idea how many times I pretended to be too drunk to hook up after proms or homecoming dances, and then later after just really terrible dates. I got to a point where I couldn't take it anymore, you know? So, as a gift to myself on my twenty-fifth birthday, I finally came out to my mom and she couldn't have been cooler about it. She told me I was her son and she loved me just the same and it didn't change a damn thing. Then I told Eddie and some friends and that was a longer adjustment period. We just don't talk about it, really. I don't think it bothers any of them, they just don't know what to say."

Luke pauses. "I think that's why when they were harassing

you in high school, it upset me so much. Because deep down I knew I was just like you. So, I stopped all that bullshit for you, but I also stopped it for me, too. That makes me less of a hero, I guess."

I laugh. "Well, it had to be easier for you. You were a lot more successful at hiding the whole gay thing, that's for sure. I didn't stand a chance. I was such a little queen. I should have just walked down the hallway in a gold lamé thong, twirling rainbow flags and coughing up glitter."

"You were cute as hell and you know it," Luke says.

"Your lies burn like fire, but I appreciate the effort," I say. "I guess the good news about those days is that both of our mothers didn't freak out about the gay thing. Dad was typical Dad, which means he just shook his head and says, 'Well, you're still an Adams.' I remember thinking, 'Was there a possibility I'd have to change my name, that he would actually disown me for being gay?' It was such a bizarre thing to say. It wasn't the beginning of the gulf between us, but it was definitely a low point in our journey to polite distance."

"At least you had a dad to come out to."

"That's true. Although when the kids in the neighborhood would make fun of me, I always wanted Dad to stick up for me, you know? But Dad's a very 'fight your own fight' kind of guy. But maybe he did the right thing. It certainly toughened me up. Those kids making fun of me was nothing compared to seeing my shows trashed in black and white in review after review. Maybe it was all just the cosmos training me to man up and take my medicine. Still, the occasional 'I love you' from Dad would have been nice."

"I get that. Believe me. So, how about you?" Luke asks. "How did you know you were gay?"

I say quickly in one breath, "Chad Michael Murray as Lucas Scott in the WB drama series *One Tree Hill*."

Luke laughs so hard he snorts wine.

I take it as a win. "I made you snort wine!"

He coughs a little between laughing. "I just . . . man, that was specific."

"The teenage heart wants what it wants and mine wanted Chad Michael Murray as Lucas Scott in the WB drama series *One Tree Hill*."

"I'll give you this, you've always got a snappy comeback at the ready."

"Spend enough time with me and you'll soon realize that's all I am. A collection of snappy comebacks and cute sweaters."

His voice softens. "You're much more than that, Noah." I watch his eyes glisten beneath the perfect night sky and wonder how I say something witty. I finally give up and just watch him tear into his burger with unabashed gusto. When he's done, Luke gives the last piece to Bosco and then hops up to clear the table.

I jump up, too. "I can help, you know."

Luke shakes his head. "I got it."

While he takes the plates and silverware inside, I stand in the backyard wondering what comes next. Fireflies amble leisurely through the air and the sky gets pleasantly dark.

Shit. Insecure Noah is back.

Do I thank him and go?

Do I stand around like an idiot?

It's been almost two years of being only with Chase and I worry I'm rusty at this dating thing. Obviously Luke likes me. He not only wore a tie, which is adorable, but also put it around my neck. He let me pet his dog and made me hamburgers. And then we had that mind melting moment on his bed. Why would I walk away from that? Things are going fine, Noah. You're just out of practice. Jesus. How am I a grown adult and a fumbling adolescent at the same time?

Maybe I should just go. Take this whole thing slowly. I can ask him out on a date next time. In some strange way, it'll make me the one in control.

The slam of the back screen door snaps me out of my mental spiral. Luke has refreshed our wine glasses. "One more?"

"Uh . . . sure."

He hands me a glass and rekindles a fire pit that I didn't even notice was there. A couple of wicker chairs and a couch surround it and Luke takes his place on the couch with a sigh. Unsure what to do, I take a chair and we both stare into the dancing fire.

"Hey, Noah?"

"Yeah?"

"You're awfully far away."

Oh, boy. Aaaaand we're back.

My stomach does a couple of chaotic somersaults, but I walk slowly over to the couch and consider what to say. I sit next to Luke and feel the heat of his body and try not to get dizzy. We stare into the flames as they send sparks swirling up into the night sky.

I decide it's time to do away with any frothy wordplay and just move things along already. "Luke?" I ask.

"Yeah?"

"Could I put my arm around you?"

He laughs and says, "I wish you would."

I shoot my arm up into the air and somehow he settles his massive frame snuggly into my side. I lower my arm around his sturdy shoulder and sigh. "What the hell is actually happening here?"

He laughs again and the weight of him against me makes me lightheaded. I wrap my arm more tightly around him like I'm his protector. And that's exactly what I want to be. I want to protect him from any and all marauders.

*Nothing's gonna harm him, not while I'm around.*

Luke slowly shifts his body until his head is in my lap. His head is actually in my quickly-growing-crowded lap and he's staring up at me. I reach down and dare to run my fingers through his incredibly soft, floppy golden hair.

"Would it be okay if I kissed you?" I ask.

"Noah. You don't have to ask."

"Well, in this day and age—"

Luke cuts me off. "I consent to everything. You can do whatever you want to me."

Gulp.

"Uh . . . would you please stop making my head explode? I need it. Especially when I want to wear hats."

With a smirk, Luke jumps up and instead of unbuttoning his shirt, rips it over his head and stands in front of me shirtless. Talk about moving things along. That torso. He's like a statue come to life. My eyes quickly take it all in. The muscular chest, the veins snaking through his forearms, the ridiculously etched abs. I mean, I'm in pretty good shape, but this is some next-level shit.

I try desperately to negotiate the waves of lust rolling through my body. Steady there, Noah. Find your sea legs.

Luke approaches me and grabs the tie dangling loosely around my neck. Slowly, he tightens it so much I can hardly breathe. "What are you doing?"

He bends over and whispers softly into my ear, "Putting you on a leash."

Is this really happening?

I manage to get to my feet and our eyes lock. Then he gives me a deep kiss that tastes like very warm heaven. When he finally pulls away and stands there, boldly shirtless in front of the crackling fire pit, I find myself saying, "Lead the way."

He pulls on the tie and I follow him into the house, somehow impossibly still talking. "Do you want to go back and get your shirt? What if it rains? It looked like it might have been dry-clean only."

When we get to his bedroom, he lets go of the tie and turns to me with a hungry expression on his face. Blood is pounding in my brain, the tempo increasing.

"Look, Noah, if this is all too soon, I totally get it. But I hope it's not. And if it isn't too soon, well, I was wondering . . ."

And then he stops himself. He just shamelessly ripped his shirt off and then walked me on a makeshift leash to his bedroom, but now he's turning shy?

"What's wrong, Luke?"

He hesitates. "Just a couple of things . . ."

"Hey, not to sound overconfident, but I'm pretty sure this is one area of my life where I don't need notes."

"It's just that . . . I've only done this a couple of times with some random guys on Grindr. So, can we . . . go slowly, please?"

I try not to swoon at his sudden vulnerability and quickly reassure him. "Oh, yeah. I can do that. Absolutely. Anything else?"

Luke hesitates again. "Um . . . some eye contact would be nice."

I take his head in my hands and stare as deeply as possible into those gorgeous green, brown, hazel eyes and whisper lowly, "Oh, fuck yeah."

# sixteen

# "Never Stop Crushing Me"

wake up the next morning feeling like I've been asleep for a hundred years. There's a slight sting of razor burn on my face and I take it as proof that last night actually happened and that I didn't dream the whole thing up. A ceiling fan makes lazy circles above me and I feel almost hypnotized as my eyes try to focus on the slowly spinning blades.

I roll over expecting to see a sleepy Luke next to me, but I'm alone in his bed.

Bosco snores from his mat on the floor and it appears that it might just be the dog and me in the house. Then it dawns on me that Luke is probably making me breakfast in bed.

Isn't that what hot guys do in movies and TV commercials?

I close my eyes for a moment and allow the events of last night to wash over me. The way our bodies quickly agreed on a rhythm. The unexpected tenderness of it all. And how, at the last second, I had to remind myself to breathe. And looking down to see Luke staring up into my eyes and the realization that we're both trembling and gazing in awe at one another like we can't believe any of this is real. And me finally collapsing on top of him as he accepts my full weight with a muffled laugh. And then the two of us lying there, almost vibrating in time with one another.

Me saying, "I'm crushing you."

And Luke saying with a sigh, "Please never stop crushing me."

And then me falling into the deepest sleep of my life.

I get up and take a good look in the mirror. My chronic bed-head is back and makes me look like a gay cockatoo, which is redundant, I know. I duck into the bathroom to throw some water on it to tame it slightly, then head into the kitchen.

No Luke.

No Luke anywhere.

I grab my cell and quickly call him.

He answers with an almost annoyed, "Hey."

"If you've fled out of fear, I can promise you that scientifically speaking there is absolutely no chance I could have gotten you pregnant last night."

He doesn't laugh. Not a good sign. "I'm kinda busy right now."

My stomach does an elevator drop into the floor. Is he mad at me? "Did I do something wrong? Because you seemed pretty happy last night. I thought we both were."

"I'm working. Some of us have to work. Even on Sundays. There's coffee in the kitchen if you want it." And then he hangs up.

What the actual fuck is going on? What's with this Jekyll and Hyde bullshit? Is he just like Chase? Do they both have evil twins that appear once they've had their fun and they're ready to move on?

No. Uh-uh. This isn't going down like this.

I go to the bedroom and angrily start pulling my clothes on. He's fucking with the wrong motherfucker.

By the time I get to the barn, Luke and Eddie are using a hay thingy to do things with hay. Luke looks almost annoyed to see me and Eddie has the surprising good sense to wander away altogether.

When I get within a few feet of Luke, he has his clenched fists on his hips and he seems to be studying a rusty weather vane as it turns sluggishly on the barn's roof. It emits a sorrowful squeal in the slow-moving August breeze. The metallic groan perfectly matches the put-upon expression on Luke's face.

Steady, Noah. Speak slowly. "So . . . am I missing something?"

No eye contact. Last night was all about eye contract. But somehow a page has been turned and nobody told me.

"What do you mean, Noah?"

"I don't know, it's like I was watching this really romantic movie, I got up to go to the lobby for some Sno-Caps and when I came back somebody switched reels and it was a horror movie. Why are you being so . . . I don't know . . . abrupt?"

"I'm not being abrupt," Luke snaps.

And then he just stands there until I say, "See that? What you just did? That was abrupt. You're being abrupt about not being abrupt."

"I really am busy, Noah." Luke turns and walks into the barn, but I'm right behind him.

"Can we at least talk? Are you angry with me? Because you certainly weren't angry with me last night."

"I get it, Noah. You know how to use your dick. Congrat-ulations."

I'm winded for a moment, but then plow forward. Without thinking, I grab his arm and turn him around and force him to look me in the eye. "It's not about the sex stuff, though. I thought, I thought we had a real connection. Forget all the fireworks. I thought what happened last night was very, I don't know . . . sweet? Tender? Remarkable?"

"Yeah, and then what? You'll leave. In a couple of weeks. I fi-nally get what I've wanted for I don't even know how many years and you're going to leave. You're not going to stay here for me. And I guess I thought I could handle that. You know, be casual and go with the flow. Take things as they come. Roll with the punches. But not after last night. Last night, everything got real. And now you're just going to go back to New York and you and all of your fancy friends are gonna laugh about how you fucked the dumb, small-town ex-jock."

My face twitches with confusion. "I would never call you dumb, Luke."

"Oh, come on, I know what you think of me."

"You are the furthest thing from dumb. First off, you saw through my mom's little eggplant emoji ruse. You re-created an entire Broadway set from scratch—"

Luke rolls his eyes. "I had pictures, big deal. I was just helping your dad."

"You basically single-handedly run this farm."

"None of that matters. The point is you have all the power. When the show is over, you're going back to New York and I'm gonna be left here just hurting and lonely. And I don't think I can take that. So maybe it's just better to stop this and call it what it was. A one-time hookup. No strings. No emotions. We're both adults, the end."

Luke turns away and starts picking up buckets and loudly stacking them as if to signal that the conversation is over. I refuse to let that happen and continue to speak over the annoying metal clanging.

"Well, if you're calling me an adult, then you clearly don't know me very well. I'm just a frightened little boy walking around in a man's body. I'm a complete neurotic mess. And after Chase, I don't think I will ever trust my own judgment again. And as for you, I had you all wrong when we were younger. I guess I just made a bunch of stupid assumptions about you and now I'm learning how wrong I've been all this time. Do you know how rare something like what we found is? So please don't tell me it has to just stop, because—"

Luke drops an armful of buckets in exasperation and turns to me as they clatter to the ground and says, "I'm fucking scared, okay?!"

We're both a little shocked at how forceful Luke's voice sounds. His eyes soften and he says much more tenderly, "I'm scared, Noah. Don't hurt me."

Luke's story about his dad leaving him flashes through my mind, and it feels like gravity just tripled around us. Luke's been rewired to think that he's easy to leave. If only he could be standing where I am, he'd understand that nothing could be further from the truth.

I walk toward him and gently push him up against the wall of the barn and lean my full weight into him. I can feel the warmth of his breath on my face. And the smell of his skin, that orchard smell again.

"There are airplanes, you know," I say. "There are such things as long-distance relationships. If we decide we want that."

"You're crushing me."

"You told me never to stop."

I kiss him as gently as I can. I run my fingers through his hair for a second.

"Noah . . . I'm sorry. I freaked out."

"I get it. I'm the king of freak-outs."

He smiles and it goes right to the pit of my stomach.

"It's funny," I say, "I've spent most of my childhood trying to avoid this dirty, creepy building."

Luke chuckles. "It's called a barn."

"A barn? And all this time I've been calling it a cow garage."

I lean into him even harder. We stay suspended like this for a few seconds until Luke whispers, "Follow me."

He wraps his massive hand around mine and pulls me toward a ladder that leads to the hayloft. There is an uptick of mooing from the cows and it feels like they're watching us and judging.

Luke starts to climb up the ladder first and I notice his ass and then I stop and notice his ass again.

"It's not going to be dusty up there, is it? Because this is a very expensive shirt."

Luke stops climbing and turns around on the ladder, feigning exasperation. "Well, if you're worried about your fancy clothes, I can just go back to work."

I borrow his move from last night and whip my shirt off, throwing it on the ground so quickly that I rip the seams slightly. "I'm an idiot. Keep climbing."

There are a few bales of hay stuck together in the middle of the loft covered by a wool blanket. Luke leads me over to it and I get suspicious.

"Is this where you bring guys when you want to hook up with them, but don't want them to know your home address?"

"It's where I pass out when I'm on a break. But that's a good suggestion."

"Wait a second, I don't want you thinking about other guys when you're with me."

Luke wraps his arms around my waist and pulls me to him. "There's no one else. It's just you, Noah. You stupid, talkative, handsome motherfucker."

"Next time, I'd like you to thin out some of those adjectives."

"Do you ever shut up?"

We fall backward onto the makeshift bed and do things to each other that the barn definitely wasn't designed for. Afterward, Luke lightly grazes his fingers over my chest. Downstairs, the cows croon out a chorus of moos.

"Jeez, Noah, where did you get this body?"

"Amazon. It was delivered last week. I opted for Prime so they sent it the next day."

And then I feel a rush of bitterness. If I do have a tidy collection of muscles, they were all for Chase. The daily rituals at the gym were all for him. The Spartan high-protein, low-carb diet. I guess I was trying to play catch up. Chase was a Greek god on loan from Olympus and I was a mere mortal.

I stop myself from going any further down that path when I realize that I'm actually lying next to Luke Carter.

Luke, who came by his physique honestly, through sports or manual labor. Not from some gym, fueled by vanity like Chase. Or, if I'm honest, like me, too.

Is it possible that Luke could erase all the damage that Chase left in his wake? I'm trying not to fetishize him. But he's just so unbelievably perfect. My newest obsession is his nose. For lack of a better word, it's strong. Noble. Trustworthy. I run my index finger over it as softly as possible and Luke smiles. And how did I not notice earlier that when he smiles he has honest-to-God dimples?

How is all of this beauty possible in one person? It should be illegal. Or he should be the arrogant douchebag that I always assumed he was. And that's the miracle of Luke. He's a musclebound, aw shucks, tender marvel. And he somehow, against all odds, has a thing for me.

"I can't believe this is really happening," I say. "How'd I end up in a hayloft with the quarterback of my high school football team?"

"Well, technically, I wasn't a quarterback, I was a wide receiver."

"I never understood football. It's too complicated."

"I could explain it to you."

"Please don't."

"So you were never into any sports?"

"I threw a Frisbee once. Does that count?"

"I better get back to work before Eddie or your dad notices I've been gone too long."

We get dressed and climb down from the loft. I grab my shirt and kiss him quickly before starting to head toward the house. I pause to consider a row of cows staring somewhat knowingly at me as I go, their cattle tags dangling like earrings. I'm pretty sure they're going to gossip about Luke and me as soon as I'm out of sight.

The moment I walk into the kitchen, Mom gives me a curious look. "Noah, honey?"

"Yes?"

"Are you currently doing what the kids call the walk of shame?"

I'm appalled. "What?"

"Somebody didn't come home last night."

"I fell asleep on Luke's couch."

"You're sure that's what you fell asleep on?"

Hold on. Was Mom trying her hand at sexual innuendos? Barf. "Nothing happened with Luke."

"Then why are you covered in hay, dear?"

I look down and realize she's right. "You know, you don't have to say every thought that enters your head, Mom."

"Where's the fun in that?"

I step onto the back porch to brush my clothes off. When I reenter the kitchen, Dad hits me with, "I don't care what you boys do in your spare time. But when Luke is on the clock here, he's working for me. And he's meant to be focused on the farm."

"Sorry, Dad. Got it."

Mom turns to me, practically giddy and all schoolgirl-y. "So was it nice? Your date with Luke? Did you kiss?"

I ignore her.

"Okay, I won't pry. Are you joining us for Sunday dinner tonight?"

"That depends. Are you planning on making something edible?"

Mom huffs. "I am roasting a chicken. Plain old chicken, so I don't want to hear any grumbling."

"Fine. I'll choke it down."

"And then for dessert I was thinking of making your aunt Sandy's Snickers salad."

"Aunt Sandy's what now?"

"Oh, you just chop up a couple of Snickers candy bars and some Granny Smith apples and then you scramble it up with a bunch of vanilla pudding. It's a celebration of textures!"

She just can't stop while she's ahead.

I'm halfway out the door when I hear her say to Dad, "Maybe I'll invite Luke!" Ay dios mío. For a Presbyterian, she is such a fucking yenta.

When Luke shows up that night, it's somehow strange to be near him with my parents around. While Mom desecrates some poor chicken's carcass, Dad and Luke are going back and forth about cars for the millionth time.

"If you look at the doorknob, you can tell the two models apart," Dad lectures. "The 1964 knob will be painted to match the interior. Whereas the 1965 knob will be chrome."

I try to join in. "So, Dad some cars go faster than others, right? I guess that's because of their engine size? Or is it the wheels?"

Dad just stares at me in confusion, then turns to Luke and asks, "What's he doing?"

"Trying," Luke answers.

Dad considers this. "Son, you don't have to pretend to be interested in things you're not interested in just for me."

"No, let's talk about cars and sports stuff. So, the Dallas Cowboys, they're a women's lacrosse team, right? And what exactly are the Pittsburgh Steelers stealing? Is it hearts and minds?"

The doorbell rings.

Mom wipes her hands on a towel. "I'm happy to answer the door, if only to get out of this conversation."

Dad continues and Luke sits there rapt with attention. "Now, the 1966 has a different grill . . ."

Mom comes back and stares at me like she's seen a ghost. Which shouldn't be a big deal because she claims to see ghosts all the time. But this must have been a scary one.

"What's wrong, Mom?"

In walks Chase. He's wearing one of his work suits and carrying an enormous bouquet of very expensive looking flowers. It's been almost two weeks since he ripped my heart out of my chest

242 CHAD BEGUELIN

cavity and here he is standing in my parents' kitchen and has the gall to look nonchalant.

The room falls into a stunned silence.

Chase puts on his usual prefabricated charm. "Um, hi, Noah. Everyone. Surprise, I guess."

There's more silence and then Mom lifts her eyes and stares at Chase like she can barely control her anger. She speaks in a low, trembling voice that I have never heard her use before.

"I cannot be in the same room with someone who has treated my son badly. So I'm going to just go paint a little, because I don't trust what I might say. But I will say this. You're a bad person and I'm just gonna hope that between karma and Jesus you will be dealt with."

And with that, she goes into the first-floor bedroom and closes the door. Chase gives a little exhale, then turns to me. "Is there somewhere we can talk? Privately?" He seems to be actively ignoring Luke's presence at the kitchen table.

"We don't have anything to talk about."

"Noah, please."

"I'm not moving from this spot," I say very slowly.

Chase throws his head up in frustration and stares at the ceiling. "So you're going to force me to do this right here? Fine. I guess I deserve that. All right, then. Here we go. I made a horrible, stupendously stupid mistake. I don't know what I was thinking. Maybe we can chalk it up to an early midlife crisis or something. It's completely over with Aleister. I started getting texts from Kiara about the lease. And she wanted me to box up your things and so I started. Your six thousand belts. Your alarmingly colored socks. Your Thom Browne sports jacket from opening night that still smells like you. And it was gutting. Absolutely gutting. I was actually crying and you know me, I don't cry. But there I was, standing in our closet, smelling your jacket and wanting you back. And panicked that I'd never get you back because of what I'd done. Because of the terrible, awful way that I hurt you and cocked everything up . . ." He trails off, clearly losing steam.

I can barely stand to look at him, but I force myself to. "So this is your power move? Showing up to Sunday dinner with flowers? With a fucking bouquet? Like that's magically going to fix everything?"

"Noah, can we please go somewhere and talk this out? I'm trying to apologize here. I'm trying to beg you to forgive me. The minute I started gathering all of your things, I was horrified at what I had done to you."

"Oh, so it wasn't until you were putting my socks into a cardboard box that you realized it? That's a little late for an epiphany, Chase."

"What can I do? Please, Noah. Just tell me."

"Well, you could build a time machine and go back to the exact moment when you were about to let Aleister Murphy put his dick inside you and then *not* let Aleister Murphy put his dick inside you."

Luke puts his hand on my knee very firmly. I'm embarrassed that he has to witness this, but I'm also glad he's there and it's not just Dad and me. I have no idea what's going on in Dad's head, but I'm sure it's not good.

"Everybody makes mistakes."

"I don't! I mean, I make plenty of mistakes. I get on the wrong subway. I call people by the wrong name. I never use the word 'nonplussed' correctly. But I don't cheat on the person I'm supposed to love and be faithful to. I don't promise someone forever and then throw it all away on a fucking whim."

Chase averts his eyes. I continue on.

"I can be self-centered and petulant and melodramatic. But I'm also faithful, Chase. Faithful to my friends, faithful to my family, and faithful to the person I'm in a relationship with. And you couldn't do the same for me. So there's no going back."

Chase's shoulders slump and it occurs to me that this might be the first time in his entire life that he didn't get what he wanted.

Out of the blue, Dad stands up at the table and grips the edges of it for balance.

He leans forward slightly and addresses Chase.

"Now you listen to me." Dad struggles to control his anger. "You listen to me right now. Because I'm going to tell you who my son is. My son is a man who makes things. He builds things out of words. Now, I may not understand what he does all the time, but I do know this: A hundred years after all of us are dead, people will still be saying his words and singing his songs. And that makes him immortal in a way that none of the rest of us are.

Now let me tell you who you are: You're just some sleazy nickel-and-dime guy trying to make a couple of bucks off my son's talent. You aren't fit to carry his boots. You're a grifter at best. And I don't like grifters under my roof. So I'm only going to say this once. Get out of my house. And do it now. Unless Noah has anything to add."

I pause, and then discover I do have something to add. "Just this. You're fired."

Chase furiously tosses the flowers on the floor and leaves.

I turn to Dad in complete disbelief. He stares back at me as if he hasn't said a word and I've just imagined the whole thing.

"What?" Dad finally asks.

"Jesus, Dad, that was dramatic even by my standards. I mean, seriously. Who are you?"

And as God is my witness, I see Dad's eyes go watery for the first time in my entire lifetime. He looks away and says, "I'm your father, that's who." And then Dad and his trusty oxygen tank exit the kitchen stage left.

Luke puts an arm around me and I let my head fall to his shoulder.

"Are you okay?"

"Yes. I'm sorry you had to see that. Did he really think that showing up here like some overdressed flower delivery guy was going to work? That I was just going to forgive him for everything? And of course it didn't work out with Aleister. I don't know the guy that well, but he's got more sleazy ambition than Lady Macbeth."

Luke hesitates. "Wait, was that the lady who killed her own kids?"

"You're thinking of Medea. Medea killed her children. But in her defense, she did it because she'd just been jilted. And as someone who has recently been jilted, I can see where she was coming from. And also, I mean, who wants to be a single mother these days anyway?"

"You're going a little dark, don't you think?"

"I can't help it. I'm sorry, but I actually hope that Aleister broke Chase's heart. If anyone deserves his heart broken, it's Chase. I hope Aleister left him for someone more handsome and more British."

"It'd be hard to be more British than that guy."

I consider this for a moment. "No, they're out there. I hope Aleister left Chase for someone with a title. A duke or a viscount, maybe. Someone who wears a top hat and possibly a monocle. That would kill Chase. He would literally spontaneously combust on the spot."

"Jeez, remind me never to cross you."

I feel my anger start to dissipate and it's replaced with a slow, creeping sadness.

"I'm also kind of offended that he thought he could get me back that easily. That I would be that stupid and just come running back into his arms, full of gratitude. We were together two whole years and it's like he hasn't even met me before. It's just depressing, you know?"

"Is there anything I can do?"

I think about it. I think about it for a long time. "Yeah, there is." I hesitate. "I know this is random, but I'd like to meet your mom sometime."

Luke nods, unsure for a moment. Then he just says, "I'll make it happen."

# seventeen

# "Heart"

The buzzing of my cell wakes me up the next morning and I blink at it in complete confusion. It's Anna Wong. Talk about random. Assuming she's dialed me by mistake, I give a sleepy moan and answer.

"Hi, Anna Wong. Why are you calling me? I fired Chase."

"Right. That's why I'm calling you."

She already knows? Of course she does. She arranges all of his travel. I hope he felt embarrassed when he asked her to book his return trip so quickly. Maybe he even went so far as to book an extra ticket for me that she then had to cancel. Chase has that kind of obnoxious, deeply assured opinion of himself.

"I'd like to pitch you something."

"Um, now isn't a very . . ." I sigh. "Oh, go ahead. What do you wanna pitch me?"

"I want to pitch you Anna Wong."

"Anna Wong wants to pitch me Anna Wong?"

"Correct. I can't take being Chase's assistant anymore. I've been slowly making connections in the industry and I'm ready to strike out on my own. And I'm asking you to be my first client."

I have no idea what to say. I mean, I technically have no agent at the moment, which fits perfectly with the fact that I technically have no career, either.

"This is a little out of nowhere."

"I know, I know, but somebody took a chance on you once, right?"

"Yes, his name is Chase Abrams and I burn him in effigy every night right after my evening prayers."

"Are you currently seeking representation elsewhere?"

I pause. Anna Wong is good. "No."

"So you really have nothing to lose, do you?"

"Oh, Anna Wong, Anna Wong, Anna Wong . . . Why do you think you'd be able to revive my rotting corpse of a career?"

"I've put together a whole PowerPoint presentation. I called it 'The Lazarus Docket.'"

Okay, I hate her for that and I love her for that at exactly the same time.

"My plan is to go out far and wide to producers and artistic directors everywhere with a very curated demo of songs which you put together. Just your absolute favorite top three songs. The ones you're proudest of. Some variety in tone would be nice, but I'll leave that up to you. In the meantime, I'm pitching you as a book doctor to every show that's in trouble. Anonymous for you, which is good. But also possibly extremely financially advantageous for us both. In the meantime, you start spitballing a new musical. Something very small and producible. Tiny cast. Unit set. Maybe even a small orchestra. Kind of like *The Fantasticks*, where they just need piano, bass, and drums. And then maybe you throw in something wacky like a theremin, just to keep it interesting. Once that's ready, I shop it to the Public, Playwrights Horizons, Second Stage. It's so scrappy and producible, how can they resist? This is all just the tip of the iceberg, Noah, and I'm running out of breath."

Wow. She's clearly insane and probably also exactly what I need right now. "You know, you have clearly given this a lot of elaborate thought and I'm intrigued. But before I make up my mind, I need to ask you one thing."

"Okay."

"Did you know about Chase and Aleister? I don't care if you did or if you didn't. I only care that you answer me honestly. That I feel I can trust you. And I'm sorry for putting you on the spot, but did you know?"

A long pause, a slow exhale and then she says, "I knew. He was my boss and it wasn't my place to get involved. But yes. I knew. And I found it disgusting."

I pause. "Well, look at that. We're already agreeing on something. You're hired."

"Shut up! I am not! I am? Really! I can still send you that PowerPoint presentation."

"We both know I'll never look at it anyway. You are now in full control of my career. All hail the Lazarus Docket. Go forth and be bold."

And then she screams in my ear for about a month and hangs up.

Hours later I gallop down the stairs and find Luke waiting for me outside in his truck. He's agreed to let me meet his mom. We ride in silence until he pulls up in front of her trailer. I'm hoping Luke isn't regretting his decision.

"So, before you meet her, you should know that Mom uses words like 'ain't' a lot. And her teeth are kind of . . . not great. But if you come even slightly close to making fun of her or embarrassing her . . . I'll . . . I'll . . ."

"Kick my ass?"

"I'll never forgive you."

And that is something I would never recover from. "The reason I wanted to meet your mother is because she raised you. And you're amazing. So I just wanted to see where all that amazingness came from."

Luke gives my thigh a squeeze and says with grave seriousness, as if we're about to storm Normandy, "Let's do this."

By the time we get out of the truck, Sue is already standing in the yard holding a tray heavy with a pitcher of iced tea and three glasses. She's surprisingly petite, but makes up for it with a no-nonsense aura that seems to radiate for miles.

"Well, there's my big boy!"

Luke looks embarrassed, but hugs his mom and grabs the tray.

"And you must be Noah," Sue says. "I hope you don't mind, but I'm gonna need to hug your neck."

"Well, what are you waiting for?" I say. And just like that, we're hugging and in an instant I somehow understand where Luke gets all of his humanity.

We pull apart and I realize that she's set up a whole little tea-time spread on her outdoor furniture.

"Oh, look. Tea for two . . . or, um three," I say like a dummy. And then, because I suffer from chronic verbal diarrhea, I keep yammering on. "You know that song 'Tea for Two'? Those weren't supposed to be the actual lyrics. They were just supposed to be placeholders. The lyricist just jotted them down quickly because he and the composer were late for a party and they wanted to pick up some girls. But the composer fell in love with the lyrics and insisted they stay. Even though they don't really make any sense. I mean, 'Picture you upon my knee, just tea for two and two for tea?' How are they supposed to have tea if they're sitting on each other's knees?"

Sue just stares at me, dumbfounded.

"He babbles when he's nervous," Luke explains.

"Why would he be nervous of me?" Sue asks.

"Oh, I'm not nervous." I laugh and then pick up a Fig Newton and say, "You know, they're called Fig Newtons because they were originally baked in a factory in Newton, Massachusetts." They stare at me some more. "Just a fun fact."

Casually, we all take our places around the table and Luke, gentleman that he is, starts to serve Sue and me.

Sue launches in. "So I don't know if he told you, but Luke let me read your script. He was so excited about it that I just had to take a look at it. But me, well, I have a couple of questions."

I heave a little sigh. "Everyone does."

Luke jumps in. "Mom, I don't think Noah wants to hear a bunch of—"

I stop him. "No, no. Ask away. I haven't gone wrong listening to notes yet."

SHOWMANCE                           253

Sue considers for a moment. "Well, you know, at first I didn't think I'd be able to follow it. But then, I really got into it. And I can't wait to hear the music to them songs."

"But?" I patiently prompt.

"Well, there's just something that really stuck in my craw."

"Mom, jeez!" Luke is embarrassed and I won't allow it.

"No, Luke. I'd really like to help your mother unstick her craw. Go on, Mrs. Carter."

She scans the horizon pensively. "Well, I get that most families are screwed up. Just like the Lears in your play."

Luke corrects her. "Musical, Mom."

"Musical. And God knows I understand that people make bad decisions in life. I mean, bad decisions are what landed me in this palace of dreams." Sue wearily waves a hand at her surroundings.

"Wait. Luke, you didn't tell me your mother did comedy."

Sue gives me a sardonic smile. "Oh, I'm a laugh riot."

Luke gets impatient. "Mom, I've asked you to move out of here a million times and all you say is that you're comfortable where you are. You know that I'm totally willing to help you find someplace else."

Sue gives Luke a shake of the head. "I ain't going anywhere. The point is, Noah, there ain't much heart in your musical."

I swallow. Hard. "Heart?"

"You know, who are we rooting for? They're all terrible people except for that one daughter."

I'm listening with laser focus. "You mean, Cordelia?"

"Yeah, that's the one. We don't care about all of those other bastards. So could you focus on her a little more? I mean, the rest of the characters have shit for brains. But Cordelia and her love for her dad and the fact that her dad don't recognize that? Well, that there's the heart of your story."

I sit in a haze for a second. Like I've just made my way down a very inspiring mountain and don't know what to do with myself.

Then Sue cackles. "Of course, I don't know anything."

I look her dead in the eyes and say, "Sue. You have no idea how much you've just helped me."

Sue sits there and I think she knows she's blown my mind and is a little bit proud of herself. Luke announces that he has to go to the bathroom by saying that he's "got to go see a man about a horse," which is a very confusing phrase to use seeing as he works on a farm. I mean, he could actually be seeing an actual man about an actual horse.

After more iced tea sipping, Sue finally says, "My Luke's pretty smitten with you."

I gurgle, I guess to limber up my vocal cords. "Well, you've done an amazing job raising him. Every time I turn around, I learn something even more ridiculously wonderful about him. What'll I find out next? That he saved five babies from an orphanage fire?"

"Oh, don't go crazy. It was only three babies."

"Careful, Sue. I don't like people who are wittier than me. I feel threatened."

Luke comes back and the three of us watch two squirrels race quickly through the yard as if they're hurrying to catch a connecting flight.

I finally ask Sue, "So you're coming to the show, right?"

Sue gives an exhausted shake of the head. "Nah. Nobody wants to see this old bag of bones parading around town. Besides, in a place like this, you make a few mistakes and you're branded with a bad reputation. Whether it's warranted or it ain't. So people are assholes. What else is new?"

"Oh, no. I think you should consider coming. Luke has worked so hard on the set. Well, he's worked so hard on two sets. And you are hardly a bag of bones. You look great!"

She gives a rousing laugh and points an index finger at me. "I like him. He's a good liar!"

I love this woman. "Well, as the kids say, 'you do you,' but it would be amazing to see you there."

Sue waves her hands in the air, clearly more comfortable being noncommittal. Finally, Luke stands up and announces, "We better get going."

Sue gets up and pulls me into a hug. While I'm there she whispers into my ear. "Think about the heart thing."

I pull away so I can look her in the eye. "Thank you for the insight."

Luke and I head back to the truck and before I know it, Luke grabs me and pulls me into the warmest hug of my life. "What's this for?"

"People aren't always so nice to my mom." And then I notice he's tearing up. And even more upsetting, he's embarrassed that I realize that he's tearing up.

I take him by the shoulders and look him fearlessly in the eye. "Well, people are going to start being nice to her."

Luke looks away, shaking his head. "How?"

"I'm sorry, have you not met my mother?"

When I get home, I find Mom curled up on the couch under an afghan. I sit down next to her and grab the remote to turn off whatever cooking show she's watching.

"Noah, they were just about to show the recipe for Hot Cheetos mozzarella balls!"

"We need to talk. It's about Luke's mom."

Mom goes right into gossip mode. "Well, you know what her story is, of course. Everybody does. She used to go down to that dive bar over on Calumet Street every single night and well, believe you me—"

I immediately cut her off. "Okay, Mom, just stop it, would you?"

We're both a little stunned that I've interrupted her, but I push forward. "You don't know her life. I don't know her life. This town doesn't know her life. The only thing we know for sure is that she single-handedly raised the best person in this entire galaxy. Someone who would run and fetch the moon for you, Dad, me, any of us. And I don't know what kind of narrative has been spun about Sue Carter, but I need you to be the one to unspin it."

Mom puts a startled hand to her mouth.

I can see her wheels turning, click-click-clicking along, slowly manifesting little tinges of guilt on her face.

I wait patiently as her brain comes to an inevitable realization.

She starts out very slowly. "Son, you have just righted your mother's ship."

I'm not sure what she means, but I can see where I get my love of nautical metaphors.

"Okay, Mom, let's go with that. Let's just say I have righted your ship. What does that actually mean?"

"It means that tomorrow morning I start working the phones."

"Working the phones?"

"Oh, would you like a little sample? I might get on the phone and say things like, 'No one is supposed to know this, but I found out that Sue Carter won a chunk of change from the lottery. She decided that there were people worse off than her and gave it all to charity. All of it. Please tell no one I've shared this very personal information with you.'"

"So it's a gossip Jedi mind trick?"

Mom nods. "If that's what you want to call it. And maybe I say to someone else that she volunteers at a soup kitchen every Saturday, while the rest of us are all out eating fancy brunches. And also, she's related to the Kennedy family, but she's too classy to bring it up! Oh, Noah, I'm just getting started. I see redemption for all of us! You know, for a town with so many churches, we've got a lot of people who aren't very Christian. Oh, let me get my planner and start writing these ideas down."

"Don't go overboard, Mom. She doesn't need to be shunned by the people of Plainview if they catch you in a ton of lies."

"I'll be slick about it. I was blind, but now I see." She pauses. "And you know what? From now on, I'm only going to call someone a great gal if they're actually a great gal."

I'm leery, but nod anyway.

———

Back at the theater, Abby has decided to start each rehearsal with a quick warm-up session, which is basically a glorified Zumba routine. While the cast devotedly stretches under her tutelage, I wander slowly backstage in hopes of finding Luke. He's on a ladder, putting a gel into one of the lights.

"You do lighting now?"

Luke shrugs. "I'm a jack of many trades."

I turn into an anxious third grader. "Did your mom like me? Did I pass the test?"

Luke hops down from the ladder and beams. "You passed with flying colors. She loves you." He pauses and then says slowly, "So, I was wondering if you'd like to come over tonight after—"

"Yes," I cut him off. "You don't ever have to wonder if I want to come over. Let's just always assume that it's a 'yes' on my part. Let's just assume I'm legally grandfathered in."

"Ha. Okay. But also . . ." And now Luke seems to be searching for words.

"Also?" I prompt.

"Also, I was wondering if, like that song from *Anything Goes*, I could be the top, if I could be the, you know, coliseum."

I take a step back and start making animated computer noises. "Bloop! Bleep! Blonk!"

Luke stares at me and is probably convinced that I'm having a psychotic break. "I'm sorry, my brain just needs a second to process this information."

Luke looks completely embarrassed and I rush to reassure him.

"No, sorry, I would very much like to formally and graciously invite you to be the, um, coliseum. It's just, you know, not my usual go-to move, is all. But, sure!"

Luke gives me a devious grin and says lowly, "Yeah, baby."

"I'm a grown man. You can't start calling me baby."

"Why? Because you might like it too much?"

I simply reply, "Stop being right about things," and stomp off.

In order to distract myself, I pull out my badly wrinkled rehearsal schedule and count. Only nine rehearsals left. It's funny how the growing Xs on the calendar used to seem like a positive thing. Now the Xs just represent what precious little time I have left here with Luke. It's with a surprising amount of sadness that I put a big, fat X over today's date.

Rehearsal winds down and I find myself getting slightly nervous about what's about to happen with Luke. Instead of driving myself to rehearsals, it's now become a habit to ride with Luke in his truck. The moon hangs low in the summer sky as I slide into the front seat and Luke starts the engine. I'm quiet as we drive. Luke keeps his eyes on the road, but reaches out to put his hand on my thigh. I quake a little as stars whiz by my window.

Why am I being so strange? This ain't my first time at the rodeo.

When we get to Luke's place, Bosco is barking up a storm and though he's happy to see us, he's happier to run out into the yard and into the night. I throw The Executive onto the sofa and plop down beside it.

"You hungry?" Luke asks.

"I think I would like a beverage of a very alcoholic nature."

Luke walks from the kitchen to the living room to confront me. "Are you okay?"

"No, I'm great. I'm super. I would just like a large amount of alcohol, that's all."

Luke sits down on the sofa next to me. "I don't have to be the coliseum, Noah."

"No, no, no. It's not fair that I always get to be the coliseum and you always have to be . . ." I search my brain for the lyrics of the song. "A toy balloon that's fated soon to pop?"

He laughs and then leans into me, rubbing his scruffy chin against my neck, which is unfair, since he knows it's my kryptonite. "We don't have to if you don't want to."

I sink back into the couch. Somewhere in the backyard, a church owl is screeching on about something. I finally whisper into his Luke's ear using my best director's voice, "Can I please have the talent move stage left toward the bedroom?"

As I take his hand and lead him down the hallway, I reiterate his notes to me from our first very official date. "And can we just . . . go slowly, please? And . . . some eye contact would be nice."

Luke stops and wraps his arms around me from behind, whispering hotly in my ear, "Oh, fuck, yeah."


When it's over I find myself falling into my usual position, crushing him with all of my might. I slowly roll over and let him nuzzle into my very sweaty side. We're both struck mute for what seems like forever.

Finally, I give an old-fashioned Midwestern, "Welp."

Luke laughs. "I'll say. Double welp."

We then assume what has become our default snuggling arrangement. Though he's obviously larger than me, I always play the role of the big spoon. I wrap myself around him like I'm a possessive koala. What is this intrinsic need I have to protect him? He's just too good for this world. Too kind. If anyone tries to hurt him, they're going to have to go through me. And Dad made me take karate in seventh grade. So be warned, marauders. I'm nothing if not scrappy. And willing to fight dirty.

We're quiet for a while and then out of nowhere, Luke says, "I was thinking. Maybe you and I have been hurtling toward one another our entire lives and we just didn't know it."

All I can say is, "You don't get to be poetic *and* have a six pack, Luke. It's like if the world found out Tom Brady did ballet in his spare time. It's showing off."

"I'm just impressed you know who Tom Brady is."

Luke quietly runs his fingers over my collarbone. It's strangely hypnotic. "Not to ruin the moment, but are you . . . are you still bothered about the Chase thing? Like, are you still hurting because of that guy?"

"Oh, Chase? Am I still bothered about that lying, dissembling, cheating garbage person I used to date? Sometimes, I guess. But mostly I just think about how great it would have been if we got together sooner. Then I never would have had to date that prick in the first place. You're so superior to Chase in every single way. It's almost laughable. I mean, I guess Chase was good for some things. Like sparkling conversation. He always had a witty, snarky comment waiting in the wings. But he could be a real dick. And cold. And he hated kissing. That should have been a red flag. Light kissing was fine, but no tongue action. He didn't like tongues. Or maybe he just didn't like *my* tongue."

All of the sudden Luke is on top of me, plunging his amazing tongue down my throat so hard and it's almost too perfect for my mere mortal mind to process. When he finally stops, I stare at him in disbelief. "What was that?"

"That," he says with complete sincerity, "is how you deserve to be kissed."

This. Fucking. Guy.

# eighteen

# "The Bravest Person I Know"

A couple of days later I decide to go for a morning run in hopes of keeping in shape. The only gym in town is inside a nursing home and called Grammy Tammy's Gym and Tanning Salon. That's a hard pass for me.

I'm just starting to break into a sweat when my phone buzzes. It's Anna Wong. I pause long enough for my breath to slow and then answer.

"I have news to report. I think I might have landed a big fish. It's a stinky fish, but it's big. Do you remember the *Barbarella* musical based on the 1968 Jane Fonda movie?"

"I know that most people would rather sit through a root canal without anesthesia than sit through that show. And that it has failed to make it to Broadway three times in a row. And that its author Valerie Wernsman is a raving lunatic."

"Well, they're giving it the old college try one more time. And they need a book doctor. Which I know sounds like a grunt job, but they want you. They want you to go out of town with the show and see if you can fix the structure and polish the dialogue. The tricky part is that it's an all-female creative team. So they're not going to be thrilled to have a man come in and 'save' them."

"Well, that sounds slightly fraught."

"But here's the upside. It's a six-figure flat fee. Upon signature and non-recoupable against royalties."

I take a second to catch my breath. "Six figures? That's unheard of! Are the producers insane?"

"Well, they're putting money into a *Barbarella* musical, so you tell me."

Would I even consider wasting my time on this dreck? And Valerie Wernsman is known to be a raging madwoman whose hobbies include baking children into pies. Anna Wong can clearly hear my wheels turning through the phone.

"I know it sounds like one long, extended headache, but the good news is that your name won't be on the project, so if it crashes yet again, you just take the money and run."

"What's the time commitment?"

Anna Wong goes silent.

"What's the time commitment, Anna Wong?"

"A year."

"What?!?"

"Because the project's history is dicey to say the least, the producers want to do two out of towns. It goes to Seattle for four months, opens there, and then you get a month off and after that they do a long slog in Minneapolis, where they're basically assuming things will have to be rethought like crazy and then, fingers crossed, rehearse and open in New York."

My heart quickly sinks into my shoes. Luke was right. I was going to leave him. But would I really leave him for a pile of money and a project that's about as fun as putting my head through the spinning blades of a turbo jet engine? Still, in the cold, harsh light of day, how can I say no? I'm financially running on fumes.

Anna Wong continues her hard sell. "Look, Noah, it's a shitty job. You're going to be treated like the enemy by the entire creative team. And it's not going to do a thing for your reputation. But it's a stopgap. A very well-paying stopgap. And while you're there helping them rearrange the deck chairs on the *Titanic*, you can be quietly working on something new. That small, producible musical we talked about."

I put a sweaty hand to my forehead and consider. "How soon would they need me?"

"Yesterday. I told them you were committed right now. I didn't go into the details, obviously. But as soon as this community theater production of *Stage of Fools* opens, you'd have to be on a plane to Seattle, ready to be accused of mansplaining."

"Ugh, I don't even know what one wears when mansplaining. I'm guessing a light cotton fabric? Maybe a gabardine?"

"They need an answer immediately. I'll email you the paperwork. So think on it. But be quick like a bunny. We don't want them to go to someone else."

I'm too depressed to continue my run, so I turn and amble slowly home. Reality hits me pretty hard. Was I really thinking that I could stay here with Luke forever? I have a career to revive and even if I don't take the *Barbarella* gig, I would have to be

back in New York networking at opening night parties and
awards shows. Showing my face so people don't forget I exist. I
can't be a Broadway writer in Plainview and Luke can't work on
a farm in Manhattan. Is everything good in my life doomed to
just explode in a blaze of melodramatic glory? Am I cursed? Is
that it? In my mind, I run through the people I know, trying to
figure out who would be most likely to dabble in voodoo. Turns
out it's a very long list.

When I get home, Luke is on the front porch and hugging
Mom. I slowly climb the stairs as they pull apart.

"What's going on?"

Luke turns to me, embarrassed that his eyes are welling up.
"I'll let your mom tell you."

He's down the stairs and off to the barn. "What did you
do, Mom?"

"Oh, nothing. Just stopped by to say hello to Luke's mom the
other day. Brought her a pie."

"So you tried to poison her."

Mom rolls her eyes. "I knew you would say something like
that, so I didn't make it myself. I bought one at the Piggly Wiggly. And we had a very nice chat and I told her that I did not remember saying anything unkind about her in my life. But I was
guilty of staying silent while other people made idle gossip. And
I told her that would not be happening anymore on my watch.
And I convinced her to come to the musical. She agreed to come
with your father and me. We're going to pick her up and I am
going to walk into that Theodore arm in arm with Sue Carter

and if anyone has anything to say about it, they'll have to say it straight to my face."

I boost myself up to sit on the porch rail and look at her in awe. "That's . . . that's really great, Mom."

"Well, as I said. I was blind, but now I see. A very handsome, sweaty young man helped me to realize that." Mom kisses me on the forehead and then says, "You stink like a heifer. Go shower."

The next day at rehearsal everyone is shocked to see Jackie and Julia McNew in two completely different outfits. Jackie guesses what everyone's thinking and addresses the room. "Yeah, we're not dressing alike anymore, so get over it. I also started my second attempt at Nicorette chewing gum, if you're all so interested in my damn personal life."

"It was Jackie's idea," Julia says, almost glumly.

Feeling bad that I might have caused this shift in their lifestyles, I try to justify things. "You know, it's kind of good for your characters. Goneril and Regan aren't twins. Think of it as an acting exercise. Sometimes it helps to do in real life what you actually do onstage."

"Great advice, Noah. Should I poison my sister in real life, too?"

"That's your call, Jackie."

As Luke and I head home, a growing dread starts to creep over me. I know it's time to come clean about the horrible *Barbarella* gig. I'd rather eat glass than hurt Luke, but keeping it from him any longer seems like a complete dick move. He deserves the truth, even if it's going to be difficult to deliver the news.

I take a deep breath and forge ahead. "So . . . the new agent I was telling you about? She kind of got me a job."

Luke is enthusiastic and supportive because he's Luke. "She did? That's great! What is it?"

"Did you ever see that campy movie *Barbarella* with Jane Fonda? There's a kind of cockleshell about her."

Luke stares blankly at the road. "I don't think so."

"Consider yourself lucky. It's batshit crazy, but this composer Valerie Wernsman has been hacking away at the musical version for years. They want me to come in and secretly help fix it. It's crazy money."

"When would you start?"

"Right after *Stage of Fools*'s opening night. Like, the day after."

Luke's shoulders slump. He pulls the truck over to the side of the road and turns the engine off. The sun shines through the window straight into his eyes and they dilate, making them seem almost emerald green. We stare at each other and it feels like we could sit like this forever, the traffic and the rest of the world speeding carelessly by.

Finally, Luke says, "Well, I knew our time was limited from the start. But it still hurts." For once in my life I'm lost for words. "So we only have one week left."

"But we could do the long-distance thing, couldn't we?"

"I don't know. You'll meet some hot chorus boy who'll probably be able to shuffle all the way to Buffalo and back again."

"But I don't want to meet a hot chorus boy. Also, there's no tap in the show, so the shuffling part doesn't apply."

Sadness hangs in the air.

"It's mostly in Seattle, then Minneapolis. You could fly out every once in a while when you have time off."

"Maybe. But you'll definitely meet someone new. And I'll be forgotten."

I turn to face Luke and solemnly take both of his hands in mine. "That's impossible. And I won't meet someone new. I'm not like Chase. My dick doesn't call the shots. I do. And as far as we're both concerned it's only Luke Carter from here on out."

Luke gives a soft chuckle. "So, you're saying your dick is exclusively mine now?"

"If you'll have him. He's very demanding, but he's loyal as fuck."

Luke looks at me and just slowly shakes his head with a smile. "Is it strange that that is the most romantic thing you've ever said to me?"

I give Luke a humble shrug. "Hey, I'm freaking Shakespeare, man."

He gives me that warm pillowy Luke Carter kiss and then starts the truck back up. As we get closer to the farm, red and blue flashing lights start flickering through the trees. Panic rushes over me and Luke gives me a worried look and guns the engine. As we pull up to the house, two paramedics are loading Dad onto a gurney while Mom looks on with fear etched across her face. Luke and I hop out of the truck and run toward them.

"What happened? Mom? Is he okay?"

Mom latches on to me, pulling me toward her in a viselike

hug without taking her eyes off Dad for one second. "He passed out on his way back from the barn. I found him sprawled on the grass."

I quickly look at Dad, whose eyes are closed, and he's breathing through an oxygen mask. As they start to load him into the ambulance, Luke says, "You go with him. I'll drive your mom."

I wonder for a second if I should be the one riding with him. Wouldn't he want Mom? But there's no time to think, so I start to climb into the back of the ambulance behind Dad. One of the paramedics stops me.

"You have to ride up front."

I nod and give Dad one more quick look. He seems so frail, eyelids fluttering and oblivious to the world around him. He also seems so much smaller than usual. Has he been shrinking all this time and I just didn't notice? And what if this is it? What if he doesn't make it through like he did on opening night? I shudder for a second but quickly try to shove the thought deep into the crowded utility drawer of my subconscious.

The drive to the hospital seems to take forever, even though we're speeding pretty fast and the sirens are blaring. Fresh guilt pours over me when I think of Mom having to go through this alone during his earlier heart attack. She's tough but having to race your husband to the emergency room all by yourself must be terrifying.

I can't stop myself from asking unanswerable questions to the paramedic as he drives. "Is he going to be okay? I mean, he's not going to actually die, is he?"

"We're going to do everything in our power to help him."

All I can do is groan quietly in response.

By the time they're unloading Dad from the ambulance, his eyes are open, which I take as a good sign. I run alongside the gurney as we head into the emergency room and his hand seems to be searching for something, waving in the air. Oh God. Am I supposed to hold his hand? Because we don't do that, Dad and me. But he's clearly scared and I have to override all the past protocols at this point. I take his unbelievably fragile hand and give it a squeeze.

"I'm here, Dad. I'm here. You're going to be just fine. You're Bill fucking Adams and there's nothing you can't handle." And then I add, "You're the bravest person I know."

I detect the tiniest squeeze from his hand before they whisk him away from me once we're through the hospital doors. I stand there stunned as they wheel him down the hall, never having felt so powerless in my entire life.

I spot Mom talking conspiratorially with some of her friends from her nursing days. She's clearly getting privileged intel, so I know not to interrupt. Luke rounds the corner carrying cardboard cups of coffee.

"How did you beat the ambulance?"

Luke shrugs. "Shortcuts. And illegal speeding." He hands me a coffee, which I don't really want, but I appreciate the gesture.

"I've never seen Dad scared like that. I wasn't sure what to say. We don't really do the whole 'consoling' thing. I'm not sure he even heard me."

"He did."

I give Luke a puzzled look. "How do you know that?"

Luke answers with unwavering surety. "He heard you, Noah."

Luke sounds so confident that I almost believe him.

An hour passes agonizingly slowly.

Finally, Mom walks over and her entire attitude has changed. Her gaze is steely and being back in the emergency room has clearly awakened her former health care professional demeanor.

"Dr. Dunbar is off, so Dr. Vohs is with him. She's a great doctor, so there's no need to worry. He probably just got lightheaded. I didn't see his oxygen tank near him on the lawn, that stubborn old coot. I predict they'll run an echocardiogram and possibly tinker with his statins. One thing is for sure, they'll definitely keep him here for a few days to make sure he's stable. He's apparently already talking—which means complaining—so that's a good sign. They said they'd look the other way if I wanted to sleep on the chair in his room tonight."

"That doesn't sound very comfortable, Mom."

"Well, he might wake up confused in the middle of the night and I don't want that."

I'm as shocked as anyone when I blurt out, "I'll stay."

A look of complete surprise flickers across Mom's face before she can quickly hide it.

"Why, Noah, honey. I think your father would like that."

Deep down I worry he might not. But it somehow seems like the right thing to do. Soon we're all standing over Dad's hospital bed and it's clear that he's too groggy to even complain anymore. The good news is that he is, in fact, stable.

Before Luke leaves to drive Mom home, he pulls me into a quick hug and whispers, "When he wakes up, just remember the old guy's a Cordelia. He might not have the right words to say, but that doesn't mean he doesn't feel things."

I make myself as comfortable as possible on the cheap foam chair and finally think I'm about to drift off to sleep when I hear Dad's voice whisper softly.

"The bravest person you know, huh?"

So he did hear me after all. His eyes are tired, but they're open. I give him an exasperated look, but deep down I'm relieved that he has enough strength to start busting my hump.

"Don't start, Dad."

"What about General S. Patton?" Dad asks weakly. "What about Abraham Lincoln or Harriet Tubman? I'm braver than them?"

I sigh. "I said you were the bravest person I *know*. I don't know those people personally. Can you just accept the compliment and move on?"

Dad chuckles softly.

"You're supposed to be resting. Do you want me to turn on ESPN or some sort of ESPN equivalent?"

Dad considers. "It might help me sleep. If the volume's low enough."

I put the TV on and the muffled murmur actually lulls Dad to sleep. Once I'm sure he's completely out, I walk quietly over and take his hand. Confident that he's far off in dreamland, I whisper softly to him. "I know you're a tough guy, Dad. I get that. But if you need to be scared for a little bit, that's okay, too. I'm right here and I'm going to do my best to be brave enough for the both of us."

I give his hand a gentle squeeze and I'm almost positive he squeezes back.

# nineteen

# "More Than Words Can Hold"

After a couple of days and endless lectures about taking better care of himself from the entire hospital staff, Dad is finally released. I was too preoccupied with Dad, and to a lesser extent with Mom, to even think about the musical. Mrs. Henson took over running things, lifesaver that she is. With Dad safely installed back at his usual place at the kitchen table, I realize it's time to head back to the theater. Luke drives and when we walk in, the houselights are off and the cast is running through the show. I take a moment to appreciate how different it feels without the dated language. It seems more urgent, simpler and yet somehow more complex. But it's also bare. There's no "high concept" for the words and music to hide behind. There are no Danielle Vincent special effects. It's just the show, out there all on its own, on display for everyone to see.

I take a seat in the second-to-back row. Luke whispers in my ear, "I'd better go help Eddie."

I grab his arm. "Wait. Sit with me and watch for a second."

We watch. They may be amateurs, but they're damn good ones.

"Man, they're really finding their groove, right?" Luke gives my knee an encouraging squeeze.

"There aren't any distracting cyborgs or blood packs or futuristic trappings. Maybe we've stripped it back too far?"

"Have a little faith in your show. Maybe it doesn't need any extra bells and whistles."

My phone buzzes and it's Anna Wong. I walk out into the lobby to take the call.

"Hey, you."

"I have news to report. Apparently some theater chat sites have caught wind of the Plainview Players production of your show. And so has Carrie Payne at *The New York Times*. She's coming to see it, Noah."

My knees start to buckle and not in a good way. A wave of nausea hits me hard. "She's coming here? To Plainview? She can't do that."

"Anyone can buy a ticket, Noah. Word is she wants to write a human-interest piece."

"But I don't want humans interested in this particular piece, Anna Wong!"

"But at least it's not going to be another review of the show."

"Of course it is! Oh, she'll disguise it with little distracting flourishes here and there. But it's another chance for her to publicly humiliate me in print and online. Why does she want to destroy my career? What did I ever do to her?"

"I can't stop this from happening. But I'll be there, for moral support, and also to try to sweet-talk her."

"That's not how it works! There is a golden rule that neither the author nor the author's representative is allowed to talk to any critic."

Maybe going with Anna Wong was a mistake. How did she not even know the basics?

"I'll be there anyway. Just for hand-holding."

She hangs up and I slump to the floor.

Luke finds me lying there in the lobby a few minutes later and sits down on the ground next to me. I put my head in his lap and tell him the whole tragic news. He strokes my hair as I talk and it actually does seem to slow my pulse slightly.

Then he kisses me so perfectly that nothing happens except that my vertebrae vibrate and fall apart like a crumbling Jenga tower. When my eyes come back into focus, Luke says, "Let them come. Let them say what they want. The show is great. And with all the changes that have been made, who knows? Maybe it'll blow their minds."

I take a minute to digest the thought and then say, "It will definitely not blow Carrie Payne's mind. She has a vendetta against me."

"Listen, the show has really grown, Noah. Maybe you can't see it because you're so close to it. But believe me, it's like an entirely different musical now."

"I don't know, it just feels like something is missing, you know?"

"Come on. You're just being paranoid. Nothing is missing from your musical, Noah."

My mind starts racing and suddenly an alarm bell sounds in my brain. I find myself shooting straight up into a sitting position. "I know what's missing, Luke!"

"What?"

"Just like your mom said. Heart."

Once the cast is gone Luke gets cuddly on the beat-up couch and closes his eyes. I sit at the piano, trying to find something Cordelia can sing that will add Sue Carter's much-needed heart to the show. I attempt to pluck a melody out of the air and try it out on the piano. Nope. I try another one. No, too syrupy. The next one almost sounds like it's a military march, which is the exact opposite of heart.

Think, Noah. Ignore the pressure and *think*.

Why did we have Cordelia's ghost come back at the end of the show? It's not in the source material. What's the point? Her sisters are dead and lying in a heap. Her father is broken, wracked with insanity and despair. And what does that have to do with her?

It's not her fault that she couldn't fawn all over her father with flattery. Deep down she clearly loved him much more than her sisters. But she just couldn't express her love so boldly. What did she say in the very first scene? "My love's more ponderous than my tongue." Which means what? Which means that though she can't say it, she loves him more than words could hold. Can hold.

More than words can hold?

More Than Words Can Hold.

Is that the song title? That's the song title! Holy shit, that's the song title! She's there to tell him what she couldn't in the first scene. That mere words aren't big enough to contain her love for him. But does she really mean that? Screw it, in this version she does.

I take a deep breath and try to musicalize the phrase. I close my eyes and attempt to open my mind to the universe. I hear it so softly in my head. A five-note melody. I carefully open my eyes and the melody comes out of my fingertips.

"That's the one," Luke says, watching me from where he's lying with a grin on his face.

By the time the sun comes up, the song is done. I call Melissa and she rushes over to the theater. When she walks through the door, it's clear she just pulled on whatever clothes she could find. Not a usual look for Melissa, who's always polished and camera-ready.

She's almost pulsating with excitement. "You wrote a song for me? For little old me?"

I'm almost nervous to play it for her. If she hates it, everyone will hate it. I give Luke an anxious look.

"Go ahead, Noah. Play it for us."

"It's called 'More Than Words Can Hold.' And I'm a terrible singer, so don't let that affect your opinion of the song."

"Enough chitchat, just play it already," Melissa begs.

"Just trying to manage expectations. Here we go."

I start lightly playing the intro and Melissa holds onto Luke's arm for balance as she slowly sinks into a chair. I can't look at either one of them as I sing. I try to give my voice a breathy quality instead of the usual strident sound that comes out of my mouth. Whenever I have to audition a song for anyone, actors, producers, directors, I always get a little flop sweaty. Time moves in slow motion, because I know that my talent is being judged right along with the quality of the song. It's terrifying and seemingly endless. But the worst part is when I play the final note and I have to turn in silence to see how the listeners are reacting. It can be brutally embarrassing for everyone involved if it doesn't go well. And then no one knows what to say. But that dreaded moment is here: I play the final note and let it hang in the air until it fades into oblivion.

I take a deep breath and turn to Melissa and Luke. Melissa has tears running down her face and Luke is just standing there beaming, his thick arms crossed and shaking his head back and forth.

Melissa has me record the accompaniment on her phone and promises she will have it memorized by tomorrow's run-through. Thankfully, it's Sunday morning, so I decide to crash for a couple of hours. There's not much more I can do writing-wise, anyway. When I wake up and come downstairs, bedhead and all, I find Mom sitting on the back porch. Still dressed in her church clothes, she's busy with a rag and paint remover, furiously trying to get paint out from under her fingernails. She's constantly either adding paint to her body or subtracting it.

I take what has become my usual spot on the porch railing. Humidity is just starting to turn the air into quicksand. Even the wind chimes sound sluggish.

"How's Dad?"

"I just took his blood pressure. It was slightly elevated, but *All Girls Garage* was playing on the TV, so that might explain it."

"Ugh, can't he just watch porn like a normal person?"

Mom chuckles softly and shakes her head.

"So, I've kind of got a job that starts after opening night. It's to be a show doctor on a really shitty show. But it's a sizable check and I can't turn it down. And Kiara's husband found me a studio rental where I can keep my stuff while I'm on the road."

"You don't sound very excited about it."

"It's based on *Barbarella*."

"That movie where Jane Fonda runs around in a fur bikini and gets bitten by doll babies?"

I groan. "That's the one."

"Good Lord, Noah. They better be paying you extra. What a colossal waste of everyone's time."

"The good news is that the movie actually has very little plot and what is there is a totally hackneyed mess. So in a way, that's kind of freeing, I guess. Maybe I can help them craft a story with some forward action and meaning."

"Or you could just have Barbarella shoot herself in the head in the first five minutes so everyone can be put out of their misery and go home."

"Okay, you can stop talking now."

Mom looks up and flashes a smile. "What does Luke think?"

"That it's bittersweet. I'm going to have to be gone for over a year."

"But he's worth it, isn't he?"

"Of course. He's just so honest and unassuming that it's hard to believe he's actually real. Like, maybe this is all a joke. And the way he exists in the world is crazy, too. It's like he has no idea that he's about as perfect as a guy can get, inside and out. And he's interested in me? I don't get it."

"Oh, don't play humble, Noah. It's boring. And for my money, I'm glad you two are going for it. After what you've been through with that Chase character, it seems like sweet Luke might be just what the doctor ordered."

"But what does Luke get out of the deal? A neurotic writer whose only redeeming quality is that he thinks that Luke Carter is the best human being that God and/or evolution ever created? I mean, am I just supposed to go on blind faith that I'm actually going to be enough for that guy?"

Mom pauses for dramatic effect.

"Well, as we say in the church basement on Thursday nights, '*Bingo!*'"

I exhale loudly. "I don't know. Maybe I'm just scared to be happy. Or, even worse, maybe I just don't know how to *do* happy."

Mom leans in for a conspiratorial whisper, "I don't mean to frighten you, honey, but you're *doing* happy as we speak."

Once again, Mom has thrown me for a loop.


The following night we fold Cordelia's song into the show. When Melissa performs it for the cast, they go completely apeshit. I allow my head to swell for exactly three seconds before I go back to cracking the whip. There's no time for patting myself on the back. It's the final week of rehearsals and haste has to be made. Dad's lingering around, having been given the okay by his doctors to inspect the new set. It's just a collection of suspended windows and random door units with a simple drop behind them, but it's somehow effective anyway. Dad and Luke have repurposed a farm backdrop from *The Wizard of Oz*, but speckled it with bits of gray paint to make it less cheery. It's eerie in just the right way.

Afterward, in Luke's backyard, he spreads a blanket on the ground and we look at the night sky. There are so many stars it feels like they might start raining down on us any minute. We both lie back and take it all in.

"This is amazing, Luke. You can't really see any stars in the city. I guess because of all of the lights from the buildings."

"Well, that's just sad."

I turn to look at him. "Yeah, I guess it is, a little."

I move over and cradle his gorgeous head and wonder at his beauty. I close my eyes for a second.

"What are you doing?"

"Just trying to imprint this moment on my brain. There's bound to be some point in the future where I'm sad or frustrated or preparing for a colonoscopy and I'll need to summon the perfectness of this moment."

"Aren't you too young for a colonoscopy?"

I shrug. "I'm a planner."

"You know what my favorite part of your body is?"

"Well, I can guess which part you're most enthusiastic about."

Luke gets adorably annoyed. "Come on, I'm being serious."

"Okay, go ahead."

"My favorite part of your body is your brain."

"But it's so squishy and wrinkly."

"But such amazing things fall out of it."

I laugh. "Oh, they don't fall out. I have to force them out. Mostly through self-torture and panic attacks."

"That new song, though . . . I love the intro . . ." And then he sings a couple of lines from Cordelia's song so softly and effortlessly that I think I might pass out or at least forget how to breathe.

> *Once angels rush me from this weary world*
> *My words won't reach you from up above . . .*

It's almost too much to bear, so I stop him from continuing.

"Okay, it's not fair that you're so perfect, Luke. It's like I filled out a survey and then a team of scientists went into a lab with it and out you came. You check every single box. Don't you have any flaws? Not even one, so the rest of us can feel less inferior?"

"I can't write musicals."

I can't help but sneer. "Consider yourself lucky."

Luke sits up, urgent all of the sudden. "No, really. How do you do it?"

"How does anyone do anything? People are always trying to figure out how to pin down the creative process, but I just don't think you can. There's this story about Michelangelo. It might be apocryphal, who knows? He apparently said, 'The sculpture is already complete within the marble block, before I start my work. It is already there, I just have to chisel away the superfluous material.' So basically his advice is to just remove any part of the statue that isn't a statue. That's not very helpful advice. Thanks for nothing, Mike."

"So it really is impossible to explain it? The stuff that goes on in your head when you're writing a song?"

"I guess I mostly just sit at the piano and pray to many unseen gods to send me inspiration. If nothing happens after a few hours, I usually think 'screw it' and go watch horror movies on Netflix. Somebody once said, 'Writing is hard, but having written is wonderful.' I always tell myself that when I'm struggling with a song. When it's done it'll be wonderful. Not the song, maybe. But the sense of accomplishment will be wonderful, at least. And I'll get to know that there's one more song in the world. And even if it isn't a great song, it might make something somewhere just a tiny bit better for someone."

Luke kisses me on the top of the head like I'm a puppy.

"I brought something else, just in case the stars aren't entertaining enough for you." He reaches into his pocket and brings out his battered paperback of E. E. Cummings poetry.

"If you think this cheesy attempt at being romantic is going to work on me, I'm here to tell you that you are completely and totally correct. You're playing me like a violin."

"Around here we say, 'You're playing me like a fiddle.' But I guess violins are classier."

"As a rule, yes." I start to leaf through the pages. "Edward Estlin Cummings. But he preferred to use just his initials. And most of the time wrote his name in all lowercase letters. I tried to do that with the first musical I wrote in college. But my middle name is Oliver. So on the poster it said, 'no adams.' And then people started calling me 'no,' which was confusing as hell. So I finally just went back to Noah."

I notice one of the pages has been dog-eared. "Oh, look. It's your favorite. 'anyone lived in a pretty how town.' The one with the guy who dies and no one will stoop to kiss his face."

"I kind of feel like that's how I'm going to end up one day."

"Well, that's just depressing . . . hold up, I'm gonna find you a new favorite poem." I leaf through the book and find what I'm looking for. I quickly dog-ear the page and hand it to Luke.

Luke reads the poem's title out loud. "'i carry your heart with me.'" He gives me a tiny grin. "Now you're playing *me* like a violin."

"But I do, you know. And I will. Carry your heart with me. It's cheesy, but it's true. Please don't feel like that guy in a pretty how town. And please stop acting like this is over. I can't take it. It's not. We agreed."

"But you're going to be so far away. It's going to hurt so much."

"We'll text every hour on the hour like clockwork. And talk on the phone every night. And once I get my schedule, we'll figure out when you can sneak away and we'll have an amazing time. You'll visit me in Seattle. We'll take selfies at the Space Needle. We'll watch them throw halibut around at the fish market. Being apart will be hard, but think how much more special it'll be when we do get to be together."

A blinking airplane plays connect the dots with the stars overhead. I stare into Luke's eyes and borrow a line from *Follies*. "If you don't kiss me, Luke, I think I'm going to die."

His arms go around me quickly and he kisses me while hugging me so tightly it's difficult to breathe and I don't care. The ground beneath us turns into a Tilt-A-Whirl and we disappear into one another. And I realize that the moment could go on for an eternity and I'd still feel shortchanged.

# twenty

# "Opening Night. Again."

Against all logic, I find myself once again at an opening night of *Stage of Fools*.

I've spent the last few days obsessing over Carrie Payne. Where the hell is she even staying? The best thing Plainview has to offer in the way of hotels is a Best Western. And that Best Western is far from the best. It's kind of disturbing that she's followed me all the way to my tiny hometown. What makes that woman tick? What makes any critic tick? I know there are fair critics out there. Critics who can give a well-considered and balanced assessment of a show. But that's not Carrie. Oh, sure, she gives the odd rave review here and there, but she does so almost begrudgingly. It's clearly more fun for her to be wittily jaded or jadedly witty. There's more entertainment in it for her to go after a particular script or score or actor or design element and put her acerbic analysis on display.

Where did she ever get a taste for that sort of thing? Was it the way she was raised? Did her mother look at her when she was a little girl and say, "Well, you're not very successful at being a little girl, now are you? I mean, what can we say about your eyes, Carrie, other than you've got two of them? And when you were talking just now, all that dialogue about your dolly? It was stiff and unbelievable. And I don't even know what you're trying to say with that hair. What's the subtext of the hairdo, Carrie? Well, I'd better type all of these thoughts up and send it to the local newspaper. Hopefully they can get it in the morning edition so everyone can read it before you get to kindergarten."

Hmm. Should I maybe feel sorry for Carrie Payne? Not a chance in hell.

Though I hadn't read her original review of *Stage of Fools*, word got back to me that she had used the phrase, "laughable solemnity at every turn."

So I won't be feeling sorry for that woman any time soon.

True to her word, Mom and Dad left early to pick up Luke's mom. I'm so nervous as I sit on the front porch waiting for Luke that I worry I might actually start to levitate from the stress. He pulls up wearing the same tie and plaid shirt combo from our first very official date. I hop in the truck and there's a small present waiting for me on the front seat cushion.

"Is this for me? Because I didn't get you anything and now I look like an asshole."

Luke grins. "I didn't expect you to get me anything. You've been distracted with tearing your show apart and putting it back together, so you don't look like an asshole. You look drop-dead handsome. Now, open it."

I tear the wrapping paper off and open the tiny box. Inside is

a silver chain with a charm in the shape of the comedy and tragedy masks. Here's the thing. I hate the comedy and tragedy
masks. They're hideously ugly and anyone who is in theater gets
gifted all kinds of garbage with those faces embossed on them.
They're obvious and cheesy. Tacky as hell. And this particular
necklace will be cherished forever and never leave my body.

We kiss and then I tell Luke, "I sometimes think that you're
too good to be true. That I might actually be hallucinating you.
Or maybe this is like one of those very bad TV movies where you
find out that it was all a dream."

"Well, if it is, let's never wake up."

"Deal."

Luke starts the truck's engine and I'm off to be crucified by
*The New York Times* for the second time in less than two months.
There's actually a huge crowd of people lining up outside when
we get to the theater. From what I can remember, it was never
like this when I was in shows as a kid.

I take a moment to consider the crowd. It's obvious that most
of these people have never been to the Plainview Players' Theater
before. Apparently tonight was just out of the ordinary enough to
make them come and bear witness.

I remember the first musical I saw at this theater. It was a
summer production of *Oliver!* I had no idea what I was in for, but
when the curtain went up I was transported to another world.
What is this place where people sing and dance and wear costumes? Where there are sets and lights and music playing? And
when it was over, I refused to leave the theater. Mom tried to
convince me that the performance was over. That they were done

for the night. I was actually heartbroken. But then she explained that I could be part of the next show if I wanted to. And that was the moment I knew without a doubt what I had to do with my life.

Luke eyes the crowd. "Let's go around through the back."

We hightail it to the back entrance. Everyone backstage looks like they're about to have a panic attack.

Allison is running around adding finishing touches to the makeshift costumes. Louis is rambling like a madman through tongue-twisting vocal warm-ups. "Betty Botter bought a bit of bitter butter, but the bit of butter was too bitter for the batter, so Betty Botter bought a bit of better butter."

Jackie and Julia are doing their disturbing mirror exercise, when Jackie looks up and sees me and shouts, "Fracture an arm tonight, Noah!"

I smile nervously and nod. "You, too!"

Then I creep silently up to the stage curtain and try to get a glimpse of the audience without getting caught. There's Mom, Dad, and Sue. Sue is dressed up and even wearing a corsage for some reason. Mom is yammering nonstop into Sue's ear and thankfully making her laugh.

I also spot Anna Wong, dressed way too well for this Podunk town. And there's a bald guy holding flowers, who I assume is Melissa's husband. I recognize Audra Bogner from her *Post-Dispatch* bio picture. And there are a bunch of vaguely familiar faces of people I probably once knew, but have now completely forgotten.

Before I let the curtain drop and walk away, I spot her. Carrie

Payne. A brittle, birdlike presence in all black and with a pixie haircut that looks like it would make your fingers bleed if you actually touched it. Her face is pinched as she scrolls through her phone. She occasionally looks up to generally scowl at the place. She seems like a supervillain from a movie, if that supervillain was really shitty at applying makeup and wore knockoff Chanel pumps.

What does it matter, Noah? In a couple of hours it'll all be over and you'll be forced to focus your efforts on the looming disaster that is *Barbarella, The Musical!*

The theater is quickly filling up to almost full capacity when Mrs. Henson whispers to me from the stage. "Noah, we're ready for you."

Ready for me? Ready for me to do what?

I notice the cast standing onstage in a circle and holding hands like the Whos from *How the Grinch Stole Christmas*. They're clearly waiting for me to make some kind of speech. I duck under a random pair of clasped hands and end up in the center of the circle.

"Well, here we are," I start out shakily. "To say that this has been a month full of surprises would be the understatement of the year. Who knew that Louis Jenkins has a voice that would make Norm Lewis want to throw in the towel? Who knew that Abby Gupta was the next Bob Fosse? Or that the McNew twins could teach my personal idol Patti LuPone a thing or two about diva-like intensity? And then there's Melissa, who makes the entire room weep until we run out of tears and our eyes turn to dust every time she sings. Although, in fairness, I really shouldn't single anybody out. Because all of you have brought every last part of yourselves to this show. Your dedication is something that even a few seasoned Broadway actors could learn from. Now, I know that the lead critics from both *The New York Times* and *The St. Louis Post-Dispatch* are out there. And that is batshit crazy and scary and, frankly, a little unprofessional on their part. But you know what? Fuck 'em. We're not doing this show for reviews. We're not even doing this show for pay, obviously. We're doing this show because we believe in the power of live theater. We're doing this show because we want to take that audience out there on a journey and make them laugh and cry and feel something. Working with all of you has not only made *Stage of Fools* better, it's also, I don't know, changed me on a personal level, somehow. Made me less of an asshole, maybe . . ."

"Let's not go overboard, Noah!" Jackie shouts out. Everyone laughs, including me.

"I walked right into that one. But seriously you guys . . ."

And of course, my voice is wavering and of course my cheeks are stained with tears, but I don't even care.

"This is the place that taught me to love theater. And now it's the place that returned that love of theater back to me. So I don't know how to thank you, I really don't."

I pause, because it's so profoundly true. How could I ever thank them enough? Maybe I can't, so I simply say, "Here's the crazy thing about theater. It's not like film or TV. It only exists for a moment when you share the same experience with an audience and then it's gone. That's the magic. It exists in real time and then it's gone forever. And all you get to keep is the memory of it. That's what makes it so precious. It's here and then it's gone. So don't waste a minute of it. Go out there and enjoy every single second. You've earned it."

There is hushed clapping and a bunch of hurried hugs and then I'm out the back door of the building.

I have a hard and fast rule to never watch my own show if a critic is there. But this is my one and only chance to see this new version of *Stage of Fools* in front of a real, breathing audience. So I circle the building and enter through the lobby. Just as the houselights are going down, I slip into the theater and stand far in the back.

My phone vibrates. It's Kiara. I made her promise not to come, but she hasn't forgotten. It's a picture of her and Stephen smiling wildly with their fingers crossed.

There's a murmur of excitement in the crowd as Mrs. Henson launches into "Who Loves Him Most?" The curtain rises and there stand my lovable collection of misfits.

Dressed in humble everyday clothing, they start singing. It's timid at first, but they start to gain confidence. And the subtle staging that Abby Gupta has added to the number helps build the tension.

By the middle of the song, they've hit their stride.

By the end of the number, they're downright triumphant. Since practically everyone in the audience is related to someone in the show, the applause is thunderous.

Things settle down and we're into the first book scene. My cell buzzes. I look down and see the name Valerie Wernsman. Anna Wong had given me her number and asked me to call her at some point. I've been putting it off. Shit! Knowing I have to take it, I hurry through the lobby and out into the parking lot.

I answer breathlessly. "Valerie, I'm so sorry, I've been meaning to call, but things have been a little hectic."

"Well, I thought we should at least speak once before you just pop up at rehearsal in a few days."

God is she frosty. Ugh. Smile pretty, Noah. She'll be able to hear it in your voice. "This is great. I'm really looking forward to meeting you in person."

"I also wanted to let you know that I'm not very happy that we're being forced into this situation, you and I."

Oh fuck. Keep smiling, Noah.

"Oh . . . I'm sorry. I know this might seem awkward at first, but I'm sure we'll figure it out."

"I'm just not sure why *you* were chosen. I mean, after all, your first Broadway show was hardly what you'd call a success."

My mouth drops open. So this is how we're going to play this? Fine by me.

"Well, you know, Valerie, my show did flop, but at least it was only once. Your show's flopped a grand total of three times. So congratulations on the trifecta and everything."

The line goes silent.

Recalibrate, Noah. Recalibrate.

"Sorry, that was shitty. I'm actually at a kind of family thing right now and emotions are running high."

"Just so I'm aware, what earthshaking ideas do you have for my show? I'd love for you to run them by me, because ultimately I will have full creative control."

That's not what I was told.

"Well, uh, Valerie, that's why I think the first day I get there, maybe the two of us can just sit down over coffee and you can tell me what it is that you're looking to, um, improve."

A deadly pause. "Improve?"

"Um, not improve. Tweak. Finesse. Sometimes, and I know this from personal experience, when you've worked on a musical for a long time, it helps to have someone with fresh eyes come in."

"That is the exact same thing my producers keep saying. But I'm not so sure you're that set of eyes, Noah."

"Well, your producers seem to disagree and they're the ones paying me."

Long pause.

"Well, just know that I don't plan on being open to any new ideas. Enjoy your time with your family."

She hangs up and I stomp back and forth in the parking lot for what seems like five years. Not only is it killing me that I have to tear myself from Luke for almost a year, but it'll be ten times worse that I have to spend countless hours with this walking nightmare of a woman who clearly has no intention of even trying to improve her broken down musical.

I take a deep breath and go back into the theater to find the McNew twins killing their duet. Killing it. The audience is collectively leaning forward toward the stage in rapt concentration. Jackie and Julia were always slightly comical in the roles before. But now, without the Shakespearean language and the over-the-top costumes, they're just two sisters competing for their father's love. And man, are they going at one another. They clearly have some hidden family issues that they've pent up over the years and they are on full display tonight. The song ends and for a moment you can hear a pin drop.

Then, another almost embarrassingly huge ovation.

And before I know it, we're near the end of the first act and Abby and Drew begin their eye-gouging movement piece. This might be tricky. It's a little avant-garde for Plainview, Illinois. But the audience actually gasps each time the red ribbons seem to get pulled out of Abby's eyes.

The act finishes and the curtain falls. The audience is murmuring loudly as the houselights come up and I go and hide outside behind a tree, because that's the kind of bravery I possess.

A few minutes later, the door to the theater opens and Mom and Sue come out both carrying wine in clear plastic cups. "Where's my sweet potato at? Where is he? Is he out here hiding behind a tree?"

I sheepishly walk around the tree and she sweeps me up into a hug, almost spilling her wine. "Oh, it's so good, Noah! It's beyond good! It's brilliant!"

When I finally extract myself from Mom's hug, I take a huge gulp of her wine.

"What do you think of the show, Sue? You can be honest. I can take it."

Sue thinks for a moment. "It's disturbing. I mean, in a good way. Makes you think about families and how they compete with each other and all. And I think that's good, if a show like this can get people thinking about how they treat other people. But what do I know? The only other show I ever saw here was *Annie* a hundred years ago. I couldn't stand it. Every time that little loudmouthed girl opened her trap to screech, I wanted to punch her in the face."

Mom bursts out laughing. "Sue is too much! We have been just cracking each other up!" Mom stops herself short and says solemnly, "Not during the show of course. We're paying very strict attention to your show, Noah."

The door opens abruptly and my blood runs cold as Carrie Payne steps out to light a cigarette. "Uh, ladies, I have to go check on some things backstage. Don't be late for Act Two!"

I run down the side of the theater and around to the back door as quickly as I can.

The cast is scattered about the wings, changing costumes and checking their makeup. Luke runs up to me. "It's going great, Noah! You've gotta know that, right?"

"I guess so."

He pulls me into a hug and I put my head against his neck and feel his familiar pulse thudding. He kisses me gently on the ear and then says, "I gotta go call places for Act Two. The house-lights are at half!"

Since when did he start using phrases like "the houselights are at half"? The other night, as we were falling asleep and spooning, he muttered, "Do you think they're holding the button of the finale too long?" A button is the final pose of a musical number. And now big, masculine Luke Carter not only knows what it is, but is using it correctly in sentences.

Mrs. Henson launches into the entr'acte, so I trace my steps back around the outside of the theater and into the building once

again. I take my place at the back of the theater as the second act
starts.

Once again, everything seems to be happening faster and
faster. Before I know it, Louis Jenkins is soaring through "Terrors of the Earth" and it seems like the entire place is fighting
the urge to give him a standing ovation right in the middle of the
song. When the final scene rolls around, it's time for the only
new song I've written for the show. I silently pray that Melissa
doesn't get too nervous or forget the lyrics.

Mrs. Henson starts the intro and Melissa steps into the light,
the crown of oak leaves resting softly on her head.

Suddenly her face goes pale.

Oh, shit. I knew it was too much to throw at an amateur.
Even a professional actor would be nervous to pull it off with so
little rehearsal. Mrs. Henson plays the intro again, as if to jog
Melissa's memory. Still nothing. Melissa just stares out into
space.

The cast starts to surreptitiously look at one another, wondering what to do. This can't be happening. My show is horrifically
tanking in front of Carrie Payne for the second time.

Melissa looks out weakly into the audience and inexplicably
says, "Henry?"

Who the fuck is Henry? Is she actually so nervous that she's
confusing *King Lear* with *Henry V*? What the hell is going on?!

"Henry . . . I think my water broke."

A gasp goes through the crowd and before I know it, I'm
sprinting toward the stage, side by side with the bald man I spot-
ted earlier.

"Turn the work lights on!" I shout out, climbing onto the stage with Henry right behind me.

The fluorescents snap on as Henry and I reach Melissa at the same time. She's trembling and her crown of leaves has fallen to the floor. We flank her, each taking an elbow.

I look down to see Mom in full-on nurse mode, pacing back and forth at the lip of the stage and calling to us. "She's all right. You're all right, Melissa, honey. We just need to get you to the hospital. This is all totally natural. Henry, do you think you're in a calm enough state to drive her?"

Henry looks rattled, but puts on a brave face. "Yes, Mrs. Adams. I think I'm good."

"Okay, then. Let's everybody move aside and make a path for them to get off the stage and into their car."

Melissa turns to me with tears in her eyes and whispers, "I'm so sorry, Noah."

I whisper back. "Don't you dare apologize! You're gonna be just fine." And then I add. "And try to have a cesarean. They're just classier."

Melissa manages to laugh as everyone moves out of the way and Henry helps Melissa toward the stage door.

I turn and bend down to pick up Melissa's crown of leaves and remember that the whole crowd is looking at me. They're waiting on me to say something. To give them all permission to go home, I guess.

I clear my throat and a few audience members take their seats, but most just stand staring at me and wondering what the hell I'm going to say.

I might as well get this over with.

"So . . ." My voice actually breaks like I'm back in the throes of puberty. I clear my throat and apologize. "Sorry, just trying out a new voice there . . . So, for those of you who don't know *King Lear* that well . . . um, what just happened was not part of the play."

A nervous chuckle or two. Great. It's going great.

"I wrote a new song for this spot in the show. The only new song that we added to this production, actually. But fate is obviously a comedian, because our Cordelia's water just broke. So I guess that's that."

I feel the weight of a familiar hand on my shoulder. I turn around and realize that Luke is looking at me with an expression of total tranquility. I stop talking as he turns and addresses the audience.

"Hey, everyone. Um, so, I was here when Noah wrote this song. I got to watch him compose while I pretended to sleep right over there on that couch. I heard that song so many times, I don't think it would be humanly possible for me to ever forget it now. Noah hates his own singing voice, which I think is crazy. But if you'll let me, Noah, I'd like to sing your song for you."

The audience murmurs and the cast looks at one another as if they're not sure this is a good idea.

I give Luke a worried glance. "Are you sure about this?"

He nods. I shrug numbly and slowly leave the stage.

Luke, now wearing the crown of leaves, signals to a stunned Mrs. Henson and she begins to play. Luke opens his mouth and there's that gentle baritone that has no business hiding out in an ex-football player. Luke's face has an almost otherworldly serene quality and the melody just floats out of him and over the crowd.

> *Once angels rush me from this weary world*
> *My words won't reach you from up above*
> *Well, that's how heaven goes*
> *And yet, heaven knows*
> *I need you to hear the measure of my love . . .*

The cast upstage of Luke stares at him in barefaced awe. It seems impossible that he's been hiding that beautiful voice all this time while he's been rewiring props and painting flats. The entire building is transfixed.

> *More than words can hold*
> *More than breath can say*
> *This helpless heart is yours*
> *Till my dying day.*
>
> *Should the moon turn black,*
> *Or the sun turn cold*
> *I will love you still*
> *More than words can hold . . .*

And though the song isn't written as an ensemble number, one by one the other cast members join in. Soon the entire stage is singing along on the final chorus. Mrs. Henson shamelessly slows the tempo and the song reaches a rafter-shaking crescendo.

> *More than words can hold*
> *More than breath can say*
> *This helpless heart is yours*
> *Till my dying day.*

*Should the moon turn black,*
*Or the sun turn cold*
*I will love you still*
*More than words can hold . . .*

There is one final modulation before the coda. Everyone sings the final lyric of the song at the top of their lungs. And to my surprise, I'm singing along with them from the audience without even the slightest hint of self-consciousness.

*More than words could ever hold*

A sensation of pure joy blooms inside my chest by the time the song finishes. And somehow it feels like I'm floating above the audience as they leap to their feet and applaud for what seems like days. And I know right then that no critic anywhere will ever be able to take that sensation away from me.

# twenty-one

# "Places!"

The curtain falls and the houselights come up. And the place immediately turns into a madhouse. People start rushing onstage or climbing over chairs to get to their family members in the cast. Selfies are being snapped everywhere. Jackie and Julia look like bookends, hugging an older woman with a walker from either side. The woman's sweatshirt has the words "Twin Baby Momma" spelled out in gold lamé letters, and she weeps majestically with pride. Louis Jenkins is crowded by a seemingly never-ending mob of family members. Kids from Abby's bus route ask for her autograph and she obliges, cackling with glee.

Anna Wong runs up to me and gives me a hug, which is very un–Anna Wong. "It's like a totally different show! I mean, I liked it on Broadway, but this version is so much more tangible, so much more sincere! I'm thinking we might be able to license this baby. We'll make it a big story for the press. 'Revamped *Stage of*

*Fools* is alive again!' Oh, there's Carrie Payne. Should I go ask her how she liked it?"

"No!" I hiss under my breath. "We just have to wait and see what she says in her so-called 'human-interest piece.' Promise me you won't even look in her general direction."

"Got it. My mind is spinning with all the opportunities this new version of the show could have! I've gotta go make notes in my phone."

To my complete horror, Mom is doing some strange little conga dance as she moves through the crowd. A sort of celebratory jig. She keeps singing at the top of her lungs, "My sweet potato's a genius! My sweet potato's a genius! My sweet potato's a genius!"

"Stop singing that!"

Mom laughs. "Well, it's true!"

She squishes me into a hug and when she lets go, Sue's caught up to her.

Sue takes my face in her tiny hands and smiles up at me. "Now that was heart."

I sigh and say, "I can't believe on top of everything else, Luke can sing like that."

Sue shrugs. "My son can do anything."

Luke appears and starts hugging his mom from behind, wrapping around her tiny frame like a massive quilt. "You ladies wanna stay for the cast party?"

Sue shakes her head. "Oh, no. This is about as much socializing as I can stand for one day."

Mom fiddles with my hair and says, "I'm going to try to twist Sue's arm and get her to come over for a nightcap and some of my fruitcake cookies. They're little cookies that taste just like little fruitcakes!"

"That should tell you all you need to know, Sue," I warn grimly.

Mrs. Henson rushes over to me, breathless and carrying a bouquet of bouncing congratulatory balloons. "I hope I didn't milk the ending too much. I didn't want to gild the lily, but I couldn't help but draw out the last few notes! And Luke Carter, you little sneak! Where have you been hiding that voice? We're doing *Sweeney Todd* in the fall and you'd make a fabulous Anthony Hope!"

Luke turns magenta and laughs. "No way. That was a one-time thing. Back to the set shop for me!"

I notice Dad sitting glued to his seat, staring blankly at his kneecaps. His oxygen machine silently stands guard as always.

I turn to Mom. "Is he okay? He's not having another episode, is he?"

Mom's voice goes soft and secretive. "No, nothing like that. I think your musical just really spoke to him."

I blink at her in confusion. "But he's seen it before. Bits and pieces, anyway. He's been to a couple of rehearsals."

"Well, now, honey, it's different when you see it all at once, you know. In one fell swoop. And with an audience and everything."

I take a moment to hem and haw, and then ask, "Should I go check on him?"

"Oh, Noah." Mom puts a gentle hand to my cheek and I can tell she's somehow trying to infuse me with any courage I might lack. "I think that would be very kind of you."

I begin walking toward Dad with an almost comical abundance of caution. Like he's a big, bald bird that might fly away if I move too aggressively. I silently take a seat next to him and he doesn't stop staring down at his knees, as if they hold some kind of cosmic answer.

Finally, Dad says, "So . . . is your show about us, son?"

Swallowing unexpectedly becomes harder than usual. And there's a strange piercing feeling in my chest cavity. But I can't lie to him. Not if he's brave enough to ask. Isn't this the conversation I always wanted to have? Isn't this the not-so-subconscious reason I chose *King Lear* as my source material in the first place?

My voice trembles, but I ignore it. "Well, it's kind of about us, I guess. I mean, thematically speaking—"

Dad stops me by placing his weathered hand on my knee. "Well, then let's clear something up right here and now."

I steady myself, not sure what to prepare for. Dad continues as sadness slowly spreads across his brow. "I guess, maybe I've let you down somehow . . ."

The piercing in my chest cavity grows more intense. Unable to bear it, I quickly fall all over myself to reassure him. "No, Dad. Not at all."

Dad gives an exasperated huff. "Let me finish, Noah."

I quickly go mute and wonder if this little scene is really what I wanted after all. "You see, son, I was raised a certain way . . . and me and my dad, well, we never . . . my generation didn't . . ."

His fumbling breaks my heart. "We don't have to do this, Dad."

Frustrated, he squeezes my knee and I once again snap my mouth shut.

"Let me finish. I'm not good at saying things. You must have got your talent for words from your mom's side of the family. I mean, I wouldn't be surprised, those people never shut up."

We share an awkward laugh.

"But, son . . . I do, you know . . . I *do*."

I put my hand on top of his. And though I'm usually an unstoppable fountain of babble, all I can muster is a simple, "I get it, Dad."

His eyes lift slowly until he's staring directly at me.

"More than words can hold, son. More than words could ever hold."

I don't spoil the moment by bursting into tears or throwing my arms around his bony shoulders or any other countless theatrical options that would make him uncomfortable. This is as vulnerable as Bill Adams is ever going to get. And I'll take it.

"Me, too, Dad. Me, too."

And as if to put a stop to any further soul baring or general mushiness, Dad wobbles to his feet and says, "I'd better pull the car around for your mom and Mrs. Carter."

He starts to head for the door, but then stops and shyly takes a program from one of the seats and slips it into his sports coat jacket. He catches me watching him and shrugs. "Souvenir."

And then he's gone.

Luke comes up behind me with a worried expression written across his face. "You okay? What just happened?"

All I can do is shake my head in disbelief and say, "Oh, nothing. And everything. Nothing and everything and everything in between."

"But you and your dad are good, right?"

I gaze into Luke's hopeful face and say with complete and total amazement, "You know what? I think we actually kind of are."

Cast and crewmembers start setting up tables on the stage and bringing out homemade snacks and booze. I put my arms around Luke's waist and notice the crown of leaves still circling his head.

"You saved the day, Luke Carter."

"You're the one who wrote the song."

We hug until we both can't breathe. I put my head against his neck and feel his pulse again. The smell of apples.

"Tomorrow's going to be horrible, isn't it? There's no denying it." Luke sighs.

"What do we do?" I ask.

"We don't talk about it."

And so we don't.

The party goes on until dawn and Luke and I sneak out onto the roof of the theater to watch the sun come up. Hidden where no one can see us, we're together under the brightening sky for what we know will probably be the last time for months.


Saying goodbye to my parents is the same as it always is. Mom is weepy and melodramatic, and Dad is neither.

Luke and I drive mostly in silence to the airport. The atmosphere is so thick with sorrow that it seems wrong to talk at all.

Luke finally breaks the general air of misery. "Are you going to be okay on the plane?"

"The fear of heights thing isn't so bad when I'm flying. Plus, the free cocktails help."

"I wish I was gonna be there to tell you that you're safe."

He reaches over and takes my hand in his. I try to imprint the image of his rugged fingers entwined with mine on the back of my brain.

"Jesus, Luke. I wish you would just turn this truck around and tell me to quit this stupid show."

"Don't tempt me, Noah. I'm trying my best to do the tough guy thing."

When we get inside the airport, the dreaded moment comes right before security. It's time to say goodbye and I find myself getting self-conscious about our surroundings.

"I guess we should just hug goodbye. I mean, this is St. Louis, not New York. People might freak out if two guys—"

Luke cuts me off. "Fuck 'em."

His magnificent lips lock onto mine and we're embracing each other so tightly that I think our bodies might meld together. I completely forget to worry if my fellow passengers are noticing or not.

Luke refuses to let me go and whispers into my ear, "I can't believe it's taken me so long to say this, but I love you, Noah Oliver Adams."

Because he knows me so well, he holds me tighter as my knees start to give out.

I whisper back, "And I love you Luke I-don't-know-your-middle-name Carter."

And then we have to break apart because we're laughing too hard. But now I definitely have to know. "What *is* your middle name?"

Luke gives me a painful look. "You're going to hate it."

"That's impossible."

"Fine, it's . . . Harlan."

I squeal, "Harlan?!"

"Stop it."

"No, I love it!" I grab the sides of his face and gaze into his eyes. "You're my lovable Harlan! Can I call you that instead of Luke?"

"Can I call you Oliver?"

"Fuck no."

"Good. Let's stick to first names."

Luke Harlan Carter gets very serious and I hate it.

"Call me when you land. And do me a favor. Once you get through security, don't look back. I'll be here until you disappear into the crowd, but if you look back it might just break me."

I'm openly weeping like a baby. "Everything about this feels awful and wrong."

"I know, but it's all going to be fine," Luke promises.

For the first time the old Carter confidence seems a little shaky.

I follow Luke's instructions and don't look back at him once I'm past security. I reach into my bag and pull out my sunglasses, hoping that if I put them on I won't look like a crazy sobbing person roaming the airport. Thankfully, Anna Wong insisted that the producers of *Barbarella* fly me business class. A bottle blond flight attendant with a name tag that reads "Juana" approaches me and points at her name tag as she says, "Juana drink?"

I respond, "Oh, you don't know how much I wanna, Juana."

Something seems so horribly final when they shut the cabin door. I'm really doing this. I'm actually leaving. Putting over eight hundred miles between Luke and me.

Since I promised to call him as soon as I land, I do. But the sadness in both of our voices is almost unbearable. Hanging up feels miserable.

Even more miserable is wandering around the city now that I'm on my own. Reminders of my past life with Chase are everywhere and they don't sting, but they do carry a tiny punch. Oh, look, that charming little café where Chase tried to make me an oyster enthusiast and failed! How fun, an advertisement for Chase's favorite cologne on the side of that bus! And what's on display at my favorite newsstand? A trendy downtown magazine with Aleister Murphy and his over-tweezed eyebrows! Isn't that just fucking swell? I used to love Manhattan, but now everything just seems tainted. It's not that I miss Chase in the slightest, it's just that reminders of our rotten relationship are everywhere. And being so far from Luke doesn't help matters much.

One particularly hideous day I find myself absentmindedly

walking in Times Square and I can't stop myself from a bit of morbid curiosity. I stroll past the Broadway theater where *Stage of Fools* went down in flames. And there's the marquee. No longer with my name on it, obviously. In obnoxiously cheery colors it reads, "*Cassatt & Degas*—a new musical by Christine Garrick."

I need to vent, but I don't want it to be to Luke. Our calls are sad enough. I consider Kiara, but she'll just give me a lecture on the pitfalls of self-pity. I decide on Melissa. I had promised to be better at staying in touch anyway.

Melissa doesn't answer with a hello, but a simple, "I just bought a bra that has breast pumps attached and it's a game changer! I'm hands-free, baby!"

"How is little Noah Jr.?" I ask.

Melissa moans. "Give that up, Noah. His name is Anthony. Anthony Nelson Fazio."

"A name that will put all the other used car salesmen to shame."

Melissa sucks her teeth. "Just because I'm hands-free doesn't mean I'm patience-free. What's up?"

"I'm standing in front of the theater where the show flopped and there's a new marquee up, which is to be expected. But it still hurts, you know?"

"Oh, Noah. I'm sorry."

"I mean, of course another show moved in, but it just makes it feel like *Stage of Fools* never even happened. As if it's been completely erased and it's simply destined to be totally forgotten. I mean, some diehard theater buffs might talk about the show every now and then. But we didn't even get to record a cast album. So there's hardly any chance that it will live on at all."

Melissa is quiet for a moment, then says, "You know what Marilyn Henson said to me the other day at the car wash? She said next to the *birth of her daughter*, getting to be a part of your show was the biggest thrill of her life. Look, I know you wanted your musical to reach millions of people worldwide. But you've got to know how much it now means to our little town. To those of us in the cast, your musical was . . . well, it made us feel alive. And that's not a small thing. At least, it isn't to us."

I note the tiny lump in my throat and say, "I am so glad I called you. Thanks for that. I'll let you get back to the baby."

Melissa feigns panic. "Baby? What baby? Oh, shit. I knew I left something at the hospital!"

"Just stop by any nursery and pick up another one. They're pretty interchangeable."

Later in the week, Kiara challenges Melissa's standing as my favorite girlfriend by magnanimously offering to help me unpack my things in the studio apartment Stephen found for me. The place is a huge step down from the swanky pad I had with Chase, but Kiara always looks on the bright side.

"It's not really that bad. Just think of it as a temporary crash pad. You know, just someplace to hold your things until you're done with the shitty *Barbarella* show."

I change the conversation to an even more depressing topic. "Valerie Wernsman is going to eat me for lunch. Daily."

"You're going to have to just stand up to her from the very start. Read her Carrie Payne's human-interest piece about your show. Tell her to suck on that."

Carrie's non-review review had actually been very kind. She

still had all sorts of issues with the musical, but she did admit that the show was stronger than it was on Broadway and wrote, "Though the revamped musical is still called *Stage of Fools*, there was not a fool to be found onstage or on the creative team." The *Post-Dispatch* review was a flat-out rave. Mom was right, no local critic would rip apart a community theater production. People know where Audra Bogner lives.

I find myself saying, "Speaking of Carrie's non-review, I wonder if Chase read it."

Kiara snorts. "Didn't you once say that the *Times*'s Arts and Leisure section was his bible? He read it. The question is, baby boy, do you even give a shit what he thinks anymore?"

I stop to consider if I really do. I perform a comprehensive scan of my brain and then my heart and come up with, "You know, I actually think I don't."

"And that, ladies and gentlemen, is what we call progress! Besides, why waste a single thought on Chase when your new boyfriend has the soul of a saint and the body of a Hemsworth? He is an embarrassment of riches."

"I know. I've just filed the paperwork to have everything below his waist certified as a UNESCO Heritage Site."

Kiara cackles and announces, "Let's unpack the books next."

I climb up on a stepstool and Kiara hands me a stack of well-worn paperbacks, including my cherished copy of *The Complete Lyrics of Lorenz Hart*. When I reach down to grab the books, Kiara notices the necklace Luke gave me dangling out of my t-shirt. "What's that?"

"Luke gave it to me on opening night."

"Oh my God. It's hideous."

I smile. "I know. Don't you love it?"

"Desperately." Kiara's eyes glance over to the wall where I've hung the Balloon Faire t-shirt Luke bought for me. Instead of saying anything, she hides a smile and wags her head.

My phone buzzes. It's Anna Wong. Why is she calling so late?

I hop off the stepstool and answer.

She sounds panicked. Very, very panicked. "I have news to report. This is . . . uh . . . I'm completely blindsided by this, but I have Elton John on the other line."

I pause. Then laugh. "That's funny, because it sounded like you said you had Elton John on the other line."

Anna Wong is practically breathless. "No time for jokes. It's actually him. He wants to talk to you."

"Is this a prank? Because it's not funny."

"It's no prank. You know how I sent your demo out far and wide? Well, this is because of that, I guess. I also might have emailed his management a bootleg of your boyfriend singing 'More Than Words Can Hold.'"

"You did what?!"

"You told me to be bold! I can't stall any longer. You have to take the call now. Elton John doesn't wait."

I'm shaking so hard that I have to use two hands to hold the phone up. "Okay, okay! Go!"

A muffled beep and then I'm talking to Elton John. I'm actually talking to Elton fucking John.

"Is this Noah, then?"

Please don't let him hear my voice shaking. "Hello, Sir Elton John. It's me."

"Oh cut the 'Sir' crap. Ms. Wong sent some samples of your work. I thought your lyrics were quite good."

"Well, that means the world coming from someone like you, sir." I quickly add, "That wasn't a 'sir' in a knighthood kind of way, that was just a regular sir."

"I don't like either, but never mind. So your lyrics I love. I hate to be a bit of a cunt, but I'm a much better composer than you."

Ouch. But, valid.

"Well, you *do* have five Grammy Awards."

"Six, but who's counting?"

"Technically, I think we both are."

He gives a little laugh. "Someone's quick on his feet. Look, I'll cut to the chase. I've had a bit of a dustup on one of my musicals. The lyricist just wasn't working out. No personal issues, he just wasn't cutting it. And I want you to take over. Immediately, if possible."

I grab the wall to steady myself, because it feels like my soul is leaving my body. Elton John wants to write a musical with me? Sir Elton John? The color must have drained from my face because Kiara gives me a worried look.

"That . . . that . . . would be dream come true."

"Good! So that's settled. I'll have my management send your agent the script with the old lyrics cut out and you can start crafting new ones and emailing them to me. I'm constantly on the road with my tour. So unfortunately we're not going to be able to meet in person that much. Why I agreed to one more tour, I'll never know. But anyway, it's going to be writing via email and Zoom for the next several years. I know that's not optimal, but the good news is you can work from wherever you like."

My heart stops beating. "What?"

"You don't have to be in New York or London, as long as the work gets done."

My heart explodes into a thousand cartoon butterflies. Luke. I get to come home to Luke.

A screeching sound, probably feedback from a speaker blares over the phone. "Listen, there's a problem with my sound check. I've got to go, but looking forward to reading what you come up with, Noah."

In a flash Anna Wong is back on the line, she's clearly been listening in.

"Oh my God, Noah!!!"

"You goddess! You made this happen!"

"Don't you deus ex machina this moment! It was your songs that did the trick. I just sent them out far and wide."

"Can you get me out of that shitshow *Barbarella*, though?"

"With pleasure!" And then in totally un–Anna Wong style, she gives me an Oprah-like shout. "*Noah Adams is working with Elton John!*"

"I'm hanging up because I might have to vomit. In a good way."

I throw the phone down and turn to a wide-eyed Kiara.

"Noah, did you say the words Elton John?"

"I'm working with him on a new show."

Kiara screams.

"And I can work from wherever I want."

Kiara screams louder.

"I have to tell Luke. I have to tell him that I could actually be with him in Plainview while simultaneously working on a new musical with Elton fucking John. That's like having my cake and eating it, too."

"That is an endless supply of cake, baby boy!"

And then the old, neurotic Noah pops up.

"But what if Luke doesn't want that? Me around all the time, I mean. And could I actually move to Plainview? I don't think they really understand my fashion choices. Does this mean I'll have to buy jean shorts?"

Kiara grabs me by the wrists and pulls down, as if hoping to ground me.

"Noah, it's okay to get what you want every now and then. This is a mean old world. Just be grateful and call Luke."

I nod. Everything is happening so fast and none of it seems real.

I call Luke and he answers with a familiar sadness in his voice. "I was just thinking about you, baby," he says. Cows moo away in the background as if to remind me how far away from New York Luke is.

"So, the brilliant Anna Wong might have saved our relationship."

Clearly confused, Luke asks, "As in how?"

"Elton John just hired me as his lyricist for a new show. But he's on tour, so I can work from anywhere. I want to come home to you, Luke." My voice breaks and I pause to take a breath. "I mean, I'll live with my parents and we can—"

Luke cuts me off. "You'll live with me."

The sentence takes my breath away for a second. "I . . ."

"You'll live with me. Please come live with me, Noah."

"Uh . . . if you're sure."

"I'm sure."

"I want to say something, but I'm afraid I'll jinx everything if I do."

"Go ahead, Noah. Say it."

"One night before rehearsal, Melissa was listening to me completely self-flagellate over all the things that had gone spectacularly wrong in my life. And, well, she said that maybe . . . maybe I was only at intermission. That maybe there was a big old second act barreling right toward me. What if this is it?" I gasp quickly. "Fuck, did I just jinx it? I did, didn't I?"

"Noah, stop talking and get on an airplane as fast as you can. The houselights are going to half and the entr'acte is just about to start. You need to get here so that I can call places!"

"Call places? For what?"

"Forever, Noah. Forever."

I close my eyes and exhale.

Let the second act begin.

# Acknowledgments

I was born in a small town in the Midwest called Centralia, Illinois.

It's about sixty miles "as the crow flies" from St. Louis, Missouri. Our high school basketball team made it into the *Guinness Book of World Records* for being the "winningest." Or something like that. Let's just say I didn't fit in.

But then one day I discovered a shimmering oasis called The Centralia Cultural Society. The community theater branch was referred to as the Little Theater Players. It quickly became my second home and even if there wasn't a show to rehearse, I would volunteer to organize their costume collection or tidy up the prom room. Also, would it be okay if I alphabetized the filing cabinets?

I was so relentless that *they gave me a key to the building.*

So this novel wouldn't exist without that place and all of the wonderful people who were a part of it. So many of these characters are inspired by real people and I don't dare attempt to list any names because I'll unknowingly leave someone out. But as a group, they took me in. They heard this short, scrawny teenager say he wanted to write musicals and they said, "Alright, buddy, you're on!"

It was stupefying.

I barely had my driver's license, and they were letting me write and direct shows and paint sets and hot glue sequins onto costumes until the cows came home. And yes, there were actual cows. It's a rural place.

It changed my life.

So if you have a place like the Cultural Society in your town, please cherish it. If you don't, please start one. Like immediately. Like right now. Stop reading and get to work!

A huge thank you to my family for all their support. And a formal apology to my siblings for the hours they had to listen to me belting out show tunes in my room. They didn't make walls thick enough to contain my impassioned and never-ending performances as Fruma Sarah. Although, to be fair, it's not my fault that I identified so completely with an imaginary dead Jewish woman's ghost. Let's not blame the victim here.

I am so grateful for my amazingly supportive parents. My dad was the kind of guy who went through his life encouraging friends, family members, and strangers alike. I used to joke that if I had told him that I wanted to grow up and hula dance on the moon, he would have said, "Well, we need to figure out how to get you a grass skirt and a spaceship."

And no character in the book is closer to their real-life counterpart than my mom. She just so happens to be named Nancy Kay, also. Thank you, Mom, for always being a good sport when I ribbed you about your dubious cooking skills. (The crockpot pizza is real, folks. Terrifyingly real.) But what more can you say about a woman who arranged for her obviously gay theater nerd son to have a birthday cake decorated to look exactly like an Evita poster? That's love. Pure and simple.

A big merci beaucoup to my theatrical agent, Olivier Sultan (he's from Paris!), for having enough faith in the book to spike it over to the literary side of CAA. Thank you to my newly minted literary agents, Mollie Glick and Lola Bellier, for patiently helping me whip the manuscript into shape before sending it off to market.

I am forever thankful to Pamela Dorman and the entire team at Pamela Dorman Books/Viking for choosing this wannabe novelist. To quote Comden and Green, "I'm so lucky to be me." And a full bended-knee royal-court bow to my editor, Marie Michels, for her brilliant notes and endless supply of optimism. Marie is such a fountain of kindness that she makes Gandhi look like a nasty old bitch. I'm forever indebted to cover designer Elizabeth Yaffe and illustrator Debs Lim. This cover art deserves nothing short of an hour-long standing ovation.

A shoutout to my amazing friends for being so reassuring throughout this whole process. It's been so much fun namechecking you in these pages. Please don't feel you owe me anything in return. (I take a size nine and a half in Ferragamos.)

But the biggest thanks of all must go to my husband, Tom. The act of writing this book possessed me in the best possible way. But it meant that I was constantly distracted from our life together. It meant me jumping out of bed a thousand times at night to write down a thought. It meant me dropping out of conversations to type a bit of dialogue into my phone. And it meant that Tom had to read mountains and mountains of endless pages, most of which ended up being cut anyway. And he did it all with the patience of Job and the dreamy hair of a male supermodel. If there's any question where the inspiration for Luke Carter's pillowy lips and hazel green eyes comes from, look no further than wonderful, beautiful Tom.

I truly believe that before I was born, I said to the powers that be, "I can't do planet Earth without Tom. You have to send Tom with me."

I am eternally grateful that the gods said yes.